Portals

A Dungeon Crawler Adventure

Portals
A Dungeon Crawler Adventure

Brian S. Pratt

Portals
A Dungeon Crawler Adventure
Copyright 2010 by Brian S. Pratt

ISBN: 978-0-9843127-1-9

Books written by Brian S. Pratt can be obtained either through the author's official website:
www.briansprattbooks.com
or through select, online book retailers.

Books by Brian S. Pratt:

The Morcyth Saga

The Unsuspecting Mage
Fires of Prophecy
Warrior Priest of Dmon-Li
Trail of the Gods
The Star of Morcyth
Shades of the Past
The Mists of Sorrow*
***(Conclusion of The Morcyth Saga)**

Travail of The Dark Mage
Sequel to The Morcyth Saga

1-Light in the Barren Lands
2-(forthcoming Spring 2010)

The Broken Key

#1- Shepherd's Quest
#2-Hunter of the Horde
#3-Quest's End

Qyaendri Adventures

Ring of the Or'tux

Dungeon Crawler Adventures

Underground
Portals

The Adventurer's Guild

#1-Jaikus and Reneeke Join the Guild

**This is for Gavin and Gabe of New York.
Great fans are much appreciated.**

—1—

Soaring high above the heat-seared sands of a desert known as *The Devil's Kiln,* a scavenger navigated the thermal updrafts with balletic ease. Its keen eyes scanned the sand's surface far below for any sign of movement.

For hours now, the airborne scavenger had looped in lazy, contented circles. Having eaten the day before, its hunger had yet to become a nagging urge. But that didn't mean it would ignore the unwary on the sands below. In a land so barren of life, a single meal quite often had to last for days. And so, it searched.

The sun baked the parched land, and would continue to do so for many hours to come. Most creatures of the *Kiln* emerged only with the onset of night, for the oppressive heat made any diurnal excursion practically a death sentence. An hour in the open would burn the skin, drawing forth precious water, water difficult to replace when one lives in the Kiln's aridness.

But despite that, the scavenger knew from past experience that certain creatures made the daylight hours their own. Snakes, scorpions, and dozens of other burrowing creatures that it had been fortunate to feed upon, could be found skittering along the sand's surface going about their business. For such signs, the bird kept watch.

Drifting along the currents, it passed over a series of undulating hills and spied something other than the monotonous, sandy expanse. The bird altered its course and flew toward the curious oddity.

Little more than a patch of brown against the sand's beige, it piqued the bird's interest. *A dead animal perhaps?* Carrion suited the bird's needs just as well as a fresh kill. Reducing its altitude, the bird tightened its circular flight until finally alighting upon the ground several feet from the brown patch.

The bird held its ground for a moment, cocked a curious, wary eye at the brown patch nestled within the sand, then glanced for rivals that may be en route. The skies were clear and the vicinity deserted. Naught but a light sprinkling of windblown sand disturbed the tranquil scene.

Twice it hopped before coming to a stop. Now two feet away, it watched to see if the brown patch would react to its presence. When it didn't, the bird hopped again. Across the remaining foot of sand, the bird strode with rapid steps until coming to within pecking distance.

The dark patch didn't look like the hide of any animal it had ever before encountered. Organic though it may be, it didn't have fur, scales, or chitinous outer casings as other inhabitants of *The Devil's Kiln* exhibited.

Reaching out with its beak, it gingerly pecked the brown patch; not once, but twice. Curiouser and curiouser; the twin pecks did little to pierce the object. The bird stepped back and gazed at the object a moment, wondering at this strange thing. Deciding to give it one more try, the bird hopped closer again, and pecked.

In a span of time that would have made a heartbeat seem long, a hand shot forth from out of the sand. So suddenly had it appeared, that the bird had scant time to react before fingers encased its body in an inescapable prison.

Squawking but once, the bird vanished from sight as the hand just as rapidly returned beneath the surface. During the ensuing minutes, a gentle wind erased all traces of the bird's presence; tri-toed tracks faded away, the surface grew smooth once more, and a lone, black feather danced its way across the dunes.

The Devil's Kiln remained quiet throughout the rest of the day. Though once the sun began sinking toward the horizon, and the oppressive heat became less so, life returned to the desert.

Small creatures scurried from their sandy hideaways, birds with large eyes took to the skies in search of prey, and on a quiet dune where a bird once pecked, sand erupted into the air.

Throwing off the blanket and layer of sand which had served to insulate him from the *Kiln's* lethal heat, Squad Leader Holk Tyre emerged from his hole. Still remaining in his diurnal burrow lay what remained of the bird. It hadn't been pleasant, consuming the bird raw as he had, but in so doing, Holk had regained a little of his spent strength, enough perhaps to reach the end of this infernal place.

For two weeks, he had endured searing heat, parched lips, and an aching belly. Though not native to such conditions as existed in this godforsaken land, Holk quickly learned that night travel would be the only means whereby he could survive.

As he folded his blanket and then slipped it within his tunic to keep his hands free, the one-time squad leader couldn't help but think of the men that had fled with him into *The Devil's Kiln* following the disastrous assault upon the city-state of Trelakan.

Seventy-five thousand men had set out under the leadership of King Redstorm, a monarch with a great vision for the future of his peoples. A two-week march brought them across the Egothian Plains to Trelakan, a commercial hub for caravans from the Far East. To take it would give Redstorm's people access to many riches and luxuries currently beyond their means.

The assault had gone wrong from the beginning. Earlier intelligence had indicated the city held a garrison of less than five thousand, a force Redstorm's seventy-five thousand should have readily overcome. Instead, they found twenty thousand men ready to sell their lives dearly to protect their city and their people.

Word had reached Trelakan of Redstorm's plans, and they were ready. In addition to the ten thousand within the walls, reinforcements over a hundred thousand strong marched from their allies and arrived three days into the siege. Redstorm's men had been obliterated.

The fate of King Redstorm remained unknown to Holk, though hope for his continued survival eluded the squad leader. It had only been through a desperate fight that Holk and his men won their freedom. Before losing sight of their King, Holk watched a force of five thousand descend upon, and completely cut off, the men personally led by Redstorm. All must have been either killed, or captured.

Holk's men had numbered three score when they originally set out for Trelakan. The ensuing rout and fight for their lives, claimed one score, the *Kiln* had taken the rest. Only Holk survived. For all he knew, he may be the *only* member of that ill-fated campaign to still live.

Desert raiders from Trelakan discovered them three days after the annihilation of the siege. Holk and his men had won the ensuing battle, though at a terrible price. Four men aside from Hold continued in their flight. Of the four, one died from his wounds not long after.

Another perished after being bitten by a denizen of the *Kiln*. None saw what had attacked the man, the only evidence the attack had even taken place was the appearance of a great swelling near his ankle. His final two men had merely collapsed from the effects of the heat, and perhaps no small amount of hopelessness. Holk was alone.

Using the emerging stars as a guide, Holk continued his quest to find the end of these infernal sands. His strength continued to diminish with every setting of the sun. Food was scarce, but water was even scarcer. He had come across but one pool during his trek across the dunes. Clear and crisp, the water did much to revitalize him. But that had been three days ago and the oppressive heat of the *Kiln* had subsequently robbed him of those precious fluids.

Throughout the night, he walked. His mind roamed paths of past joys as he sought to put the direness of his situation behind him, even if for only a moment. Family, friends, times of joviality spent with men now lying dead amongst the desert sand, all this he concentrated on as he forced his body to put one foot in front of the other. For though his body longed to keel over and rest, he knew that to succumb but once would be a death sentence. Holk doubted his ability to ever get moving again should he allow it.

Cries of birds accompanied his desert odyssey, the scurry of small animals aided to break his sense of isolation, and Holk trudged onward. Not until the eastern sky began to lighten with the coming of dawn did he finally bring his trek to a halt.

I can't go on.

Exhaustion and despair sought to sap what will he had remaining. Turning dry, sandy eyes toward the predawn light, he dreaded the time when the sun would emerge. The air was cool at the moment, or at least relatively so. But once the sun peeked over the horizon, the air would once again turn searing.

With an unknown distance yet before him, parched nearly beyond endurance, Holk realized that should he again bury himself beneath the sands to avoid the heat, the burrow may very well become his grave. It had been all he could do to muster the strength of will to crawl forth the last time. Would he be able to rise again? Whether he could or not, Holk had little choice, he must dig and bury himself or the heat would assuredly kill him before the sun reached its zenith.

Dropping to his knees, he began the arduous duty of creating a hole large enough into which he could readily fit. It couldn't be too deep, or excessive sand would accumulate atop him and he would suffocate. Not deep enough would cause him to bake like bread in an oven. The perfect depth allowed for two inches of sand to settle atop his blanket. Most of the heat would be radiated away while still being porous enough to allow oxygen through.

Both hands worked to remove the sand. He prayed that his efforts would have the added benefit of uncovering water, though knew he would not be so fortunate.

The eastern sky continued its journey toward dawn. Having grown much brighter, he could feel the temperature already beginning to rise.

Dig, scrape. Dig, scrape. His hole steadily grew, yet with each action of sand removal, his will to continue diminished. Halfway completed, his arms grew still and he stared blankly at the hole. Holk hadn't even realized he sat there motionless until the sun's first rays peeked over the horizon like bolts of fire. When realization hit, he knew this day would be his last.

Memories of his young wife and child left behind nagged at him to go on. *What's the use?* Mind clouded by fatigue, belly aching with hunger, lips cracked from dehydration, he simply hadn't the strength or will to continue. He tuned his face toward the sun. *You win.* Toppling over to the side, he hit the sand and didn't move.

How long he laid there as the unrelenting sun rose into the sky, he couldn't be sure. But a time came when consciousness returned and eyes opened. At first he thought he had gone blind until realizing that he must have unconsciously drawn the blanket over him at some point. Reaching a hand to move it aside, his fingers discovered the material to be extremely hot. Uncaring, he thrust it aside.

The heat hit him like a physical blow and he gasped. Drawing in the hot air caused him to gasp all the more. Heat waves made the world a disorienting place. With vision distorted and disorienting, Holk gazed across a hellish landscape. About to succumb once more to the desire to just give up and die, he caught sight of a disturbance in the unchanging, undulation of the dunes. A dark spot.

At first, he doubted what his eyes told him. Heat radiations made the dark spot indistinct, but from somewhere deep in his fatigued mind, surfaced the thought that this might in some way be shelter.

Hope sprang anew and he surged to his feet. *Shelter!* Clouds of sand exploded upward with each staggering step he took. His eyes fixated upon what gradually grew to be a dark spire of jagged stone rising out of the sand. Further steps drew him closer and he came to realize that more than the lone spire rose from the desert.

The dark spot turned out to be a group of four, stone monoliths. Three tapered off to become more mounds than spires, while the fourth peaked at twice the height of the others. Formed of dark stone, they looked to be natural rock outcroppings rather than manmade.

Holk increased his speed as visions of water and caves filled with sheltering coolness drove him onward. He stumbled but once, tumbling down the slope of a dune. At the bottom, he dragged himself back to his feet and by sheer force of will, pushed his wearied body forward.

High expectations met bleak reality upon his arrival at the first up-thrusting monolith of stone. Its height provided some break from the unrelenting sun. And though its base could have encompassed several homes and still have room for a mill, it failed to hold the internal cavity he so desperately needed.

Pausing within the monolith's shadow, Holk gazed across to where the next one rose from the sand. Similar in height and width, it too bore little in the way of welcoming openings. His eyes scanned the others until finally falling upon the smallest of the stone projections. Nearly half the size of the one in whose shadow he now stood, it nevertheless bore a sliver of shade that could very well be the entrance to a cave.

His mind worked overtime as to what he might find within. Would there be an underground pool of water; crisp, cool, and deep enough to wallow in? Perhaps stocked with fish, edible lichen, a cord of wood, ale, mutton, a good sized wo… Snapping out of his delirium, he shook his head to clear away such errant thoughts and concentrated on the distance to the cave, if cave it be.

A quick run. He could do that. His strength would assuredly hold out that long. After taking but another moment to compose himself and prepare for the entrance back into the searing heat, he lurched into motion.

Instantly, the sun began sapping what little strength left to him. Its blistering tentacles of light ravaged and sought to bring him down. One step, a quick second, then followed by a shuffling third, he began working his way toward the promise of relief. Relief from wandering, relief from having to put one foot before the other, but most of all, *relief from the sun.*

Midway there, he began making out the inner contours beyond the opening. No doubt remained about it being a cave. He could almost feel the coolness of its inner core reaching out to lend him strength against its age-old enemy, the sun.

His pace quickened. Sweat would have run in rivulets down his back had his body any to spare. Each step was hell; so close, yet still to be weighed down by unrelenting heat. Sand flew as his lack of strength prevented him moving beyond a shuffling gait. Plowing twin furrows, he continued on.

Five feet before the opening, he felt it: a drop in temperature. Six more quick, shuffling steps and he passed from the hell of *The Devil's Kiln*, to that of blessed coolness. He had but a moment to enjoy this new world before it begun spinning out of control. Fatigue, dehydration, and perhaps a touch of heatstroke could be held at bay no longer. They would have their will.

Holk pitched forward and passed out.

How long he remained unconscious he may never know. When he awoke, Holk discovered himself in a world of darkness. Disoriented at first, he couldn't recall why he felt stone beneath him instead of sand. Also, part of his forehead throbbed. Upon closer examination, he discovered a rather large goose egg just above his right eye.

Further disorientation came when he found no stars in the sky above. The only indication he had not gone blind came in the form of a sliver of dark, slightly lighter than the rest. When he came to understand it was the night sky being silhouetted by the narrow entrance, memory returned.

Unable to discern anything about this new environment, he carefully found a spot against the wall where he could sit and keep watch on the outside world. The coolness of the cave wall brought a welcomed comfort. Nestled up against it, he laid his head back and gazed at the stars.

I'm going to die here.

If death did come calling before the sun rose, at least they could share this cool refuge. Perhaps death would be thoughtful enough to bring along a cask of ale. Holk grinned at the thought of sharing a mug of frothy goodness with the *Stealer of Souls*. One last mug of ale, he'd give anything to be able to slake his raging thirst.

Sighing for things that could never be, he watched the stars. Before even realizing it, the black thief of fatigue came and scampered away with his consciousness.

Cracking open eyes red as the fires of hell, and drier than the sands of the *Kiln*, Holk returned to the world. No longer shrouded in cool darkness, he found night having fled and that dawn had come.

Rays from the tormenting sun penetrated his bastion. Already, the temperature within the cave had increased twenty degrees. Not exactly hot as yet, the air retained only the faintest memory of coolness remembered from before.

At least the position of the sun in relation to that of the cave entrance had prevented the rays from falling directly upon him. Holk could feel the heat radiating outward from where they did land, less than a foot away. He knew it wanted him, could see it in the way it maliciously inched its way closer to him with the rising of the sun.

"You'll not have me," he croaked. Throat parched beyond belief, he laughed. Not the normal laughter one would find at the local tavern, or perhaps the sort that bubbled forth when the person you despised the most acted in an embarrassing, and much ridiculed manner. No, this laughter boiled forth from another source. Holk wished to believe it came from the fact that he lived, but feared it may be the beginning of madness.

As the sun crept closer across the floor of the cave, the laughter continued, only winding down when his stomach cramped and seized up on him in a most painful spasm. Doubling over, Holk wrapped his arms around his middle, fell to the side, and writhed in agony. By the time the pain had stopped, the sun peeked around the edge of the opening and fell upon him.

His eyes flashed with hate toward the burning orb, and he rolled deeper within the cave, away from its murderous clutch. Coming up against the other side of his small enclosure, Holk came to a stop. Eyes focused upon the light that could no longer reach him, he felt the return of the laughter. Fearing to allow it free reign once more, Holk balled his hand into a fist, and struck his leg a painful blow. The interjection of pain halted the laughter, and he grew calm once more.

Hoping that if he ceased gazing toward the sunlight, the laughter would remain in its lair, Holk, turned to take in his surroundings. Last night, the cave had been steeped too deeply in darkness to make out more than vague outlines. Now that the sun had infiltrated his refuge, he could see its every detail.

Small would be the best description of the cave. If he and three other men laid down head to foot, the line thus formed would be hard pressed not to touch the walls. The entrance through which the bright invader shone proved to be the only way out. Above, the ceiling rose to twice his height before tapering to a close. Around him, the walls formed a ragged excuse for a circle.

No water. Not even the barest hint of a drip cascaded down the sides. His hope of a wet sanctuary had been dashed upon the dry rocks of despair. The one consolation he had was that he remained out of the sun, and the rock protecting him drew coolness up from the depths below as a man would water in a well.

Not a bad place to spend one's final hours, especially considering the alternative. Glancing once again to the patch of sunlight spread across the cave's floor, he tried spitting contemptuously at the light, but his mouth held no saliva.

Sighing, he laid his head back against the rock and closed his eyes.

Take me.

But death turned a deaf ear to his plea and left him to suffer a few moments longer. Moments turned into minutes, minutes passed into hours, and the sun marched in steady progression across the floor. As time passed and the sun rose to its zenith, the amount of sunlight entering the cave diminished until naught but a small sliver remained.

Holk watched that sliver during its last moments of life. Ever smaller it became, thinning and shortening until it was but the width and length of a man's finger. Just before vanishing altogether, a strange thing occurred; an iridescent refraction. Lasting no more than the flutter of a raven's wings, a miniscule explosion of light blossomed forth.

So quick, and lasting such a short time, Holk hadn't thought much about it at first. Minutes passed, and he found his mind returning to the starburst of light. Maybe due to the isolation of the cave, or perhaps because boredom had set in, his mind continued replaying the flash of light. Finally, he roused himself sufficiently to crawl over and see what it could be, if for no other reason than to quell the insistent obsession his mind had with it.

The temperature rose dramatically as he neared the cave's entrance. Perspiration would have formed, had his body held a sufficient quantity of water. He wanted to quickly satiate his curiosity and return to the cooler, inner confines of the cave. The air had already increased fifteen degrees in such a short span of distance.

As he neared the area whereupon the sun had shone, Holk found the stone floor to be heated to an unpleasant state. Testing indentations and raised, sand dusted imperfections scoring the floor, he found placements for his hands that didn't burn as much, and came to the source of the flash.

Blowing away a thin layer of sand, he discovered something shiny encased within the stone of the floor. Intrigued, he tried using a fingernail to pry it loose to no effect. Next, he tried using the tip of his belt knife. But that too failed to produce results.

Being unable to win its release from the stone only piqued his interest all the more. Turning his attention to the area encompassing the shiny object, he began chipping away at the stone. He found a hand-sized rock and used it as a hammer to drive the knife-point into surrounding imperfections.

Chips flew. Small though they may be, he gradually made progress and soon, a cavity began to form around what turned out to be a many faceted stone. Unlike any stone he had ever seen before, it was clear, translucent, and incredibly small. The skill involved in its construction had to have been of the highest kind.

Further excavation revealed the stone to be part of a larger, silvery object lined with other, similar stones. Intrigued, he continued widening the hole. Even though his efforts pitted the blade and warped it out of shape, still he kept pounding away.

The silvery object turned out to be rounded, a corner of something larger perhaps? With the hole now four inches deep, he chipped away another piece that revealed a shiny surface, one as smooth as glass. Clearing away the debris and blowing away the dust his efforts had created, he realized it was glass, a mirror in fact.

Such a realization shocked him. *A mirror? Buried in stone in the middle of the Kiln?* How could it have survived? Assuredly, time spent thus entombed should have seen the glass shattered, or at the very least, cracked, long ago.

Tapping ever so gently with his stone and knife, he carefully chipped away more of the cave floor from in front of the glass. If the dimensions of what had thus far been revealed gave any indication, the mirror had to be quite sizeable. Once his excavation exposed another three inches of the mirror's surface, he removed as much of the debris from the hole as he could. Then, after a short period of blowing away the finer particles, he could better see the reflective surface.

Dust clung to the glass like honey on a child's hand. Reaching out with his fingers, he began wiping the surface clean. No sooner had his finger touched the glass, than sight left him and darkness consumed him, or so it felt.

Death had come!

Overcome by a feeling of weightlessness, Holk cried out. For the first time since coming of age, fear overcame him and forced a sound from him he never thought to utter. So primal was its intensity, that it felt as if it would tear asunder his already parched and ill-used throat.

A sudden plunge into ice-cold water cut his cry short as his feet, followed by the rest of him, went under. The unexpected submerging in frigid temperature shocked him back to his senses. At first flailing about in disorientation, he quickly brought his actions under control and kicked for the surface. When his head broke the water, he sputtered and coughed, expelling a lung full of water.

Not a light could be seen. No shades of gray or deeper shadows could be discerned. The darkness was absolute. Holk didn't care, he had water! Precious, life-saving water. Crisp, cool, and wonderful, he kept himself afloat while drinking his fill. Tempted to fill his entire being with the wonderful liquid, he brought his urge under control after the fifteenth swallow. No need to get sick by ingesting too much, too soon.

The uncontrollable laughter returned. He splashed. He played. He laughed with complete, unrestrained giddiness. On the brink of madness, he didn't know if he were alive or dead. Did it matter?

—2—

Giddy euphoria only lasts so long. For Holk, it had lasted long enough that a shiver, produced by heat loss due to his continued immersion in cold water, coursed through his body. What an odd feeling. He was cold!

When another shiver prompted a brief period of teeth chattering, he came to the realization that he may not have expired. Unless of course, this really *was* the Realm of the Dead. He gave the idea little credence since in all the stories heard throughout his life, never had death's realm been described as never-ending water devoid of light.

Sipping more of the water in which he treaded, he came to the conclusion that if he weren't dead, he had to be somewhere. How he came to be there, or where this somewhere was, were questions in need of answering.

"Hello?"

Shouting, he listened for a reply. All that returned were echoes of his own voice.

"Anyone there?"

Again, no reply other than a rapidly diminishing, echoing refrain.

A mental picture emerged based on the echoing replies. Could he be underground? An underground lake, perhaps? The way his voice reverberated back to him made such a theory plausible, however unlikely it might be.

I've gone mad. That was the only explanation that seemed to fit. He had heard of people undergoing terrible situations who lost their minds. And if what he had experienced in the last weeks couldn't be termed, "terrible," then what could?

This would be the sort of place a sun-maddened man's mind would create for itself, a suitable refuge from the heat. Splashing, he thought it a rather vivid dream world. Thinking perhaps his mind may have stocked this land with more than just water, he began swimming to set out in search of it.

Using lazy strokes, Holk made slow progress. He had been at it several minutes when one of his feet encountered something solid and unyielding.

Being rather firm and encompassing a wide area, Holk attempted to stand. Coming upright, he found the water to be waist high.

It turned out to be the beginnings of a knoll rising from the surface. Small, with a diameter slightly less than six paces in width, it at least afforded him freedom from the frigid water. He cleared a spot of loose rubble and lay down as fatigue still plagued him. It would take a long period of recuperation before he would ever again feel rested.

Minutes passed as he lay upon the rocky knoll. The circumstances of his situation gnawed at him. Shouldn't madness introduce other elements of a more odd and unbelievable nature than water and rock? Where were the fantastic beasts, the glowing swords, maidens with three breasts?

Sleep remained unattainable despite gnawing fatigue. He sat up and again tried to pierce the darkness surrounding him. There was not even the barest softening of the stygian blackness. He wouldn't mind so much being in a world created by his madness if he could but see his environment.

Maybe, if my mind created this world, I could use my mind to change it?

With that thought urging him into action, he formed a vision of a lamp sitting upon the knoll next to him. "Let it be!" Using every bit of concentration and forced thought at his disposal, he willed the lantern to be. All he received for his effort was disappointment. No lamp materialized.

He tried again with food, with a woman of exaggerated proportions, with a single blade of grass. Yet each attempt met with failure. If his mind was the true creator of this realm, he couldn't do anything to change its aspect.

"Hey!"

Shouting once again, he willed for there to be an answer. None came. *Frustration!* Taking a rock from off the knoll, he vented his aggravation by giving out with an inarticulate cry and throwing it as hard as he could. About to break into a steady stream of expletives, he was shocked into silence when the rock, launched so angrily into the air, struck something. The *crack* of its impact echoed repeatedly until finally dying out.

Holk stood perfectly still until the last echo faded away. The sound of impact jarred his thinking from that of this being a realm of madness to one where his situation may be a bit more real. Picking up another rock, he hurled it in the opposite direction.

Silence hung in the air as he waited for the expected crack. Instead, he heard a *plunk* as the rock impacted the surface of the water a fair distance from the knoll. Excited by the disparity in the two results, he gathered more rocks.

One by one, he began sending them out over the water. Alternating between those that *plunked*, and those that *cracked*, he built a mental image as to the dimensions of this reality. In short order, he soon had a good idea in which direction the closest "wall" lay. Of course, he couldn't be certain the rock had in fact hit any kind of wall, but could come up with no other rationalization.

Perhaps he was within an enclosure of some kind? He no longer worried about the incredulity of such incongruous happenings, like his being where logic assured he could never be. The rocks were hitting something, and that something was different from the knoll. Different enough, perhaps, to offer the prospect for a change?

Stepping to the water's edge, he readied himself to return to the cool water. With no light to guide him, he waded out until the water reached a little above his waist, then dove forward.

He had always been a good swimmer. Days spent as a youth along the *Catalyst's Stream,* supplied enough experience for him to easily make this swim. Taking long strokes, he felt his body course through the water at a respectable speed.

...seven...eight...nine...

Counting each stroke, he waited until reaching twenty before pausing to see if he could touch the bottom. When his first attempt proved premature, he counted another ten strokes before trying again. This time, his toes touched the bottom, barely. A few more strokes brought him to a depth whereby he could walk with relative ease.

Holk streamed water as he carefully made his way up the slope to dry land. Still unable to see even the most miniscule spec of shadowing, he held his hands out before him and took small, searching steps.

His feet encountered a beach equally as rocky as the knoll had been. The loose rubble shifted beneath his feet, but considering how slow he moved, it caused him little trouble.

As he had with the strokes through the water, so too did he count his steps across the dry land. At seventeen, his hands encountered rock, a rock wall as it turned out. Moving his hands along the surface, he discovered it rose higher than he could reach, and extended outward to either side. He shuffled first one way, then the other without encountering an end. In his mind's eye, he came to think of himself being within some kind of cavern. One way being as good as another, Holk decided to try his luck to the left.

Sidestepping along the wall, he kept his hands in constant contact with the stony surface. The feel of its rough, irregular texture helped cement this into reality, as well as giving him something to focus upon.

He thought about how real all this felt; the wall's rough surface, the shallow depressions, even an abrupt outcropping three paces in length he had to maneuver around in order to continue. Holk had truly become a believer in the reality of this place, up until the moment his hand passed onto an area smooth to the touch. The unexpectedness of the encounter brought his exploration to a sudden halt.

Smooth and cool, cooler than the rock to which it was attached, this new surface protruded an inch from the wall. Holk used a finger to trace the outer circumference and discovered it to be oval, roughly two feet tall and a foot and a half wide. Unsure exactly what he had come across, he began working his finger toward the object's center. Two inches in from the outer edge, the surface dropped a quarter of an inch. Then it was gone, and so too was the stygian absoluteness of this newfound dark world.

No longer in contact with the object, Holk now stood in a dimly lit room. Two narrow windows in the wall before him, one to his right and the other to his left, allowed moonlight to filter in.

Apparently, his madness was not done with him. Trying to resolve the incongruities of the sudden shift in surroundings, Holk remained still as he took in his new environs.

The room, for room it definitely was, complete with the pair of windows already noted and a door to his right, had been constructed with blocks of stone set one atop another in an alternating pattern.

To his left was perhaps the most incongruous thing of all. An upright, rectangular field of shadow bordered by a golden area, stood at roughly eye level. Such was its out-of-placeness, that he took three steps toward the object before even realizing it.

It was a mirror. The rectangular field of shadow turned out to be the mirror's reflective surface. Holk's mind tried to grasp what he saw. Nothing made sense, the madness seemed to be spiraling out of all control.

Now that his curiosity over the field of shadow had been satisfied, he turned his attention to the two narrow windows. Each bore a pair of thick bars, effectively keeping anyone from passing through. As he approached, he caught the scent of salt upon the slight breeze wafting in. Placing his face between the bars, he saw moonlight reflected off a great expanse of water beginning some hundred feet below where waves crashed upon rock.

From desert, to a world of water, and now this. Holk shook his head. At least his madness wouldn't bore him while it ravaged his mind. After staring at what he believed to be an ocean for an extended period of disbelief, he turned his attention to the only possible way from the room; the door.

Made of stout wood and banded in three places with iron, it proved quite solid. When it turned out to be locked, he was hardly surprised. After all, why should his madness make things easier for him?

"Now what?"

Mumbling to himself, he wandered back to the window and stared out. "Hello?" he shouted. When no answer returned, he wondered if he would have been more surprised had he received a reply.

He stood at the window staring out at the unchanging waters for what seemed hours. When the sky began to lighten, he came to realize that the windows looked westward, though he doubted if such information would prove useful in his present condition. With the onset of dawn, the added light enabled him to better inspect his new prison, for prison was how he had come to think of this place. Locked door, iron barred windows, if it wasn't a prison, it was close.

His newly brightened world revealed four wall sconces set about the room. Three were empty while the fourth held a two and a half foot haft of wood. As the light grew in intensity, he discovered it to be a torch, unused by the looks of it. Reaching up, he pulled it from the sconce and held it in his hand. For madness, his world sure had the heft and feel of reality.

Clasping the torch gave him a sense of comfort. Why, he wasn't sure, but just having it did much for his morale. Most of his equipment had been lost during the flight through *The Devil's Kiln*. Other than a belt pouch wherein he kept his most basic requirements for survival such as his flint stone and a handful of coins, everything else but the clothes on his back had been discarded. Even the blanket with which he had covered himself during the oppressive heat of the *Kiln* was gone. At least with the torch, he would have light for a short duration once the sun went down. After that…?

Wondering what ravages the *Kiln's* oppressive heat may have wrought upon him, Holk moved to the mirror. In the burgeoning light, he found it to be medium-sized and rectangular. The outer frame looked to be gold with fancy filigree worked into all four corners. Turning his attention to the image in the mirror, he saw how his skin had turned very dark, his lips and the area around his nostrils showed moderate crackage. What a sight his visage had become. It would take some time before healing erased the damage.

Running his fingers over his face, he traced the outline of a scar upon his jaw line, one that he couldn't recall having acquired. Most likely it had happened during, or subsequently after, the disastrous siege.

His mind wandered back, trying to place the precise point in time. Minutes passed as he wandered along memory's byways, moving from the siege, to times before the siege, and to other instances captured from a lifetime of experiences, as one's mind tended to do when not micro-managed.

During an episodic recollection of his youth, Holk realized that his complexion in the mirror had altered slightly. Snapping back to the present, he discovered the face in the mirror looked subtly different than it had but a few moments ago. The sun-fried cracks seemed less pronounced, and the redness of his skin had lightened a shade.

Reaching fingers to again tactilely inspect the damage, they told him the damage remained despite the evidence reflected in the mirror. He closed his eyes, and shook his head. When he looked again, the face in the mirror had returned to normal.

It must be the madness. Madness, after all, often played tricks on the mind. Wasn't that the basic definition of madness? Grinning, he returned his gaze to the mirror to see if the madness would repeat itself. Sure enough, his reflected image began altering after but a few minutes of unrelenting watching.

Holk continued to gaze at his reflection, fascinated as to how far his mind would take this. He tried moving his head to see if the image would follow suit, and it did. After a bit, he began to grow tired of this game. About to turn away, he saw the barest shadows of vertical lines appear in the mirror, beyond the image. Running the height of the mirror, they remained out of focus, looking almost like trunks of trees as seen through a dense fog, only without the fog.

Reaching out his hand to touch the image, he was again engulfed in total darkness.

He groaned. "Not again."

To his surprise, the wall which had stood before him but a moment ago had vanished. Stretching his arms out to the sides and behind him as far as they would reach, he encountered only empty air. The air however, felt different. Slightly warmer and carrying an undertone of something unfamiliar, it didn't elicit feelings of danger, or unpleasantness. Actually, it reminded him of nature, just not anything he recognized.

At least he still held the torch, and in his pouch rested his flint. Now, if he could find a stone to use in conjunction with the flint, he could light the torch and see just what sort of environs his madness had constructed for him this time. A quick search of the earthen floor located a suitable specimen adequate for spark production.

Schtk...schtk.

Twice he struck the flint to the rock, each time generating a bounty of sparks. On the second try, the torch's flammable material began smoldering. A couple soft breaths encouraged the embers to life. As they caught and the fire spread to engulf the torch's head, Holk slipped the flint back into his pouch, took the torch, and stood.

What met his eyes caused him to blink several times as he couldn't believe what they saw. Before him rose a mushroom stalk to a towering elevation twice his height. Atop the stalk, the cap spread wide in a bright red display. Other mushrooms, some even taller, spread out like a forest in all direction. There were a multitude of smaller varieties consisting of the very small, to those that equaled him in height.

Their plethora of stature was equally matched by their kaleidoscopic array of colors. Varying degrees of reds such as the giant one before him, purples, gray, green, and still more; it was as if a maddened painter had been let loose with an endless palette.

"Wow."

Taking in the scene, Holk was suitably impressed by the world his mind had crafted. He reached out to test the reality and found the giant stalk quite solid. Stepping forward, he thumped it, producing a deep tone indicating a dense core. *Yes, quite solid indeed.* Solider, in fact, than what he had expected.

The mushrooms grew in an underground cavern. Overhead, the ceiling arched to a height well over fifty feet. Dirt covered most of a floor that undulated throughout like a hillside in miniature. Rocks were very few, poking from the dirt in isolated communities.

He held the torch high as he took in this latest environment his mind had crafted. Turning to the right, a flash of light drew his attention to the cavern wall beyond the forest of stalks. Intrigued, he moved closer only to find the flash had come from another mirror. Round, small, and most likely made of brass, it felt completely out of place in keeping with the room's mushroom motif. The brass frame held subtle undertones of oceanic waves coursing along the edge. Holk admired the craftsmanship that had gone into its construction.

Unconsciously, he reached out to give the mirror a tactile inspection. Holk abruptly yanked his hand back before it could come into contact with the border. Something wasn't quite right. Hadn't the last thing he did in the previous room was touch the mirror?

Holk nodded. "Yes, it was."

Come to think of it, back in the cave among the monoliths, after escaping the early morning sun of the *Kiln*, he had dug stone from around a mirror too. Dragging memories of a watery room to the surface, he remembered the last thing he did, after swimming across to dry land, was to touch a smooth surface. *Another mirror?* Perhaps. The result of touching that mirror, had delivered him to the room where he found the torch. From there, another mirrored encounter brought him to this room of mammoth fungal growths. Perhaps there was a method to his madness, or at least an underlying theme…the mirrors.

There was really only one way to test his theory. He had to touch the mirror. But dare he? Just because previous encounters had turned out benign, could he afford to assume another would? His hand hovered before the mirrored surface as indecision warred with curiosity. Finally, Holk determined he had nothing to lose. He was mad anyway, right? Moving his hand forward, he felt his fingers touch the mirrored surface.

Instantly, the world about him changed and he stood upon a knoll surrounded by a wide expanse of water. He couldn't help but laugh, for this had to be the same room he had been in earlier.

"Hello!" A familiar echo reverberated back. Holk turned to gaze at the room now revealed in his torch's light. As he had earlier figured, it was an underground cavern. Remembering the area of dry land beyond the water's edge, he sought, and found, where he had emerged from the water.

There loomed the outcropping of rock he had maneuvered around during his spate of blind groping. Not far past that protrusion stood the mirror. Its dimensions matched what he recalled from his earlier experience. "If I touch you, will I be returned to the room with the twin windows overlooking the ocean?" Such had been what happened the last time.

Turning his attention from what he knew, he began scanning the rest of the outer fringe of the underground lake. Could there be more than one mirror? Sure enough, on the cavern wall abutting another area of dry land, stood a second one. It had a silver, oval frame and was much smaller.

Holk gazed at it with curiosity. "Where do you lead, I wonder?" Not quite ready to trust his fate to an unknown, he continued his search of what he consider to be the "Lake Room," but found no further evidence of a third mirror.

He really had no desire to get wet again, but wished to test his theory about the mirrors. Holding his torch high, he entered the water and swam with great care to avoid dousing the flame. He one-armed stroked toward the landing of dry ground and the mirror he had touched the time before.

Upon reaching the dry land, he climbed from the water and approached the rectangular, golden-bordered mirror. Steeling his courage, he marched straight for it and without hesitation, laid his hand full upon the reflective surface.

—3—

It worked!

When two windows, lit with early morning light appeared, Holk grinned. He was back in the room overlooking the ocean. Turning his attention toward the mirror with the golden border adorned with fancy filigree, he figured a touch should take him to the room of the giant mushrooms. With confidence high, he marched straight to it and placed his hand upon the center of its reflective surface.

In an instant, the wall vanished and the forest of mushroom stalks took its place. There had been no feeling of having been moved. One moment he stood in the Prison Room, and the next he was surrounded by gigantic, fungal growths.

Such translocation shouldn't be possible. He had never heard of such a thing, yet he couldn't very well dispute his own senses. Or could he? Madness… *No.* This was all too real. Madness should be chaotic, emotionally taxing, and well, maddening. This had the feel of reality, though a reality with which he had little experience.

Okay, if this *was* real, where was he? More importantly, how could he get out? Standing amongst the mushrooms, a thought occurred to him. If he had entered this, uh, realm, by way of a mirror, then logic dictated another would get him out.

As he pondered his next course of action, his stomach growled. Hunger having been forgotten in the complexities of his current situation, it could no longer be kept at bay. The last nourishment that had passed his lips had been the bird caught back in the *Kiln*. Though having assuaged his hunger, it had been less than satisfying.

Gazing at the red cap of the giant mushroom before him, he wondered if it would be edible. Back home, his wife would use mushrooms on occasion. After a good rain, they would sprout in the forest near their home. Taking in the brightness of its reddish hue, he couldn't recall her using a mushroom of such coloring. Those she harvested tended to be beige or gray.

A quick glance at his immediate surroundings revealed others of a more familiar hue. He didn't know much about mushrooms other than they tasted good in his wife's stew, though he did recall how she commented once on the poisonous of certain varieties.

Again, his stomach growled, insistent in its need to be satiated. With hunger prodding him forward, he selected a specimen that closely resembled those his wife had used having an off-brown coloring. It came easily from out of the ground, a spiderwebbing of small roots breaking off as he pulled it free.

The cap was soft and malleable. Taking a hesitant bite, he found the flavor akin to what he knew. The taste was rather bland, but the texture seemed right. He took a second, larger bite. Once that had been chewed and swallowed, he decided to wait before consuming any more. His stomach didn't care for such a cautious course of action and gave out with a rather noisy declaration that said, *"Feed me!"* Holk ignored it. Should the mushroom prove toxic, it would be best if he ingested as little as possible. *An hour should do it*, he told the vociferous rumblings. If after that time he felt no ill effects, he would eat his fill. A glance around the room revealed many of the small, gray variety that waited to be gathered.

Water he had in plenty, the Lake Room held enough to last him a lifetime. Should the mushrooms prove benign, hunger would not be a problem either. There were still two main concerns which needed addressing; getting out, and light.

Of the three areas; the Lake Room, the Mushroom Garden, and the Prison, only the Prison had any source of light, and that would only last as long as the sun was up. His torch would not last forever. He needed to find the way out, and soon.

Recalling how he had discovered a second mirror in the Lake Room, Holk turned his efforts in discovering if this room also held a second mirror. Giving a quick, cursory examination, he soon found a second mirror a hundred feet farther down the wall to the right of the small, round brass mirror he encountered earlier which took him to the knoll of the Lake Room.

This one was just as small as the room's other mirror, only with swirls of crystals surrounding the reflective area in lieu of a traditional border. Holk admired the craftsmanship of the crystals, figuring it to be worth quite a tidy sum if he could get it back home.

He tried removing it from the wall, but found it to be firmly in place. He longed for the knife inadvertently left behind in the cave back in the *Kiln*. With its blade, perhaps he could have pried it from the wall. Since he didn't have it, removal was a moot point.

Would it take him from this place? Based on past experiences with the mirrors of this place, he figured it would take him somewhere, if not necessarily away. Thus far, the areas connected by the mirrors have been fairly benign. But in the back of his mind lurked the thought that placing his hand upon this mirror might take him some place he didn't want to go. Had he a choice?

This was the only mirror he knew of that he had yet to try. True, he hadn't completely explored the Lake Room, and there was the door that defied every attempt to open back in the Prison Room. Another way might be available, but in each instance, an element of unknown danger would still remain. Coming to a decision to take the chance, Holk reached out his hand and placed it against the mirror's cool, reflective surface.

Instantly, sunlight bathed him as he again stared at the twin windows of the Prison Room. "Why back here?" Musing to himself, he crossed over to the right-hand window and gazed out.

Sunlight sparkled on wave crests for as far as the eye could see. The sky above was a brilliant blue marred only by a few wisps of clouds drifting by on lazy currents of air. No boats, nor any other sign of life, just water. Disappointed, he turned his attention back to the door.

It remained resolute in its desire to balk him. Unable to budge it, he tried placing the burning end of the torch against it. All that did was leave a black mark. Maybe if he had a bonfire going he could burn the door down, but considering the barrenness of the rooms he'd been in, such a course of action lay far beyond his reach.

But was this the only remaining avenue to be tried? He yet had to give every room a thorough look. Perhaps there may yet be another mirror? Only one way to find out. Turning about, he crossed over to the gold, filigreed mirror and laid his hand upon its center.

Immediately, he was back among the mushrooms. A thorough search revealed that the two mirrors he already knew about, the small round brass one that would take him to the Lake Room and the one bordered by crystal swirls that would return him to the Prison Room, were all the room offered. Having already inspected the Prison Room, Holk touched the small brass mirror and found himself once again on the small knoll of the Lake Room.

Holding the torch high, he scanned the walls, readily seeing the reflective surfaces of the two known mirrors, one bordered by a rectangular field of gold and the other a silver oval. He knew that the former would take him to the Prison Room, and the latter to the mushrooms.

As his eyes followed the cavern wall in its trek around the subterranean lake, they lost it at one point when it passed beyond the reach of the torchlight. The area of shadows lasted but twenty feet before the wall reappeared. From there, the wall remained in sight until reconnecting at the first mirror again.

Holk turned his attention back to the shadowy area. If there was another mirror, then it must assuredly be hidden in there. He didn't fancy another immersion in the cold water, but had little options. His torch wouldn't last forever and he needed to discover whether or not the shadowy area held something beneficial, like a way out.

Bracing for the icy touch of the water, he stepped into it and upon reaching a suitable depth, began one-armed swimming; the other being otherwise occupied in keeping the torch high and dry.

Torchlight rolled back the shadows with every stroke. The cavern narrowed to a watery tunnel barely fifteen feet in width as it curved toward the right. Maintaining a steady rhythm, Holk entered the tunnel and followed the curve until the main cavern passed from view. After completing a half-circle, the tunnel's end came into sight.

Not far past where the tunnel continued straight once again, rose a jagged area of exposed rock. It held no flat area larger than the palms of his hands setting side by side, merely a conglomeration of broken rock protruding outward at every angle. Above the rocks, set flush against the wall, was another mirror; triangular with a cracked and time-worn wooden frame.

Will this take me home?

With only one way to find out, Holk swam toward the up-jutting rock pile. The climb from the water and up to the mirror left hands and arms with nicks and scrapes. To avoid the worst of what the rocks could do to him, Holk took it slow. When he at last reached the top and stood before the mirror, he searched it, and the immediate area, for any clue as to where it might lead. Unfortunately, if there was a rhyme or reason correlating the mirror's construction to where it would send him, he was unable to discern it. Feeling like a man rolling dice with everything riding on the outcome, he reached out and touched the mirror.

Translocation, though unnerving, created no ill feelings, nor any kind of sensory anomaly. Holk started out atop the pile one moment, then stood among an array of rock formations the next. Shadows danced around him as a slight breeze caused the torchlight to flicker and dance off dozens of stalagmites and 'tites.

Towers of rock rose from the cavern floor, while others cascaded down from the ceiling. Every 'mite had its 'tite. Some had even grown together, forming complete columns of stone. Small sounds of drip-drip-drip could be heard from all around.

Off to his left in a small, cavernous recess, torchlight was being reflected. Moving around the rocky spires, Holk made his way toward a mirror unlike any of the others. It had a blue, shimmering field that seemed to flow around the reflective surface in a clockwise manner. Intrigued, he came closer and gave the blue border a closer, visual inspection, preferring not to touch it until ready to depart. With a border like that, who knew what it might do.

The blueness did indeed seem to be in motion, though it could easily have been a trick of the erratic light being given off by his flickering torch. Curiosity satisfied for the moment, Holk turned his attention to the rest of the cavern. Since the other areas contained more than one mirror, he figured this one would as well.

He made a circuit of the room, its dimensions being about half that of the Lake Room, and came back to the blue-bordered mirror without finding another. *Maybe the 'Tite Room didn't have more than the one mirror?*

While bolstering his courage to try the mirror, his attention was again drawn to the flickering of his torch. It occurred to him that the breeze causing its erratic behavior had to come from, and go to, somewhere. *A way out perhaps?*

Putting some distance between himself and the wall, Holk used the torch as a guide in search of the elusive egress. Since the flame was being blown toward the center of the room, he moved against the current toward the wall.

He made his way around the stalagmites. Upon reaching the rock wall marking the edge of the room, he came to a confused stop. A breeze could be felt, but there was no avenue through which it could be passing. Placing his hand against the wall's rocky imperfections failed to bring to light the breeze's origin. That's when he realized the breeze was flowing down the side of the wall from the upper reaches of the 'Tite Room. A glance to the upper reaches of the wall and adjoining ceiling failed to reveal the source of the airflow.

If he couldn't find the inflow, perhaps the outflow would be more readily discernible. With that in mind, Holk moved from the wall and allowed the fluttering flame of the torch to lead him. Step by step, he moved toward the center of the room. At ten paces, the flame began fluttering wildly in all directions. Upon reaching fifteen, the flame had settled down but now blew in the opposite direction.

Bewildered to say the least, Holk retraced his steps back to the cavern wall. Once again, and this time taking it very slowly, he inched his way forward.

At roughly the same point as before, the flame was again blown about in every direction. Holk came to a stop as he watched the flame dance. Creeping forward, he again reached a point where the wild gyrations of the flame settled down and fluttered back toward the center of the room.

The room's center was naught but stone and towering columns where 'mites and 'tites had grown together to form columns. He returned to the center, that area where the flame danced the most wildly, and this time worked his way perpendicularly to his original path. Once he moved beyond a certain distance, the flame settled down and was drawn to the center.

He tried it along half a dozen points, and each time, the flame was blown toward the same point of the room. Not the exact middle, but close enough to be considered such. Intrigued and befuddled, he came to stand upon the spot where he believed the air currents converged.

Now, what is it about this spot that causes such a thing? There is no fissure or opening through which it could be drawn.

Holk was at a loss. There was a mystery in that room, one which may very well lead to his deliverance from this place if only he could figure it out. Intrigue and befuddlement rapidly grew into irritation and annoyance.

The walls held no fissures, the floor bore no cracks or other openings, so where...? Raising his gaze, he turned them up toward the cavern's ceiling. *Could it be?* He raised the torch as high as he could. The flame whipped about and the residual smoke emitted by the burning material twisted into a spiral as it rose to the cavern's shadowy heights.

At this point, the ceiling was beyond the reach of the torch's light. Holk's gaze tried piercing the shadows but had little luck. He had heard of such things, boreholes miners would delve in order to maintain a fresh supply of air in the nether reaches. Could this be what it was? A borehole would extend all the way to the surface. Excited and wishing to know for sure, Holk tossed the torch up into the air.

End over end it rotated as upward it flew. Peaking in its arc, the torch at last revealed a dark space crouched in-between three of the massive, rock columns some distance still farther above.

That might be it!

Once the torch fell back and landed upon the ground, Holk picked it up and this time, threw it with every bit of strength at his disposal. It quickly reached the point where it peaked the previous time and continued on. The sound of wind whipping the flame grew in intensity the farther up it went. As it peaked, Holk's hope of an avenue from this place was quickly dashed. The dark area turned out to be another mirror with a bordering of dark red, and where the reflective surface should have been, a black vortex churned.

Holk couldn't believe someone would put a mirror way up there. While pondering such incongruities, he came to realize the torch hadn't begun its descent. In fact, it appeared to be hovering several feet beneath the mirror's black vortex. The torch remained so for several moments before beginning to rise.

Moving very slowly at first, it picked up speed as it drew closer to the black vortex. Unable to stop the torch's ascent, and in awe that this could even be happening, Holk watched as his torch, his only source of light, was drawn inexorably toward, and then into, the black vortex. Being too far away, he couldn't be sure if the torch vanished upon touching the mirror, or had merely been drawn into it. Either way, the result was the same. Holk was plunged into darkness.

"Damn."

Giving out with a stream of expletives that would make any soldier proud, he began making his way blindly toward the wall. As hands passed from one stalagmite to the next, he tried to bring his anger under control. No sense berating himself over the loss of the torch. How could he have known throwing it up there would have resulted in its disappearance?

He couldn't help but think about the difference in how this mirror reacted to the ones already encountered. It wasn't passive, it drew in what whatever happened to be close. That would also explain the odd behavior of the wind that had blown the torch.

Upon reaching the wall, he worked his way around the room's edge in search of the mirror. He would have thought the mirror's shimmering blue border would be discernible in the darkness, but it must not have its own, internal light source.

He went round and round in his attempt to locate the mirror. It seemed he had gone around the room at least twice before his hand finally encountered its smooth border. Bracing himself for wherever he may be sent, he reached a finger out and touched the reflective surface.

Instantly, the darkness was no more. He was back in the Prison Room where light from a setting sun streamed in through both windows. Relieved to no longer be in the dark, he slumped down against the wall opposite the windows and allowed the sun's rays to purge the chill from his bones.

All rooms seemed to connect back to this one, while the only outbound mirror in the Prison Room led to the mushrooms. A hub of some kind? He wasn't sure if any correlation actually existed, but it was worth considering.

Exhaustion and frustration took its toll. He watched the sun as it descended below the window sill. Too tired to do anything about his situation, Holk laid his head back and closed his eyes. His stomach growled, but it would have to wait.

There were certain challenges he had yet to overcome. First and foremost was locating a light source. In the Prison Room, he at least had the daylight, but that did him little good in the other enclosed, underground rooms. Could they even be called rooms? Probably not, but that's how he thought of them.

The only area that held anything remotely organic that might have a chance of being combustible, was the room with the mushrooms. He didn't think the smaller ones would be of much use, but the larger? The one he thumped had felt more solid than fungal, kind of like a tree. He would make that his number one priority when the sun came up.

For now, his mind was shutting down, fatigue taking over. Before realizing it, he was asleep.

—4—

Holk stood with forehead pressed to the bars of the window. Outside, another beautiful day had dawned, a day he was prevented from sharing. For the last two hours, he had looked out over the wide expanse of ocean stretching away to the horizon. Birds there were aplenty, but no sign of people. He wondered how remote this place could be.

A growl disturbed his quiet solitude, an incessant need that could no longer be ignored. He was hungry, yet still hadn't figured out a viable solution to his lighting problem. The only course of action he had thus far come up with was to tear strips from his leggings to use as fuel. But that would be a short lived solution, and over time, would render him less able to keep the cold of his new environs at bay.

Turning from the window, he again glanced to the locked door that had so far resisted every attempt at opening. What he wouldn't give for an axe right about then. The wood, drawn from a very hardy variety of tree, gave up little more than tiny splinters to his efforts. After ripping off a fingernail during his latest attempt at prying a section loose, he gave up trying to use it for fuel.

Again his stomach voiced its need for sustenance. He could put this off no longer. He reached down to the bottom of the legging around his left ankle and ripped off a two inch swath. Holding it in his hand, he contemplated what would happen when he lit it. If he held it in his hand, it would burn him; allowing it to dangle free while it burned would only allow the fire to consume the material all the faster. He needed a way to carry it so the flame would last the longest possible time while avoiding serious burns.

Something in which to hold it...

Catching sight of a torch sconce upon the wall, the idea came that it would be ideally suited for his purpose. After a quick inspection revealed the sconce to be securely fastened to the wall, he turned his attention to the other three. The next sconce tried was just as securely attached to the wall, the third wiggled slightly, and the fourth resisted all attempts at movement.

Returning to the one that wiggled, he took hold with both hands and wrenched it forcefully back and forth. Aside from acquiring a holder for his burning material, the effort afforded him a much needed avenue to vent his pent-up anger and frustration. Back and forth he pulled, each wrenching loosening the sconce from the wall a little bit more. Finally, it came free.

Wadding the swath of cloth taken from his leggings, he set it within the base of the sconce. He then took his makeshift torch over to the mirror, removed his flint and knelt. Using swift strokes he began striking sparks. Following the third strike, he was able to encourage one of the sparks to ignite the cloth. Immediately, he stood and placed his hand against the mirror. The mirror and wall vanished only to be replaced with a forest of mushrooms.

Holk knew his "torch" would not last long as the material was being consumed rapidly. Looking about, he scanned the room for something to add that would keep the flame going.

Unlike a forest of trees, this expanse of mushrooms held no dead material. If Holk would have been less pressed for time, he would have thought it odd. With no ready fuel available, he turned to the large, red-capped mushroom before him. It had the consistency of a tree, perhaps it would have a tree's combustibility as well.

After setting the makeshift torch upon the ground, he picked up a hand-sized rock bearing a somewhat-sharpened edge, and proceeded to drive the rock's edge into the side of the mushroom. His first strike sank in an inch. Using the rock as a wedge, he worked a section of the mushroom's outer skin loose. Taking hold of the loosened piece, he pulled and peeled off a strip all the way down to the stalk's base. Two inches wide and four feet in length, the strip had the consistency of softened leather. A thick moisture oozed from the recently bared area of the bole. It looked akin to tree sap.

His light was burning out fast. Now little more than a small, flickering flame, it had consumed nearly all the material torn from his trousers. Holk quickly balled the strip of the mushroom's outer skin into a loose package, then set it into the top of the torch sconce.

Pushing gently, he pressed it closer to the dying flame. At first, when it came into contact with the fire, the mushroom skin did little more than smolder. But with a little spate of gentle, encouraging breaths, he managed to get it to catch. Darkness rolled back as the flame spread to engulf the ball of mushroom skin.

Sweet. He had light!

Mighty proud of himself, Holk returned to the mushroom stalk and proceeded to remove every bit of outer skin the mushroom held. Using his rock, he hacked and peeled until seventeen separate strips lay on the ground near his flickering torch. By the time the last strip had been peeled away, he added another to the torch as the first strip had been all but consumed.

After that, he set about eating his fill of the little gray mushrooms. Not the most appetizing of meals, it at least satisfied his hunger. He took a dozen with him when he returned to the Prison Room.

For the remainder of the day, he set to meticulously search the rooms of this world for a way out. During his search he used ten of his "mushroom strips" for torch-fuel, all of which proved futile as he failed to uncover a means of escape. Before returning to the Prison Room, which had become his base of operations, he gathered more mushrooms.

Now, as he stood at the window looking out over the panoramic scene created by the setting sun, Holk was at a loss as to what to do. His thoughts kept returning to that mirror positioned in the ceiling of the 'Tite Room. He couldn't shake the memory of how the torch had been drawn into the mirror's black vortex. Could that be the way out?

During his recent exploration, he had sought a way to scale the walls of the 'Tite Room in order to reach the mirror. But the walls had proven too sheer and his climbing skill insufficient. There was no other way he had yet to try. It was either that, or the door that withstood his every attempt to breach. Even using the torch sconce had been ineffectual.

Sighing, Holk looked out through the barred window to a world unattainable. Wisps of clouds went from brilliant scarlet to a deep purple as the light continued to fade. When the first stars appeared and night set to with a vengeance, Holk turned in. Sleep, however, was proving to be an elusive goal. But by the time the moon had risen, and its ethereal light fell upon him, sleep came.

Why get up?

Time dragged by as he grappled with that question. What was there for him to do? Gather mushrooms, perhaps? Take a dip in the lake? Stare out a window? He was certain he would be doing all three before the day was through.

Morning's light had dispelled night's hold upon this world, but he didn't care. When a man is trapped in a place from which he can't escape, it sucks all life from him. If only there was a way out. Correction, if only there was an obtainable way out.

There were still two possible avenues, the door, and the mirror with the vortex that drew in his torch. Neither one, unfortunately, could he avail himself. Hours of early-morning brain-wracking over a way of reaching the mirror and its vortex had birthed no viable solution.

Holk glanced to the window, could see the blue sky, and birds flittering far out over the water. How he longed to be out there with them. But such was not to be. Sighing, he reached for the torch sconce and the strips of mushroom skin that together, would form his makeshift torch.

The skins had shrunk during the night and no longer had the consistency of softened leather. Instead, they felt like tough rawhide. He took hold of a piece in both hands, and snapped it hard. It didn't break. Trying again, Holk was surprised at its ability to resist coming apart.

"This could come in handy." A quick inspection of the rest revealed how each had also become like rawhide. It was definitely an odd occurrence, especially seeing as how the strips had come from a mushroom.

Tearing off another strip of cloth from the right leg of his trousers this time, he set it within the base of the torch sconce. With his flint, he struck sparks and soon had the material smoldering. A few short breaths encouraged it to life, after which he added one of the toughened, leather strips wadded into a loose ball. The dried strip caught much more readily and didn't appear to be consumed nearly as fast as when newly peeled from the mushroom stalk.

During the igniting of the material, the idea came to him that if he were to twine three strips fresh from the stalk, after they dried he would have a very durable rope. He could even secure several strips end to end in order to form one of sizeable length. Such an item would assuredly come in handy.

He glanced to the window. If there was but a way to remove the bars, he might be able to make a rope long enough for him to climb down to the water below. How he would remove the bar remained to be seen. At least this gave him not only a tentative hope of escape, but more importantly, something to do. With makeshift torch in hand, he quickly went to the mirror and translocated to the Mushroom Room.

The tall, red-capped mushroom from which strips had been harvested the day before, had been seriously affected by the loss. No longer did it stand erect and proud. Where it had been bright red and ramrod straight, today it was splotched, bloated and no longer able to support its cap. Bending beneath its weight, the stalk had sagged to such an extent, that the cap now rested upon the ground.

But there were dozens of the tall mushrooms, more than sufficient for him to harvest all the strips required to make a rope, roughly a hundred feet in length. Choosing one of the taller specimens, he used the same rock as before and climbed up the stalk as far as he could go. Once there, he began hacking into the stalk.

Since he planned to weave three strands together, he ensured that each strip removed measured roughly an inch. Together, the tri-ply stalk-rope should allow for adequate grippage as well as making it lightweight.

Once he had completely stripped the tall mushroom, he laid the strips out near the makeshift torch. He added one to the fire burning within the torch sconce to ensure the light would continue, then moved on to the next. It took him a solid hour before he had enough to form the rope.

He was one big, gooey mess when he gathered the bundle of strips and lantern for the return trip to the Prison Room. During his harvesting, once a strip had been removed, a sap-like discharge would begin to be secreted. Unable to avoid contact, it now covered most of his exposed surfaces. A trip to the Lake Room would definitely be in order once the rope had been completed.

Back in the Prison Room, he set about weaving the strips into a tight cord. When he finished the first trio, he tied three more strips to the first, then continued. Each addition added a knot to the rope, but it would hardly prove a hindrance. In fact, since every strip was roughly the same length, it gave him a marker, something to use to gauge length if that should ever prove needful.

The weaving process took much longer than he had thought it would. Where it had been late morning when he began, it was early evening when the task had been completed. He looked with pride upon the rope coiling about the room. Satisfied with a job well done, he relit his sconce-torch and adjourned to the Lake Room for an extended period of washing.

From there, he returned to the Mushroom Room to gather the smaller variety for his evening meal. Upon arrival, he noted how the tall stalks stripped of their outer shell had already begun to droop and splotch, and that the one from the day before had completely collapsed. A pungent odor now permeated the room, and after a few minutes, Holk started feeling a little queasy. Hurrying up his harvesting, he gathered a score of the smaller mushrooms then beat a hasty retreat back to the Prison Room.

Once there, he went to the window and pressed his face against the bar. It took a period of breathing the crisp sea air before his head cleared and stomach settled down. The decomposition of the tall mushrooms after having their skin removed must have put something unpleasant in the air. Tomorrow, when he went to collect his morning meal, he would have to be in and out fast.

Now that his hunger had been satiated with an unappetizing feast of the smaller mushrooms, he turned his attention to one of the narrow windows and its pair of bars that prevented his escape. Using the torch sconce, he struck one of the bars to test the strength of the metal. It proved quite strong. Twice more he struck it, hoping that repeated blows would loosen the bar from the stone which held it in place. The stone failed to relinquish its hold.

When he turned his efforts to the stone, he made little headway. A score of strikes did little more than chip away a marginal area and leave his hand raw and throbbing. The metal of the torch sconce was not constructed to accommodate such use. Each blow did more damage to his hand than to the stone. The torch sconce soon buckled beneath the inappropriate treatment. Holk was forced to give up.

Hopes dashed, he left the window and returned to his place against the opposite wall where he sagged to the floor. The last vestiges of the evening sun found him curled up against the wall, depressed and saddened. He was never going to get out of there, and with the availability of food and water, his imprisonment could be long indeed.

The following morning, the rope was ready; a hundred feet of sturdy, rawhide-like material. He tested its strength by tying one end to a bar and yanking several times. It held up with no sign of fraying or wear. Now, if he but had a way to use it.

Later on, around noon as he figured it, he again stood at the window watching the waves flow across the surface of the water and the birds dance upon the breeze when a dark spot appeared far out on the horizon.

At first he took it to be a bird in flight, but as it drew closer, realized a ship moved across the water heading northward. He shouted and waved, but it was much too far away to hear or see him. But that didn't dissuade him from continuing his efforts until the ship sailed out of sight.

There had been a ship! Where there was one, more were sure to follow. Excited, hope of escape restored, he considered his options for alerting them to his presence. Obviously, unless they were much closer, what he had done earlier was a waste of time. He needed something more spectacular, something which would pique their interest and prompt them to take a closer look. But what?

Fire!

He could make a signal fire. Doing it during the day would have little affect, but at night? From as high above the water as his prison stood, it was sure to be seen for miles and miles. Ideas and plans coursed through his mind. The one he settled upon involved using the now-battered torch sconce, his newly created rope, and a whole lot of freshly harvested mushroom strips.

The mushroom strips burned best when freshly harvested, so he waited until the sun was low on the horizon before he returned to the Mushroom Room and began removing strips from the tall mushrooms. The air in the room caused his nose and eyes to burn, his stomach to roil, but he persevered. As bad as the air in this room made him feel, he wanted to be rescued even more.

Once two dozen strips had been torn away, he returned with them to the Prison Room and waited for the stars to come out before implementing his plan. It was simple, really. Secure one end of the rope to the torch sconce. Loosely weave the strips in and around the metal of the sconce, and light it. He would then shove it out the window, allow twenty feet of play in the rope before bringing it to a halt. After that, begin rocking it back and forth like a giant, fiery pendulum. Such a sight would have to draw the interest of any ships in the area.

When the light faded and the stars began to appear, the rope, sconce and strips were all in readiness. All he now had to do was light the small bit of cloth torn from his trousers that was nestled within the base of the sconce, and begin. This he did with a few strikes of his flint. Once the cloth caught and began to burn, he quickly brought the sconce to the window and waited for the flames to ignite the strips. First one then another burst into flames; the fire quickly spread throughout the interwoven mass.

Pushing it through the window, Holk lowered it to a spot twenty feet below. Gently at first, but then progressing to an ever increasing arc, he rocked the fiery mass back and forth.

"Come on," he mumbled as his eyes scanned the inky darkness that overlaid the oceanic expanse. There had to be a boat out there!

Lying upon the floor behind him were enough strips for another two tries. He figured to make three attempts a night until all but the last half-dozen of tall the mushroom stalks remained. No point in ruining all of them at this one attempt, he might be in this place for some time.

Minutes ticked by and no lights appeared upon the water. Holk prayed to the gods that someone would see his signal. Put it down to fate, or perhaps the gods were feeling uncharacteristically mischievous this night, for his signal did attract someone's attention. Or perhaps it would be better to say, some*thing's* attention.

A shriek sounded from out of the night. So animalistic in its intensity, the cry made Holk's blood run cold. Massive in shape, a shadow flew from out of the night and struck the burning mass at the end of the rope.

Holk stood dumbfounded for only a split-second before a second cry broke him from his paralysis. The second cry heralded the emergence of a second shadow from the darkness. He had no idea what they were, gigantic birds of prey perhaps? After the second one attacked his signal fire, he began pulling it back with all speed. He couldn't afford to lose it.

Again, the calls of the nocturnal aviators broke the stillness of the night. As one dove for the rapidly ascending burning mass, Holk was able to see what it was; a bird with leathery wings, completely devoid of feathers. It had a wingspan that easily reached thirty feet, deadly claws designed for ripping and tearing upon each foot, and perhaps the most terrifying aspect of all was its elongated beak. It alone measured three feet in length with a trio of nasty "teeth" at the end, one jutting down between a matching pair that projected upward.

Its taloned feet struck the fiery mass, the resultant, spark-filled collision jerked the rope from Holk's hands. He managed to reacquire his hold after losing a solid ten feet of length. Drawing in the rope again, he once more strove to bring it within the safety of the room.

The second bird emerged again out of the night. *"Hyah!"* he shouted, attempting to scare off the monstrous bird as it swooped in for its attack. But his shouts had little effect. Once more, the fiery mass was struck. This time he retained his grip. Jerking hard, he yanked the rope from the bird's taloned feet and resumed drawing it ever closer to safety.

Twice more the fiery mass was attacked. Twice more he braced himself and managed to retain his grip. Now, it was but five feet below the window. Scanning the darkness, he saw a shadow detach from the greater blackness of night. Midway in its flight, it split into two. It looked like the birds planned to attack in tandem.

Holk failed to comprehend why these birds were attacking the flames. Weren't birds supposed to be afraid of fire?

Pulling for all he was worth, he brought the flame-shrouded torch sconce the rest of the way to the window and pulled it in just as the birds struck. Holk jumped backward, he went one way and the fire went another. With a crash of sparks, the burning mass slammed into the back wall. Holk hit the ground just below the window. Sensing more than seeing the attack, he rolled to the side just as an elongated beak thrust through the window toward him.

A shriek reverberated throughout the Prison Room as the bird voiced its displeasure. Stretching in farther, the bird sought again to sink its trio of "teeth" at the end of its beak into him. Holk rolled out of reach.

"What are you?" he shouted. Coming to his feet, he saw the malevolent glow in the creature's eye. It wanted him. Whether as food, or plaything, it wanted him bad.

A second cry drew his attention to where the bird's partner, *or mate?,* had its head stuck in through the other window. With the twin bars in place, neither were able to squeeze its bulk through the opening. For the first time, Holk considered the possibility that the bars within the windows weren't necessarily designed to keep him in, but perhaps, to keep them out. If so, that put a whole new spin on his situation.

"You want me, huh?"

Moving closer, he taunted the bird only to jump back as the neck of the bird stretched to impossible limits and almost allowed the deadly beak to fulfill its lethal intent.

He waggled his finger at the bird. "Not nice, now. Here you come for a visit, and right off you want to play." A shriek that sent his ears ringing was all the reply he received. He went over and collected what remained of the torch and the much diminished mass of burning strips.

Taking hold of the rope three feet from where it was tied to the torch sconce, he returned to stand before the bird, only this time at a more reasonable distance. The bird's eye tracked the flame.

Holk held it up. "Oh, you want this?" Dangling it before the bird, he almost lost it when the beak unexpectedly shot forward. "Why?" A glance at the bird's partner showed it to be watching the proceedings with keen interest. *Intelligent interest?*

As he rocked the burning torch-sconce, he saw how the bird's eyes followed the fiery arc. When his empty stomach growled its desire to be filled, he got to thinking how right before him stood a hefty chunk of meat. How he wished he hadn't discarded his sword back in the *Kiln*. Despite his lack of weaponry, his mind slowly crafted a plan that might yield results.

Bending over, he began gathering slack in the rope with his other hand. Once he had sufficient length, he rocked the torch sconce away from him. The bird's head swiveled to follow, and Holk tossed the coil of rope around its head.

A momentary flinch was all the reaction the bird gave as the rope draped across its neck. Its attention was firmly fixated upon the fire. Repeating the process a second time, he managed to put a second loop around the bird's neck. This time he placed the burning sconce just out of the bird's reach and slowly drew in the slack until the rope fit snuggly about its neck.

With a rope in each hand, Holk yanked with every bit of strength at his disposal. The neck didn't snap like he had hoped it would. Instead, the sudden jerking of the rope caused the bird to duck out of the window.

"No you don't!"

Dragged off his feet by the bird's sudden withdrawal, Holk slammed into the wall beneath the window. Refusing to let go, he held on.

Shrieking, the bird tried to escape, but Holk had too good a grip. Darting up and down, the bird sought to break free. When the bird's gyrations allowed slack in the rope, Holk quickly tied one end around the bars. It took him three attempts before a suitable knot was produced.

The bird's partner hadn't sat idly by throughout this unfolding drama. Adding its shrieks to the chorus, it joined its comrade in the aerial ballet. Holk thought perhaps it would attack the rope, fortunately though, it didn't think of doing so.

With the one end now firmly secured to a bar, there was but one rope with which to contend. During momentary lulls when the bird's erratic, panicked flight created slack in the rope, Holk managed to wrap the other end once around the second bar. It was easy to maintain his grip now that the bar took the brunt of the beast's efforts. Whenever slack developed, he hauled it in. Bit by bit, the bird was drawn ever closer to the window.

Once he had it within a few feet of the window, its great wings no longer had the room needed to keep it airborne. Unable to provide adequate lift, the bird finally lost the fight and fell. The rope snapped taut. Outside, the world grew quiet.

Holk held still for a minute as he tried to ascertain where the bird's companion had gone. But the darkness was absolute and silent. Figuring it had flown off with the death of its comrade, Holk began hauling up the bird.

It was within arm's reach of the window when the second bird attacked. Having taken a stance out of sight just above the window, it shot its beak through with a blood-curdling cry.

Taken completely by surprise, Holk was knocked backward when the beak struck his chest. Snapping with its three teeth-like protrusions at the end of its beak, it caught hold of his tunic.

Panicked, Holk let go of the rope and used his fists to beat against the side of the bird's head. When it discovered the inability to draw him through the window, it snapped its beak again in an attempt to acquire a better grip. In that instant, Holk used his legs to thrust backward off the wall.

The beak shot forward and narrowly missed sinking its teeth in the fleshy part of his calf. Upon hitting the ground, Holk rolled until he was completely against the far wall and out of reach.

Suddenly, the torch sconce jerked across the floor and slammed into the wall beneath the window. The blow against the stone caused the remaining burning material to fly apart in a shower of sparks. With the bird in the window shrieking at him, Holk watched the sconce move up the wall and out the window. The releasing of the rope had allowed the dead bird attached to it to plummet. Without a secure knot about the bird's neck, the rope continued to slip around its throat, drawing forth all slack until reaching the torch sconce, which was then drawn through the window.

An hour, maybe two, the surviving bird remained at the window voicing its displeasure as to the outcome of their contest. It would fly away for a moment only to return and renew its shrieking. Sometime around midnight it finally flew off and failed to return.

Holk remained where he was against the far wall until the sky began to lighten with the coming of dawn. Even then, he waited a full hour before daring to brave the window. Approaching hesitantly, he came to where the one end of the rope was still attached to the bars. Pausing a foot away, he hollered, "Hey!" When no response was forthcoming, he moved closer. "Are you there?"

Neither shrieks nor aerial displays answered his inquiry. Tentatively, he reached his hand out between the bars until it had gone a foot past. Waving it, he snatched it back. Again, no response.

Maybe these creatures are nocturnal.

That would make sense as he had never before seen their like during the day. Hoping that to be true, he took hold of the rope and found it to be taut. Looking out, he saw how the one he had killed was still attached to it a hundred feet below. Its fall must have been halted when the torch sconce reached the rope looped around its neck and jammed. Birds were already flocked around it, trying to get their share. Taking hold of the rope, Holk pulled it up.

It was a grisly mess that he drew to the window. The carcass was still far too large to fit through the bars. So, after tying it off, he scurried off toward the Mushroom Room, retrieved the rock with a semi-sharp edge, and returned.

It took him some time, but he managed to acquire the first real meal he had had in days. After that, he used the rock and several well placed yanks of the rope to sever the bird's neck. He would have liked to have kept it, but without salt, it would not have kept well.

He put together a fire of freshly cut strips and roasted the meat. The aroma given off as the flames did their work caused his stomach to cramp with hunger.

—5—

Though the meat hadn't fully cooked, it still satiated his hunger in a way the mushrooms had never been able. During his meal, he would eat while gazing through the window out over the water. Memories of the day before, especially his fight with the birds, had reawakened the desire to escape this place. The problem of how to affect his escape remained elusive.

He considered trying the flaming beacon again, but thought better of it. To do so blindly, without foreknowledge that it would be effective, could possibly cost him his rope and torch sconce as it almost had last night. Also, the stalks from which the strips were harvested wouldn't last forever. Should he use the last of them needlessly, it could take years before more grew to maturity.

A way out *had* to be possible. There remained only the two possible avenues which he had already discovered; the door that defied all attempts at opening, and the mirror high above the 'Tite Room that had drawn in his torch.

Holk's thoughts returned to the mirror time and again. It seemed the logical way to go; he just needed a way to reach it. The more he considered it, the more the memory of how the torch had been drawn into the mirror by an unseen force kept coming to the fore. Finally, he gave in and made his way back to the 'Tite Room.

Standing in the area beneath the mirror, he felt the flow of air that circulated throughout the room. In his hand he held the torch sconce. Its light failed to penetrate the darkness of the room's upper recesses, but he knew the mirror was there.

He picked up a rock, figuring to test whether the force that drew in his torch had been a one time instance. Tossing it to where the mirror was set in the room's ceiling, he felt a sense of satisfaction when the rock failed to reappear.

It had worked. Now, if he could but find a way up there. He briefly considered tossing the torch sconce up in order to get a better idea of what the area surrounding the mirror was like, but thought better of it. He didn't wish to risk losing it as he had the torch.

Wait a minute…

The beginnings of an idea began to take shape. If he tossed up the torch sconce, it would be drawn into the mirror. What if the rope was tied to it, and in turn, tied to him? Would it draw in the torch sconce, rope, *and* him? If the rope held up under the weight of the bird, assuredly it would have no problem with him.

Excited that he may have a viable solution, Holk immediately returned to the Prison Room. There he collected his rope and all the loose strips acquired the day before. If this crazy plan worked, he may not be able to come back. Stuffing the strips in his belt, Holk quickly headed back to the 'Tite Room.

Once there, he dumped out the burning material upon the floor and tightly secured one end of the rope to the torch sconce. The other end, he wrapped twice about his chest then tied it off. There was a solid ninety feet of rope remaining, plenty to reach the mirror.

Holk took hold of the rope three feet from the sconce. Slowly at first, he began swinging it back and forth. Once he had it arcing sufficiently, did two complete circular rotations. On the upswing of the third, he gave it one final burst of speed to launch the sconce upward. It sailed past the reach of the light. A second later, it fell back into sight.

Didn't do it hard enough.

Catching it, he again moved into position and began swinging the sconce. This time, he rapidly increased the rate of revolution on the second circular rotation, and with a grunt of effort, launched it upward.

"This will make it for sure."

Speeding along quicker than before, the sconce vanished into the darkness. Seconds ticked by and the sconce failed to return. When increasing tension began to be felt upon the rope, Holk gave a cry of success.

With incredible slowness, the rope tightened. He held on with both hands as the pressure steadily increased. When it had tightened to such an extent that he began to feel his feet leave the ground, Holk started questioning whether this was such a good idea. Who knew where that mirror led, or even if he could survive once there?

Feet now adangle, he was being inexorably drawn upward. His rate of ascension could be measured in feet per minute. A snail racing across the floor would have moved faster. But, slow or not, progress was being made.

When it drew him into the inky darkness of the upper reaches, he knew he was close. Holding onto the rope with one hand, he reached his other upward in an attempt to find the mirror.

Wind whipped around him in ever greater agitation as he drew closer to the mirror. When an icy sensation seemed to strike the fingertips of his searching hand, he tried to pull them back only to discover he could not. Panic ensued.

The iciness descended his arm. He knew the mirror had been reached. It was drawing him in. Faint swirls of silver interposed with a deep amber could now be seen. His arm was frozen to the elbow.

Unable to escape it even if he wanted, Holk felt the top of his head go numb. Fear now ran rampant. Caught like a rabbit in a snare, there was naught he could do. The coldness spread to his forehead. At that point, his mind grew fuzzy. Screaming from sheer terror, he felt the iciness reach his eyes. The terror lasted but a moment more before consciousness fled.

Slowly, the mirror drew the rest of him into itself until nothing remained within the 'Tite Room.

Consciousness returned, and with it came pain. Worse than any hangover, his head ached as if fiery daggers were repeatedly being plunged into his skull. Groaning, he opened his eyes. Either he had been blinded by his passage through the fluxing mirror, or where it had sent him lacked a source of light. The later possibility seemed more likely.

He lay there, listening to his environment. To his right could be heard the sound of falling water, the ensuing splashing indicated that a pool of some sort was located nearby. Holk turned onto his belly with the intention of crawling over to it in hopes that partaking of the cool liquid would in some way tame the thunderous pain.

Even so small a maneuver as rolling from back to front increased the pain tenfold. Holding his head with one hand and taking deep, measured breaths did little to still the pounding. Aside from inflicting greater pain upon himself, the maneuver did reveal the fact that his rope was loosely twined about his body. A brief search revealed the torch sconce remained attached for which he was thankful.

The presence of the rope failed to hinder him in the least as he crawled across the stony surface toward the water. He had to be in another subterranean cavern. The musty and earthiness of the air, coupled with the tinkling of the water and the feel of stone beneath him told him that.

Though his head objected painfully to his moving toward the water, he failed to give in to its demands that he remain still. Once at the water, he cupped his hands and drank deeply of the crisp, coolness. Immediately, the pounding in his head began to subside. Not greatly, just enough so he no longer felt in danger of passing out. After slaking his thirst, he splashed water upon his face which further aided to improve his condition.

Feeling better, he rolled upon his back and laid an arm across his forehead. Now able to give in to the pain, he kept motionless for some time. Holk slipped in and out of consciousness, at each reawakening found the pain lessened. When he regained consciousness for the fourth time, the pain had subsided to a manageable level.

Now to discover where it was the mirror had deposited him. In the dark, removing the torch sconce from the rope proved tricky, but not impossible. After it was freed, he tore another strip from the bottom of his trousers and set it within the sconce's cup. He then took one of the dried strips stuffed in his belt and loosely wadded it atop the cloth.

Sparks momentarily pushed back the darkness as flint scraped across the stone floor. During the brief illumination, the small pool was illuminated as well as two stalagmites rising on either side of the water. He was definitely in a cavern.

The cloth ignited. As the fire spread to the dried strips of mushroom stalk, he took up the sconce-torch and surveyed his new environment. It resembled the 'Tite Room in many ways. Stalagmites rose from the floor, yet no 'tites descended from the shadowed upper reaches, which led him to believe the cavern roof must be quite a distance above.

He didn't see a mirror, though since the cavern continued beyond the light's reach in two directions, Holk figured to find one at some point. First off, he coiled the rope into a uniform bundle that he draped over his shoulder and across his chest. He then headed off to see what this cavern held, and what he found shocked him.

Not more than twenty feet beyond the small pool of water, a boot, and then the tattered leggings of what had once been a human, came into view. Pausing, Holk glanced curiously around at the darkness for others, but the remains before him proved to be the only one.

The bones had been stripped clean. The clothing it wore was tattered and torn, as if the man had worn these same clothes for an extended time. Perhaps due to a prolonged period within the mirrored labyrinth as Holk now found himself?

"What happened to you?"

Coming closer, Holk found the skeletal right arm extended above the head, while the left arm lay against the side of the body. From the skeleton's position, it looked like whoever this had been, had died in the midst of dragging himself across the floor. Kneeling down, he gave the remains a cursory look

An empty knife scabbard was attached to the belt. A single pouch rested next to it. Holk opened the pouch and found three small gems, two silver coins bearing an unfamiliar design, and a key.

"Yes!" he exclaimed as he took the key and examined its teeth. "It just might fit." They were of a size comparable with the keyhole in the door he had been unable to open. If it fit...

Excited, he removed the scabbard and pouch from the skeleton's belt and secured them to his. Even though the scabbard was empty, it still might prove useful at some point, like if he should come across the knife that went with it.

Further searching failed to reveal anything else of value. Holk considered building a cairn for the man, or perhaps burying him, but there were insufficient rocks available and the ground proved to be far too rocky for digging.

"Sorry, old chap. But you'll have to remain as you are."

Holk was about to rise when something about the man's clothing caught his eye. He hadn't noticed it at first, but more than one of the holes were vertical slits, such as what would be created by the insertion of a blade. Looking for others, he rolled the body onto its back and found six altogether; four on the main torso, the fifth on the left arm, and another on the right leg. Moving the clothing to reveal the bones beneath, he saw how directly beneath the openings, several of the bones showed tell-tale nicks, nicks such as what a sword would make.

This man had not died from starvation of the elements, he had been *slain*! Suddenly, the cavern felt small and less secure. There were others in this subterranean place, and from the evidence in front of him, hostile.

"Where were you heading?"

A glance to the ground around the skeleton's feet revealed how the stone was darker than the rest of the cavern floor. The darkened area extended in a wide swath for a short distance before coming to an abrupt halt. Perhaps the "stain" was in fact the dried remains of a bloody trail left behind as he crawled.

Holk surmised that where the stain-trail ended must be the point at which one would appear after using a mirror to travel to this place. The man had appeared on this spot, then crawled to where he lay now. Why?

Searching the area where the dark stain began, he noticed a rectangular object not far off. Roughly four inches by six, it bore the color of the rock upon which it laid. Interest piqued, Holk picked it up and turned it over. His face gazed back at him.

It was a mirror!

Its wooden frame bore cracks, and the glass had a slightly silver hue to it. Could the man have dropped it upon arriving? More importantly, would it work just like the wall-mounted ones? A portable, translocation mirror? Only one way to find out; he placed his thumb against the reflective surface.

At first, it appeared as if nothing had happened. But then realization came that he now stood upon the beginning of the stain trail. *It had worked!* The mirror had brought him to this room in the exact same spot as the man. Desiring to test his theory once more, he moved off a short ways and touched the mirror. Instantaneously, he was returned to the beginning of the stain-trail. This could come in handy.

Returning to where the skeleton lay, Holk said, "Wherever you were, you were attacked and used the mirror to return here. Then, you began crawling." He raised the sconce-torch high as he gazed at the floor of the cavern extending outward from the skeleton's outstretched arm.

Following the invisible line along which the man would have crawled, he came to one of the larger stalagmites in the room. There upon the 'mite, were etched three small vertical lines.

"Was this where you were heading?"

Holk brought the sconce-torch close and ran his finger along the three lines. Moving to the rest of the 'mite, he searched an ever growing radius, unsure as to exactly what to look for. Searching first the side bearing the etching, he then gradually worked his way around until having tactually inspected it in its entirety.

When that proved ineffectual, he turned his attention to the cavern floor adjacent to the 'mite. He immediately noticed how three rocks were stacked in a less than natural way, though certain it was meant to appear so.

Two the size of a man's fist rested upon a third that was wider and flatter. Holk moved aside the top two, then lifted the flat rock. A small depression barely six inches deep by five wide was revealed. Within the depression laid one solitary item; another mirror.

"Well, well, well. What do we have here?"

Taking the mirror, he held it up next to the other. They were practically an identical match. The only feature to distinguish the two mirrors apart was a single, red dot in one corner of the second.

Holk glanced to the skeletal remains of the precious owner. "Where did you get these I wonder? And are there more?" Curious as to where the mirror with the red dot led, he placed his thumb upon its mirrored surface. When twin windows filled with the light of day appeared before him, Holk gave a whoop and holler. He was back in the Prison Room.

Activating the first mirror again, he instantaneously returned to the Dead Man's Room. Touching the red-dot mirror, he again appeared in the Prison Room.

This certainly beat having to go through a series of mirrors to move from room to room, not to mention how he would now be able to avoid the need for swimming through the underground lake in order to leave the Lake Room. All he had to do now was use the portable translocation mirrors. His situation had definitely taken an upturn.

Careful to not again touch the reflective surfaces, he set the mirrors upon the stone floor. He then reached into his pouch and drew forth the key. "Let's see if this fits what I think it does."

Moving to the door that had thus far prevailed against every attempt at breaching, he inserted the key into the lock. It slid in smoothly. Holding his breath, he turned the key. Tumblers moved, a click sounded, and the door cracked open.

"Yes!"

Replacing the key within the pouch, Holk pulled the door open to reveal a small alcove with four tiers of shelves ringing the three walls. His excitement increased upon seeing the items resting on the shelves.

There were two lanterns, a stack of twelve torches, a small cask, a pile of cloth that looked liked the remnants of a dozen different garments, a bulging sack that clinked with the sound of coins when touched, a score of rotting mushrooms, and a picture of two men sitting in a library before a roaring fire.

Sitting upon the center shelf directly opposite the door was a worn, leather bound book. Next to it were three hollowed-out mushroom caps and a thin stone, three inches in length, whose end had been fashioned to a point. On closer examination, the mushroom caps were revealed to contain a dried substance; one being black, another red, and the third, blue.

Holk carefully removed the book from the shelf and took it back into the other room. He moved to one of the windows where he could take advantage of the sunlight and opened the cover.

The first ten pages were filled with drawings of birds, each having a brief descriptive narrative at the bottom detailing habits, diets, and so forth. The depictions were masterfully crafted and the words flowed beautifully. It wasn't until the eleventh page that the aspect of the book changed.

Instead of pictures of birds and descriptive phrases, the page held writing of a more hurried look, though still crafted in neat, well formed lines and characters. The narrative sounded quite similar to Holk's own experiences since his arrival.

The man's name had been Kieran Grayson, a scriber from Portsmith, a town Holk had never before heard. Kiernan was an avid lover of birds and had been on a three-day overnight to add to his growing catalog of native avians, when he spied something glistening in a pool of water at the base of a waterfall. Curious, he reached in to discover what it was, and found himself freefalling into the Lake Room just as had Holk.

Skimming quickly through the next couple of pages that were filled with a letter Kiernan wrote to his loved ones in the event he didn't make it out, he came to information of a more interesting topic.

...the mirrors allow movement from room to room...

...for some, if you stare into them long enough, it will give you a foreshadowing of what you will find on the other side...

Intrigued, Holk went to the mirror that translocated to the Mushroom Room and stared at the reflective surface. Seconds passed before the barest shadows of vertical lines appeared as a background shadow within the mirror. The lines ran the height of the mirror, and though remained out of focus, looked very similar to the trunks of the towering mushrooms. His face, too, began to alter. Scars from his ordeal in the *Kiln* gradually healed over until his face became as new.

Holk glanced to the book, wondering if it said anything about the alteration of his appearance. Skimming through, the only thing that might have pertinence was a reference to a particular variety of mushrooms.

...the small, red-capped mushrooms appear to have healing properties. Attempting to try them earlier today, the abrasion upon my calf that had been giving me such problems the last two days vanished over the course of an hour. Will have to keep in mind...

This had definite possibilities. But as the journal stated, it only happened to *some* mirrors. Returning back to where he had been reading, he continued.

...two kinds of mirrors. Those on the wall are indestructible. Tried repeatedly to destroy one without producing so much as a scratch. The handheld ones are less forgiving and can be broken. I already lost two, much to my chagrin. Probably an aspect incorporated by the Merchant...

Holk paused. *Merchant?* "What do you mean by, Merchant? Is that someone from before you came here...or after?" Interest piqued, he skimmed through the pages until finding another reference.

...Merchant is wily. There is a price for everything. Managed to get the brace of torches for three of the red-capped mushrooms. Most of the minor things can be exchanged for mushrooms. When asked what the price for escape from this place, he replied 'Your soul of course.' Have to remember to be extra careful when dealing with him...

Further skimming found:

...Merchant talks incessantly about the most trivial details. Discovered that if I remain patient and listen long enough, he'll let slip information that he didn't intend. That's how I found out about Streyan. Saw him once, but he vanished. I believe he has many of the handheld mirrors in his possession. Wish to hook up and partner with him. Maybe together we can...

The Merchant, and now someone named Streyan? Curiouser and curiouser. Searching for mention of this Streyan, he skimmed further.

...almost caught up with Streyan at the waterfall. He was swimming, but when I hailed, he quickly dashed for his pack and vanished. Before vanishing, though, I saw a bulky leather wallet-like item from which he pulled forth a mirror. May be a way to carry the handhelds without inadvertently triggering their latent magic. Have to see what price the Merchant wants...

Several pages after that reference, Holk came across a picture of a bestial creature. Walking upright as a man, it bore the visage of a tusked boar. Twin tusks protruded upward from the lower jaw. Eyes similar to that of a man, it was bipedal and heavily armored with helm, breastplate, greaves, and shield. A curved-headed axe was gripped in its right hand; it looked very formidable.

...Ti-Ocks is what the Merchant calls these hostile denizens of this place. Came across two today, tried to hail them and was immediately attacked. If not for my trusty handheld mirror, my death would have been assured...

Turning the pages, he scanned the writing for further interesting information. Most of it was comments describing various rooms Kiernan had encountered. Some were denoted with a curved blade signifying the presence of the Ti-Ocks. From the number of such annotations, the Ti-Ocks were in more rooms than not. Two-thirds through the book, he came to a drawing of an arch with a starburst engraved in the wall above.

...only place I have yet to search. Been here six months now and have gone through scores of rooms. Had to sneak through a Ti-Ock mine in order to reach the mirror that sent me to the arch. Appeared twenty feet in front of it and was immediately set upon by six Ti-Ocks...

...a week's recuperation and a dozen of the red-capped mushrooms has restored my vigor. The Merchant has been less than helpful of late. He has stopped talking about the Ti-Ocks, a fact I take to mean I am close to escape. He has made repeated offers for my soul, says he has a "quota" and I am just being obstinate. If my situation wasn't so dire, I would have laughed...

...going to try and see what's on the other side of the arch. I'm leaving everything in the storage room and taking but one mirror. With any luck, I'll be home soon...

That was the last entry.

The Ti-Ocks must have cut him to shreds when he tried making it through the arch. That would explain the wounds on the skeletal remains, and the fact that Kiernan had been crawling toward the other mirror. He had been trying to reach the mirror stashed beneath the rock next to the stalagmite and return to the Prison Room. The decomposed mass upon the storeroom shelf had probably been his cache of those red-capped, healing mushrooms.

Gazing at the arch, Holk now had a goal. But where the scribe had been cut down, Holk would not be so readily overcome. Maybe if he can find this Merchant, he could barter for a sword. And what of Streyan? What information might he know concerning the Ti-Ocks and the arch?

Making himself comfortable, Holk settled in beneath the window and returned to the beginning of the journal. Somewhere within these pages, he hoped to discover the whereabouts of the Merchant, the Arch, and anything else that would prove vital in his bid for escape.

—**6**—

Further reading failed to divulge the exact route through the maze of mirrors either to the Merchant, or the Arch of the Ti-Ocks as he began to think of it. Kiernan's journal hadn't been written for others, but for the scribe's own use. Information that would have proven useful to Holk, Kiernan must have felt unworthy to note.

The journal had made it very clear that he was entrapped within a vast labyrinthine maze of some scope. Kiernan himself had been six months in trying to find a way out before the lethality of the place consumed him. Holk vowed that he would affect his escape before meeting such a fate, and within a substantially refined timeframe.

Before heading out to explore, Holk deposited his strip-rope, the spare strips he had been using for fuel, and the torch sconce within the small storage room. The lanterns held a small amount of oil, which he augmented with oil found within the small cask. One of the lanterns was a regular glass oil lamp that provided illumination through all four sides. The other was a hooded lantern with a bull's-eye opening that could be closed so as to prevent any light from escaping. He took the bull's-eye lantern.

He also used two cloth scraps located within the storage room to wrap his portable mirrors. Without the cloth, he ran the risk of inadvertently triggering their translocation properties.

With journal in hand, he left the storage room, shut the door and locked it. The key he deposited within his pouch alongside his flint. He lit the wick and then adjourned to the Mushroom Room. Once there, he harvested one of the little red-capped mushrooms Kiernan had stated held healing properties. Popping it within his mouth, the first bite produced a euphoric feeling that radiated outward through his tissues, bringing an ease to the aches that plagued him. Two more, and he felt better than he had since that fateful day he and his comrades had fled into the *Kiln*.

The small red-capped mushrooms grew in great numbers, and before he left, eight found their way into his pack. He planned to make it a point to always have a few with him. From there, he used the small, wooden-bordered mirror, the one without the red dot, and translocated to Kiernan's Room.

Coming to stand next to the scriber's remains, he said, "You may not have made it out, but together, we'll win through. When I make it out, I'll do my best to find your family and let them know what happened." He then took up the lantern and began searching the room for the mirror that had to be there. Sure enough, he found one at the tail end of the cavern.

A full length mirror with a narrow, iron border, it was by far the largest mirror yet encountered. Holk took a moment to gaze upon his features and found that the remnants of his experience in the Kiln had been removed by the mushrooms.

"Now, let's see if you'll tell me anything about where you go."

He kept his gaze fixed unblinkingly upon the mirror. When after a full two minutes the image failed to alter, he figured this to be one that showed nothing. Reaching out, he touched the mirror.

Instantly, he was assailed by oppressive heat. The air was hot, but not painfully so. A vaporous cloud of steam filled the room. He had been brought to another cavern, of that there could be no doubt, though it lacked the stalactites and 'mites of previous rooms. Much narrower than the others, it couldn't have been more than ten feet wide. Droplets of water fell from the cavern's roof only to vaporize in a hiss of steam upon striking the floor. Seeing the water's reaction made him aware that his feet were growing uncomfortably hot.

Behind him, the cavern came to an abrupt end while the way before him extended farther into the steam. Moving ahead, he stepped quickly as the discomfort his feet felt increased.

The tunnel continued only a short distance before dead-ending at a much wider area. Two mirrors were discovered; a circular one with a gold frame on the wall to his right, and a silver-framed, squarish mirror to the left.

He entered the wider expanse and stepped quickly to the mirror to the right. His eye caught sight of two red, horizontal lines painted upon the rock alongside the mirror. Curious to see if the other mirror might have similar markings, he moved to the silver-framed, squarish one and discovered no markings of any kind.

Holk was fairly certain that it had been Kiernan who had placed the markings near the gold-framed mirror, for there had been three such lines etched upon the stalagmite signifying the location of the second, handheld mirror he had found. Yet the question remained, what did this marking signify? Was it a warning, or maybe a trail marker of some kind? There had to be something special about it, or why mark it at all. Holk decided to see where the marked mirror led.

After removing and holding at the ready the handheld mirror that would take him to the Prison Room, he reached out and touched the one on the wall. The heat vanished and was replaced by a warm, yet somewhat cooler, humid environment.

He had been taken to another cave. Sunlight streamed in through a large opening less than a dozen paces away. From beyond came twitterings of birds and the rustle of wind-blown leaves. *The way out!* Moving to the mouth of the cave, he took in the panoramic view.

The cave resided upon a hill overlooking a valley. Trees occluded a valley floor that stretched for miles with towering cliffs bordering it on either side. Excitement surged within him as he realized he had found the way from his imprisonment. A split-second later, his exuberance fled as experience gleaned from a lifetime of military service screamed that this was far *too* easy. Kiernan had to have discovered this way from the maze, after all it was but two mirrors removed from where Holk had found his body. Yet, the scribe had failed to make good his escape.

Pausing near the opening, he searched the journal for any mention of a forested valley, but failed to find any. The mirror that brought him there had been marked with two lines, as a warning perhaps? The panoramic view suddenly became a lot less enticing. What danger might lurk within that canopy of trees? Did he have a choice but to brave the unknown? This may very well be the only way to win his freedom.

He couldn't turn his back on this chance. Stepping forward, he maintained the highest level of awareness. From the cave entrance, the hillside dropped at a steep angle for well over fifty feet before reaching the tree line. Holk took it carefully.

Five paces from the opening, a sparkle from his right drew his attention to where another mirror lay partially exposed upon the stone wall some distance from the cave entrance. All but a forearm's length was encased within the rock, the border glistened silvery in the sunlight.

After casting a quick look to his surroundings, he quickly made his way to the mirror. Just as the one before, this mirror also had a pair of red, horizontal lines painted alongside it upon a prominent outcropping.

Holk shook his head. "Not this time."

Unwilling to take the chance of again becoming entrapped, Holk turned his back on it. Freedom lay in the woods, not through another mirror. Stepping forth, he started down the hill toward the trees, ever alert for the sudden appearance of danger.

What he really needed was a weapon of some kind. Searching the forest's edge, he spied a fallen tree and made his way toward it. A few well placed blows with his foot succeeded in breaking off a limb that would be suitable, barely, as a staff. It took several minutes to trim the extra branches from it, but when it was done, he held a seven foot staff that was only slightly gnarled and bent. Though not his preferred weapon, he was not completely without skill in its use.

From the tree, he entered the woods and set out for the far edge of the valley. It would most likely take him a couple hours to forge through the dense underbrush. By the position of the sun, he should clear the valley before nightfall.

Ten minutes into the trees, a sense of foreboding settled over him. At first he was unsure of the cause, but then came to realize that the sounds of the forest had died. Birds no longer sang, and the wind-blown rustle of leaves in the boughs above had stilled.

Holk paused by the side of a gnarled, old oak. Cocking his head to the side, he sought even the slightest trace of sound. All he heard was his own breath and the beating of his heart, such was the stillness of the forest.

Shaking off the uneasy feeling, he attributed it to time spent in the caves and continued on. Not far from the oak tree, displayed between the two halves of a tree split by lightning, stretched a leathery tapestry adorned with many oddly shaped bones. Holk came to an immediate halt.

The sight of the object before him gave him pause. Scanning the trees, he sought the presence of others. Upon failing to detect any, he went to investigate the tapestry, though it could only be considered a tapestry in the broadest of terms. Closer examination revealed it to be made from a skin of some kind. The bones weren't just attached to it, rather, they looked to be an integral part of the construction.

Wary in the extreme, Holk came to stand directly in front of the split trunk supporting the unusual item. After casting a quick glance to the quiet forest about him, he moved the end of his staff toward it. Before it could come into contact, a ripple coursed through the leathery tapestry.

The movement so completely took him by surprise, that he darted backward two steps in shock. *What was that thing? Could it be alive?* He couldn't see how. It was thin as parchment and the bones were bare of any type of muscle or sinew. Thinking that perhaps the momentary shudder that had rippled through it to be a product of his own over-active imagination, he decided to put it to the test, but not with the staff.

Retreating a good five yards, he picked up a stone from off the ground and tossed it toward the leathery object. The reaction produced when the rock struck was anything but what he expected. Hitting dead center, the rock was immediately enveloped by the leathery object. Letting go of the split-trunk of the tree, the *thing* wrapped itself tightly around the rock as it, and the stone, fell to the forest floor.

Holk hurried to acquire a better vantage point to view what the *thing* was doing. To his horror, he found its outer surface undulating like waves rippling across a pond's surface. The bones moved back and forth, producing a grinding noise as they worked against the stone. For a full minute, he remained transfixed by the sight before the motions of the *thing* stilled. It then unfolded itself from about the rock and expanded back to its original shape.

To his utter surprise, it began rising in the air. The outer edges of the *thing* rippled in rhythmic waves as it rose. Holk had never seen anything like it. Coming off the ground, it returned to its previous position between the two halves of the split trunk. Reattaching itself, it grew still.

Seconds passed as he kept watch upon the *thing*. When it looked as if no further movements were imminent, Holk cautiously made his way to where the rock lay on the ground. Holding the end of his staff out toward the *thing* in the event it made any sudden movement in his direction, he alternated the focus of his gaze between where the *thing* sat in the crook of the split tree, and the rock on the ground.

As he drew closer, he saw where pockmarks scored the surface of the stone that hadn't been there before. Making sure the *thing* remained in its position, he knelt next to the rock and examined it more closely.

An unpleasant odor wafted up from the rock that caused his nose to wrinkle in distaste and his sinuses to burn. "Gah!" he exclaimed as he back-stepped quickly away. He didn't stop until the noxious scent could no longer be detected.

Holk turned an uneasy gaze upon the *thing*. "What are you?" But an even more important question plaguing him was whether or not it was alone in the forest. He scanned the nearby trees and turned up a second one attached between a bush and a fallen log; a third was positioned high in another tree. Altogether, he found six more of the *things*. To his horror, he found one lying prone upon the ground not far from where he had entered this part of the forest. Had his path taken him but two feet more to the right, it would have...

A shudder coursed its way through him at the thought of his foot being treated as had the rock. That which would leave pockmarks upon stone, would assuredly have ruined his flesh. Holk was beginning to reconsider the wisdom of trying to escape along this particular route.

Movement off to his right drew his attention to a seventh *thing* floating among the trees. Still fifteen feet away, it didn't look as if it was heading in his direction, merely floating along. Deeper in the forest, another came into view.

He could now understand why Kiernan had not fled this way. They were everywhere. Better to take his chances back in the underground rooms, than to attempt to go any farther. Turning about, he came to a sudden halt. One of floaters was en route toward him and was less than a foot away.

Instinctively he struck out with the staff. When it struck, the *thing* wrapped itself around the staff's end and began working on it as the previous one had the rock. Its body spread along the wooden length, coming ever closer to where Holk held it. Unwilling to surrender his weapon, he slammed the *thing*-covered end against the bole of the tree.

Upon impact, an intense waft of odor, similar to what he had smelled when examining the rock, exploded into the air. The *thing* failed to relinquish its hold. ***Whack!*** He again slammed the end of the staff against the tree. The subsequent discharge of odor from the *thing* made his eyes water and burn. It remained firmly attached to the staff.

Movement from around him brought home the sudden change in the gravity of his situation. Dozens of *things* were now airborne and making their way directly toward him. One floated in the air between where he stood, and the cave.

Holk tossed the staff toward the floater. When it struck, the *thing* wrapped itself around the wood, and Holk raced back through the trees toward the cave.

He easily outdistanced the floaters and they quickly disappeared behind him. Realizing danger was no longer an immediate concern, Holk came to a stop and glanced back to the trees. Several minutes passed before one of the floaters came into view. The *thing* was moving in his general direction, but not in an absolute straight line. It looked as if it was hunting, like a hound that had lost the scent. When a second one appeared behind the first, Holk turned about once again and took off for the cave. This time, he didn't slow until he broke from the tree line.

Though a bit peeved at the loss of his staff, at least it had only been the staff he had lost, and not something irreplaceable like a foot, hand, or head. After putting further distance between himself and the forest, he paused to again search the trees. Several moments passed with no appearance made by the *things*. Satisfied that either he had lost them, or they had broken off the chase, he made his way up the incline to the mirror by the cave.

Once there, he glanced again to the tree line to make sure none of those leathery, tapestry-like *things* were in sight. His gaze roved over the leading edge of the forest, then scanned the treetops. How many of them might the innocent canopy of leaves conceal? He didn't want to find out.

From the treetops, he turned his attention to the hills surrounding the valley. Rising steeply, they would make for an interesting climb should he dare make the attempt. Fighting Ti-Ocks would be much preferable than facing those *things* again. An opponent wielding a weapon he could handle. But those *things* that floated through the air…they made him shudder.

Putting them out of his mind, he glanced back to the mirror. The pair of horizontal markings upon the rock face next to the mirror somehow gave him comfort. In a small way, they meant he was not entirely alone. Kiernan had made those marks, and so the mere sight of them gave him the feeling that the scribe was there with him. Holk reached out his hand and touched the reflective surface.

A dazzling display of light greeted him on the other side. Crystals of varying sizes and colors jutted forth from the cavern walls. Before him, a mosaic of blues, purples, and reds refracted the lantern's light in a prismatic explosion of color. It was perhaps the most beautiful sight he had ever encountered.

The cavern itself wasn't all that big, the lantern's light easily illuminated it in its entirety. To his right loomed a single mirror, bordered by bluish crystals. Another set of red, horizontal lines had been painted upon one of the larger bluish crystals next to the mirror.

Giving the room only a brief inspection to reveal the mirror to be the only one, and that the room lacked any other form of egress, Holk went to the mirror and placed his hand upon it.

The explosion of light vanished. In its place was darkness broken only by the light from the lantern. He stood in a wide hallway of sorts. Stone blocks had been used to form the floor, walls, and ceiling. Before him, the hallway extended past the reach of the lantern; a few paces behind him, it came to a dead end.

Now, maybe we're getting somewhere.

He took a step toward the unknown then came to a quick halt. What if this was an area in which the Ti-Ocks held dominion? Without a weapon of his own, he wouldn't survive against them. Taking a moment to ready the small, handheld mirror that accessed the Prison Room, he continued, but at a much more cautious pace.

Fifty feet from where he had arrived, the hallway made a sharp turn to the left. Rounding the corner, Holk saw a light flickering directly ahead off in the distance. He immediately closed the shutter of the lantern.

Seconds ticked by as he stood in the dark, utilizing every sense in an attempt to discover what may lie ahead. The flickering light he took to be a torch mounted in a wall sconce. But of smells, sounds, or other optical discoveries, there were none. Sensing no immediate threat, he proceeded toward the light.

His footsteps made the barest of noises as he crept forward, eyes straining as they sought to pierce the dark. As he drew closer, the area illuminated by the torch grew in clarity. It did in fact reside within a torch sconce as he had first surmised. The wall upon which it was mounted was of the same stone-blocked construction as the rest.

An object that sat upon the floor beneath the light was quickly revealed to be a plain, wooden table of modest dimensions. The sight of the table gave him pause. Aside from what he had found in the Prison Room, it was the first man-made construction he had encountered. Or perhaps, should he say…Ti-Ock construction?

Continuing forward slowly, ever alert for signs of the bestial slayers of Kiernan, he passed from the hallway and into the room. Though unable to accurately determine the room's dimensions in the limited light emitted by the solitary torch, Holk felt it to be rather large.

No shadows moved, nothing indicated the presence of another. Keeping to his cautious pace, he made for the wooden table. Constructed of plain, time-worn wood, the table was in every way nondescript. Sitting alone, bathed in the glow of a solitary torch, its presence gave off an ominous, foreboding feel.

Holk couldn't shake the feeling, and it grew the closer he approached. When he was but ten feet from the table, an explosion of light erupted before him. So bright was it, that the transition from almost absolute darkness drove needles of pain into his brain. Covering his eyes, Holk quickly back-stepped away.

"Welcome, human."

—7—

"Oh, I am sorry. I did not mean to frighten you. No, that was not my intention in the slightest."

The blinding light vanished and the ability to see returned. What he saw, however, made him wonder if the sudden flaring of light hadn't in some way damaged his vision. For there before him was a sight that he had a hard time reconciling with reality.

It was a man, or at least he might have believed it to be a man had the being before him been less translucent and not floated six inches above the floor. Dressed in bright blue pantaloons with a shirt to match, it boasted a handlebar mustache that extended a good five inches to either side before ending with an upward curl reminiscent of a pig's tail. It wore a smile both friendly and inviting.

Holk gazed at the man with wary trepidation. "Who, or what, are you?"

"To answer your question in its entirety would assuredly take far longer than your frail existence has. Suffice it to say that I am me, just as you are you. Of course, if you are not you, that would still mean that I am me. Perhaps I should phrase that another way."

There was little in the being's demeanor to indicate hostile intention. Though Holk's wariness subsided, it did not depart altogether.

"At this point in time, I would think to say that I am a provider of sorts. Yes, provider, that would be an ideal term. For you see, I provide items that humans such as yourself require. Do you require anything, human? I can supply nearly anything."

This must be the Merchant Kiernan had mentioned in his journal. Holk continued to relax in its presence as the being's rambling nature put him further at ease. "Would you also be known as the Merchant?"

The being's mustache quivered as it assumed a surprised expression. "Why, yes. I have been known to be addressed as such. Merchant, Provider, Shopkeeper, and many others, though I suppose each in their own way describes my function in this place and time. Call me what you will, just don't call me late for dinner." It paused a moment as if expecting a reaction and appeared slightly disappointed that it hadn't materialized.

"Was that funny? Another human I had dealings with once claimed that when used at the right moment, that compilation of words would prove quite the side-splitter. But alas, I must have misunderstood. A human's reaction to laughter stimuli is something that I have striven to understand and perfect, but I'm afraid my skill in this endeavor remains imperfect. You are a strange people."

"So, you could provide something that I want?"

"Yes, absolutely." Moving forward in its excitement, it accidentally floated into the table so its upper torso was effectively divided by the tabletop from its lower. Realizing what it had done, it backed off so to once again appear whole.

"Do you want a third eye? I can do that. Put it anywhere on your body you wish. One human opted to have one placed on the back of his hand so he could see around corners. Of course, he later complained that whenever he wiped sweat from his brow, his eye would sting."

Holk shook his head. "No. I do not need a third eye. But I could use a sword."

Instantly, the table elongated to three times its former width and a score of weapons appeared upon its top.

Gazing at the array of blades, he refrained from touching them as he feared what the being might do should he try. In the back of his mind, he couldn't help but recall how Kiernan had mentioned this being had a quota of souls in need of filling. The exercise of caution would be well advised.

The weapons ranged widely from a paring knife hardly bigger than his thumb, to that of a sword as large as himself that he could never hope to lift. Some were in excellent shape while others were rusted to the point where they would shatter during the first passage of arms.

"As you can see, I offer nothing but the best. I can also imbue any sword with any ability you desire." Picking a curved saber off the table, the being held it aloft as it burst into flame. "A flaming sword could prove most beneficial. Or perhaps, one of the purest adamantine." The flames vanished and the blade transformed into a shiny, black metal. "With this, nothing would stand in your way. It will cut through anything."

And probably cost me my soul?

"What's the price?"

"Price?" the being asked as the saber returned to its original form and appeared back upon the table. "Each has its own price. Nothing costs more than what you can give, I assure you. Everything is within your means."

Looking skeptical, Holk returned his gaze to the weapons displayed before him. "Can I touch them without entering into a deal?"

"Assuredly so. Touch them, wield them, why, even throw them against the wall if you so desire. I have been placed here to service those humans who were fortunate enough to find their way to my room."

Picking up a longsword that appeared serviceable, Holk asked, "*Your room?*"

"So I have come to think of it. I've been within these walls a very long time. Humans come, humans go, yet I remain; but not for long. Soon, I shall be allowed to leave this place and find work elsewhere."

"Why can't you leave now?" Discovering that the sword lacked the proper balance, he returned it to the table and picked up another.

"Providers, uh, Merchants, such as myself have a quota they must realize before the terms of their service have been met."

"And what do you need to fill your quota?"

"Why, human souls of course. I need but two more, then I can move on."

"Well, you'll just have to wait a little bit longer. You aren't about to get mine."

The being took on a sad expression. "So true. You humans are a tight-fisted bunch when it comes to your souls. It's not like they are doing you any good as it is. Can you touch it? Does it feed you when you are hungry? Of course not! Yet each and every one of you hangs onto them as if your lives depended on them…which they don't."

Holk wasn't convinced, but kept his thoughts to himself. Replacing the second longsword back on the table, he took up the third and final one that was close to the length and heft that he was used to.

After sighting down the blade, he held it at arm's length, then put it through several complex maneuvers. "The balance is just a touch off."

"It is?" The being came around the table and peered closely at the sword. "How can you tell?"

"There is too much weight in the hilt."

"Hmmm."

The sword suddenly felt…different.

"How is that?" the Merchant asked as it brought its attention to bear upon its human customer. "Better?"

Holk repeated the maneuvers then nodded. "It's perfect."

Beaming, the being's smile practically glowed with happiness. "Do you wish to acquire that sword?"

"Perhaps. What are you asking?" When the being gazed at him in a calculating manner, Holk quickly interjected, "I'm not giving you my soul."

Waving away the statement, the Merchant shook his head. "That blade, perfect for your needs though it may be, would not require such a price."

Remembering how Kiernan had written that many of the minor items available through the Merchant could be purchased with the small, red-capped mushrooms, he reached into his pouch and removed the ones he carried.

"Will these do as trade?"

Its eyes widened upon spying the red bounty. "Why, yes. I would be more than happy to trade that blade for those mushrooms." Snatching them from his hand, the Merchant quickly gobbled them up.

"I take it you like them?"

"Oh, yes. They are an exquisite delicacy not found where I come from. To use a term you humans are fond of, *they are worth their weight in gold.*"

Holk grinned as he admired the blade he now possessed. But there was one slight problem. He didn't have a scabbard. "How about a scabbard, too?"

One appeared on the table, a perfect match for the blade.

"Do you have any more of those delectable mushrooms?"

"Uh, no."

He definitely didn't relish the idea of holding the sword all the time. "How about another trade?"

The Merchant eyed him quizzically.

"I have an empty knife scabbard. How about we make an even swap? The knife's scabbard, for the sword's."

"I don't know." Eyeing the empty scabbard belted around Holk's waist, the Merchant didn't look too enthused by the deal. "It's not comparable in size or weight." The being turned its gaze upon Holk. "But, seeing as this is our first meeting, and I wish for you to return to purchase further items, I will accept the terms."

The knife scabbard vanished from around Holk's waist only to be replaced by the sword's. When Holk sheathed the blade, he found it to be a perfect fit. "Thank you."

"Always glad to be of service. Would there be anything else you desire?"

"Actually, yes." The being's eyes lit up but Holk held up his hand. "Unfortunately, I have nothing further with which to trade."

"Oh, that is not a problem, not a problem at all. Why, there have been many humans who found their way here with little more than the shirts upon their backs. By that I mean, they had nothing with which to trade, for they often had trousers, boots, undergarments, and so forth. By saying they had naught but the shirt upon their backs, I didn't want you to think your fellow humans wandered around half naked with their, uh...." The Merchant then pointed to its nether region. "...exposed."

"I understand."

"You do? Excellent."

A moment of silence ensued. Holk finally asked, "You said it wasn't a problem?"

"What wasn't a problem?"

"That I had nothing with which to trade?"

"Oh! That's right. There are always ways in which a human can be of service to one such as myself. Having to remain within this room until my quota has been filled allows for little opportunity to gather things that I may wish to possess."

"Didn't you just say you could provide me anything I wanted? Wouldn't that mean there was very little you don't have?"

The being shook its head. "I'm afraid you have developed an erroneous assumption. Perhaps due in part to my inability to accurately understand every subtle nuance of such primitive linguistics. The items I have to barter with are not mine. No, they are most definitely not mine. They have been made available to me, but I do not own them, cannot take them with me when I leave."

"So, you want me to get something for you?"

Shrugging, the Merchant asked, "First, what is it you want? Perhaps a dagger to go with your new sword? Or a whetstone? Swords don't sharpen themselves you know."

Holk produced the pair of cloth-wrapped mirrors. "I would be interested in a leather pouch that would easily carry these." Unwrapping them, he held forth the two travel mirrors.

The Merchant was quite surprised to see them. "Where did you get those?"

"Found them."

The swords atop the table vanished as the tabletop returned to its original size. A leather pouch, divided into eight thin pouches, each large enough to hold one mirror, appeared upon the table. "Would this do?"

Holk picked it up and looked it over. Taking one of the mirrors, he saw how it slid easily within, yet wouldn't come out on its own. "Yes. What do I have to do to get it?"

"Nothing much, really. Merely acquire an item that was lost to me. Or should I say, stolen by a tricky human. Alas, the human no longer survives and the object rests where the thief met his end. All you need do is to go and retrieve it for me. Bring it back here, and this is yours."

"What if I enter into the agreement, but am unable to acquire the object you want?"

"Why, then you are out nothing, other than the ability to gain this wonderful pouch for your mirrors."

"You mean, once I make a deal for an item, another deal for the same item cannot be agreed upon?"

"Oh, you are a most perceptive human. Yes. Once you agree to the terms, those terms must be met in order to acquire the item and no other terms are allowed to be substituted."

"But, I could still get other items?"

Nodding, the Merchant said, "Absolutely. I am not as strict as some Providers. Loose, that's me. Or would flexible be a better term? Your language has too many different words with the same meaning, or similar meanings. Either way, I am much better to deal with."

Holk was surprised at the possibility of others. "How many are there like you in this place?"

"None. I am as unique to these environs as, well, actually, there is nothing more uniquer than myself to be found here."

"Very well. I agree to your terms."

"You do? Excellent, excellent."

"I don't suppose you can tell me where it is?"

The Merchant looked surprised as if the thought hadn't even occurred to him. "Do you need...now what is the word...a hint?"

"At least point me in the right direction."

Nodding, the being said, "You may be correct in that to find the item in question would prove difficult in the extreme without the knowledge as to where it is." Turning about to face the wall, the Merchant raised its hands. An image appeared upon the wall, a tree-filled valley bordered by hills.

Holk immediately recognized it as the place wherein the *things* resided. "In there?"

"Yes. But more precisely..." the image focused upon an area near the center around a series of ruins. "...here."

A building, barely perceptible through the canopy of trees, alternately flashed red and orange. What he could see of it showed the structure to be in an advanced state of collapse.

"You will find the item within." Turning back toward Holk, the being smiled. "Easy. Simply go there, retrieve it, and return."

Holk met the smile with a visage of stone. He definitely didn't wish to return to that forest. While it was true, the carrier for the mirrors would prove beneficial, was acquiring it worth the risk? There was also the consideration of what he may yet have to do before making his way from this place. Should he encounter the Ti-Ocks, battle would ensue. He dared not risk having the mirrors remain loose. They afforded him a much needed escape route that he would be remiss to put in jeopardy. In the heat of battle, they could slip out of his shirt, be inadvertently left behind, or broken. He finally came to the conclusion that the carrier was in fact worth the risk.

"I don't suppose you could tell me what those *things* are that inhabit the forest?"

"*Things*? What sort of *things* are you speaking of? There are many *things* within the forest. Is it an animal, vegetable, or mineral?"

"Uh, not sure entirely. Probably animal." He then described the leathery, tapestry-like creature.

"Oh, yes. I know what you are talking about."

Holk waited for further explanation, but none was forthcoming. "Well," he said after a few moments, "what are they?"

"Do you expect me to give you something for free? Out of the goodness of my heart?" The being chuckled. "Of course, since I don't have an actual heart as you know it, that phrase may be somewhat misleading. But I'm sure that if you take it in the spirit that it was intended, you will understand my meaning. What do you have to barter for the answer?"

"Barter?"

"Well, yes. I am, after all, set here to trade, wheel and deal you might say. Our discussion thus far has been one of minor inconsequence, a lying out of the rules so to speak. I am not allowed to simply *give* anything away, be it information or material items, at least not anything of any worth. And the information of which you inquired would be, I'm afraid, considered as having worth."

Holk shook his head. "Could you at least tell me when it would be best to make the attempt? Night or day?"

The Merchant gazed at him as if considering the question for several moments. "I think telling you that would be stretching the rules a bit farther than I am allowed." When Holk frowned, the being added, "However, if we should enter into an agreement that you would, say, bring three of those delectable red-capped mushrooms when next you stopped by for a visit, I think the broadest sense of my operating guidelines would be satisfied."

"Three of the mushrooms?"

The being nodded.

"Done."

Smiling, the Merchant clapped its hands. "Excellent. Those *things* as you call them are most active during the nocturnal hours."

About to reply, Holk noticed the Merchant's eyes flicked momentarily toward the room behind him. Turning around quickly, he caught sight of a light for only a split-second before it vanished.

"What was that?"

"You really must be more specific. 'That' is a rather vague word and could be referring to almost anything."

Retuning his gaze to the being before him, Holk pointed to where the light had been. "There. I saw a light."

"Oh, that. Yes, that was a light, I believe it came from a sunstone."

"Sunstone?"

The being nodded. "A very rare type of mineral, sunstones possess the ability, when struck, of emitting light that will last for several hours."

"But who was holding it?"

"Ah, that I cannot say. Bound by a previous agreement."

"Was it Streyan?"

"Again, I can't say."

I bet it was. Had it been a Ti-Ock, it would have attacked. Or, could there yet be others entrapped as was he? That was a definite possibility.

"Do you have a sunstone for trade?"

A dozen lumps of rock, ranging from a pebble to the size of Holk's head, appeared on the table before him. Veins of bright scarlet ran through the black, coal-like rock. He selected one that would fit comfortably in the palm of his hand. "How about a dozen of the red-capped mushrooms for this?"

"Twelve? Or are you referring to a baker's dozen, which of course everyone knows would in truth make the count thirteen?"

"Twelve."

"That would be satisfactory."

Holk nodded, then turned back toward where he had seen the light.

"Are you leaving?"

Again, Holk nodded. When he glanced back to the being, it was gone. "But I'll be back."

Leaving the tableside, Holk walked over to where he had seen the light. Not finding any evidence of another's presence, he took out the mirror lacking the red dot and returned to the Prison Room.

—**8**—

Early the next morning, Holk stood at the mouth of the cave overlooking the forested valley. Having arrived just before the sky began to lighten, he now waited for the sun to crest the eastern hills. During the wait, he had sought, and believed to have found, the area to which the Merchant indicated he must go. From this distance, he couldn't make out any trace of the building hidden within the trees. It should take only an hour or so to reach the place. If everything worked out well, he'd be out of there by noon. Once the first rays hit the treetops, he made his way down to the tree line.

He again acquired a staff since he didn't wish his sword to be ruined should an encounter develop with another of the *things*. The image of what one had done to the stone remained very much on his mind.

Along with the staff, he collected half a dozen, fist-sized rocks and three smaller sticks, each roughly a foot in length. Those he stuffed in his belt. Between the stones, sticks, and staff, he hoped to keep any of the leathery, tapestry-like creatures at bay while recovering whatever it was the Merchant had sent him there for.

As he made his way between the forest's outer fringe, he realized for the first time that the Merchant hadn't stated what Holk was to recover. He would just have to bring back everything found at the location, just in case.

The presence of birdsong eased his anxiety, for if memory served, it hadn't been until the sounds of the forest had stilled that the first of the *things* appeared. Considering the way they positioned themselves like spider webs, they more than likely snared anything that happened by.

Even though he felt their presence was unlikely, he kept constant vigil; eyes roving the ground before him, as well as the trees and bushes. During the first quarter hour, his progress remained steady, and he covered ground quickly. Soon, the sounds of the forest quieted and an ominous pall settled over him.

Not long after that he sighted the first *thing*. It had positioned itself between two young saplings several feet from the ground. Holk paused and scanned the area more thoroughly; from the ground all the way to the tops of the trees above. Upon seeing that the *thing* was alone, he made sure to give it a wide berth.

As he continued, others came into view. Some were situated between trees such as the first, while others lay prone upon the ground. There was even one that had wrapped itself about the trunk of a fallen tree. His pace slowed to a crawl as he wended his way among them.

Making his way between two that had taken position among limbs of neighboring trees, Holk couldn't help but recall how the day before, when he had brought the tip of his staff close to one of the *things*, it had reacted. Now, would they react more strongly to a warm-blooded human than a dead piece of wood?

As he made his way past the pair, the leathery, tapestry-like bodies remained motionless. Not even a ripple did they make. Once past, he turned his attention once more to the forest before him, and paused.

They were everywhere. Easily two-score were stretched throughout the forest. All were relatively the same size and color, which struck Holk as odd. Were there no young? Didn't they grow larger the longer they lived? Perhaps the Merchant could answer those questions, but doubted if he wanted to pay the price.

From this point on, he had to plan his route with much greater care. One misstep and he'd be in a world of hurt. Continuing on, he worked his way around entire trees that were virtually encased by the creatures. Swaths of the forest floor were covered with them, and it took some time for him to find a safe avenue through.

Was a carrier for the mirrors really worth this? He was beginning to seriously doubt whether or not he should continue when from up ahead, he saw a dilapidated structure all but overgrown with flora. It wasn't the one he sought, but it indicated that he was close. Steeling his nerve, he scanned the area between where he stood and the structure, found a path, and made his way toward it.

The forest was absolutely silent at this point. He heard not so much as a frog croak, bird chirp, or even the rustle of leaves blown by the wind. The air was still and slightly stagnant, almost as if even the breeze feared to enter this *thing*-infested area.

One broken wall was all that remained of what had once been a small building. The rest lay in an overgrown crumbled heap with only intermittent sections lying exposed. Making his way around the structure, he had to step carefully as several of the things were laid out across the ground. Forced to make a wide detour in order to avoid having to leap across them, he finally reached the far side of the broken wall and continued on to where he saw three more edifices rising from the forest floor.

None were the one he sought. Each lay broken and shattered. Holk began to wonder if perhaps it had been something other than time that had brought these buildings down. Having recently come from a siege, he could very well imagine stone-hurling siege engines raining death upon the long ago inhabitants. Further speculation would have to wait, however. He needed to keep focused on the task at hand.

As he made his way toward the three structures, he caught sight of a *thing* adrift upon a non-existent breeze. Its body rippled as it floated along a parallel course some distance away. Holk gave it little heed since it wasn't moving in his direction, and cast only periodic glances toward it as he continued on his way.

What he had taken to be three, separate structures, turned out to be the remains of a single, enormous one. The *things* were in high concentration in and around the walls, forcing Holk to proceed in a wide arc. So numerous were they, that the actual stone of the building's construction was all but covered. For a fleeting, gut-wrenching moment, he contemplated what he would do if they would, en masse, rise and float his way. He prayed to the gods that such an event would never come to be.

At a point several yards from the remains of the large building, the structure he searched for came into view. Surprisingly, it was not covered in *things* as the others had been. In fact, beginning six strides from its walls, it was encompassed by a *thing*-free area.

Pausing a moment to scrutinize this irregular occurrence, Holk realized that the six pace radius was fairly even around the structure. It was almost as if an invisible, circular line completely enclosing the building had been drawn in the dirt, one that the *things* were unable, or unwilling, to cross.

Moving closer, he threaded his way through the *things* spread out upon the ground. They were quite numerous and twice he was forced to step uncomfortably close to them. One rippled briefly, but otherwise remained still.

The structure was as dilapidated as he remembered from the look the Merchant had given him. About the size of a small house, it lacked one wall yet still retained a third of its roof. As he drew close to the "ring of safety" that seemed to protect the place, he had a fair view of the interior. All that was visible were bushes and trees in and around the rubble.

"This better not have been a wild goose chase," he mumbled. Stepping carefully around the ground-hugging *things*, he passed the invisible line and breathed a sigh of relief. In the back of his mind, he feared that what kept the *things* out, might also react harshly to his incursion.

A glance back at the ground-huggers revealed them to be as inactive as before. Now, to locate what it was that the Merchant wanted. Moving quickly he approached the building and stepped through the crumbling remains of the wall. Inside, he glanced about and was met by a sight he hadn't expected, but should have. A mirror.

Attached to the wall through which he had just passed, sat a mirror barely two feet by three. It had an ivory-like border that looked to have been made from femurs. Whether human or otherwise, Holk couldn't tell.

Remembering the words of Kiernan, he stared into the mirror. At first, nothing happened, but then his reflection began to alter. His hair shriveled against his head and skin began to peel. A look grew in his eyes, one of unremitting horror. When tremors of fear began coursing through him, he turned away.

Sweat had broken out on his brow and it took some time before the mirror's effects subsided. He definitely would *not* be seeing where this particular mirror led. To get his mind focused on something else, he turned his attention to hunting for the Merchant's item.

If it had been conveyed to this spot by a human, and that person had died, then there should be evidence to that affect. It was a certainty that no wild animal had made its way in there and made off with the carcass. The *things* would have gotten to it long before it could have reached this point. So, where was the body?

He used his staff to poke through the underbrush and turn over some of the smaller pieces of rubble, all to no avail. He even got down on his hands and knees to sift through the dirt with his fingers. There was nothing. No bones, no coins, nothing one might expect to be left behind after someone had died. He had risked his life for nothing! Had it not been for the numerous hostile creatures surrounding this place, he would have vented his anger in a more vociferous manner.

His gaze returned to the mirror. If what he was supposed to retrieve lay on the far side of that mirror, it would forever remain so. The Merchant would just have to wait a bit longer. A second was all it took for the fear to once again rise within him. Shaking his head, he looked away and the fear subsided. No, he wasn't about to go through there.

Taking out the handheld mirror that led to the Prison Room, he unwrapped it and touched his finger to the reflective surface. Nothing happened. Placing his hand full against the mirror, he grew anxious when he failed to return to the Prison Room.

Why isn't this working? His anger almost got the better of him. *The Merchant! He must have done something to it!* Trying his other handheld produced no better results. Neither would work. There was nothing for it, he would have to return through the *thing*-infested forest.

Casting his gaze outside the building, he found everything to be as quiet as it had been on his way in. The ground-huggers remained immobile and no floaters made their way through the ruins. Holk returned to the point where he had entered the circle of safety that surrounded the broken-down structure. Finding the path, he carefully threaded his way between a swath of creatures so thickly laid, that it looked like a brown carpet.

The path felt narrower than it had been before, and each step caused ripples to course through the neighboring *things*. Holk had never been so nervous in his life. With at times less than half a foot of clearance, he came perilously close to drawing unwanted attention.

Each step was placed with care. Staff held at the ready, he moved the end toward any of the *things* that reacted to his presence. So long as they were content to do nothing more than ripple, he would keep the staff away.

The narrow path began moving off in a direction other than the way he had come. He was certain that the cave resided at the southern end of the valley, yet he was moving in a more easterly direction. The ruins remained a constant companion, the ancient city stretched farther to the east than it had to the south.

Above, the sun still sat low in the eastern half of the sky, thus he had most of the day before him. Upon reaching an island of safety in this sea of leathery *things*, Holk paused to determine if a more southerly direction was possible. There were areas clear of the creatures, each roughly the size of stepping stones, that dotted the forest floor to the south. However, in order to move from one to the next, he would be forced to step over and perhaps even leap across many ground-huggers. One misstep and it might very well be the last step he ever took. No, he had to keep to the path, at least for as long as it lasted.

Anxious minutes passed as he continued eastward. At one point, he tried the hand-held mirror again, thinking that perhaps the reason it hadn't worked was due to it being in the remains of the building the *things* avoided. Unfortunately, his theory failed to yield results.

When the sun reached its apex, he reached the final structure of the ancient city. Naught but a pile of broken stones, the building lay in crumbled ruin. From that point on, there were only trees, and *things*. The forest floor grew less populated with the *things* and a more southerly course could be taken. Tree-huggers remained a problem, but they were easily avoided. Passing quickly beneath three that stretched between overhanging limbs, he came to a latticework of the creatures stretching throughout the boughs of a score of trees. It had to be the single, greatest concentration of the creatures yet encountered. Easily fifteen foot in height and at least thirty wide, it was truly a fearsome sight.

Holk had a fleeting urge to fling a stone into its center just to see what would happen, but knew such an action could possibly create a situation from which there was no escape. Instead, he worked his way around the *things* and continued on.

For the next half hour, other latticeworks appeared to block his southern path. Time and again he was forced more to the east. After having to alter course for the fifth time due to a high *thing* concentration, he noticed a white structure within the trees ahead. Curiosity piqued, he threaded his way between the tree-huggers and the ever more infrequent ground-huggers to get a closer look.

It turned out to be a stone obelisk. Fairly overgrown with vines, it rose to a staggering height of fifty feet before tapering off to a point. The surface facing him was smooth with not a mark other than those caused by the ravages of time. He worked his way around to the right in order to see if the other sides were equally devoid of markings.

On the far side, there were no markings, but there was a hollowed out, arched cavity in which sat a hand-held mirror, identical in every way to the two he already carried. His excitement at finding it was quickly dampened by the notion that this could be a trap to the unwary. He had experienced enough strange occurrences since leaving the *Kiln* to be wary of something placed so invitingly.

Unlike the structure avoided by the *things*, this one had them in abundance. Over half its surface was covered by them, there was even one in the niche with the mirror. Attached to the right side, it rested less than two inches from where the mirror sat, a distance much less than others that had caused previous *things* to ripple and react. Any attempt on his part to retrieve the mirror would most likely result in awakening the creature.

He considered using his staff to knock the mirror out of the niche, but the recollection of a notation made in Kiernan's journal as to the fragile nature of the hand-helds stayed his hand. If not remove the mirror, then perhaps the creature? Deciding the risk was worth it, Holk picked up a stick from off the ground and moved one end slowly toward the *thing*. Once he saw it ripple, he quickly pressed the stick to its side and watched as it wrapped itself about the stick.

Withdrawing it from the cavity, he flung the stick through the air. Before it even hit the ground, he reached in and snatched the mirror, ensuring to grip it only by its wooden frame. "Got you."

The thought of seeing where the mirror went crossed his mind, but with his other two inoperable, there may be no way to return. It might be best to wait and see if the Merchant had indeed done anything to the other two, and if so, somehow get him to remove it. Holk slipped it carefully into his shirt between the other two.

From off to the side came the sound of the *thing* working on the stick. He glanced to the forest about him, fearing that his actions at the obelisk may have provoked others from their lethargic repose. Fortunately, the forest remained still and quiet. Happy with his latest acquisition, Holk quickly set out on the most southerly path available. Soon, the obelisk disappeared in the forest behind him.

During the next hour, the number of *things* encountered gradually tapered off. No longer having to head east, he kept to as southerly a heading as possible. There were still both ground and tree-huggers present, though the number of the former had reduced to only one every now and then.

To his left, the cliffs bordering the forest rose quite high. They were very sheer and he doubted his ability to scale to such a height. The ground had taken to sloping upward to meet their base. When he happened to cast a look farther up the eastern slope, the sight of movement brought him to a halt. The trees were too dense for him to get a good look at it, but it was definitely too large to be one of the *things* floating about. Besides that, it walked upright on two legs.

Holk came to an immediate halt and ducked behind a tree. Peering around the trunk, he watched as it continued to move in a lateral trajectory. Based on the description of the Ti-Ocks Kiernan had written in his journal, Holk was fairly certain that what he looked upon was one. Scanning the upper slopes for signs of further movement, he discovered the creature to be alone. This was too good a chance for him to learn more about the creatures to pass up.

Dodging stealthily from one tree to another, he worked his way closer to the creature atop the slope. Where had it come from? Where was it going? Perhaps more importantly, *what* was it doing?

Holk worked steadily closer, narrowing the gap marginally with every mad dash from one tree to the next. When the Ti-Ock stopped and knelt, he was able to come to within twenty yards without being spotted.

From this distance, he could easily see the bestial face and pair of tusks protruding upward from its lower jaw. It was heavily armored just as Kiernan had said, and bore a wicked looking battleaxe strapped to its back.

The Ti-Ock used a small hand tool to dig in the ground. From his vantage point behind a tree trunk, Holk was unable to determine what exactly it was the creature was doing. After several minutes of digging, it stood, turned, and headed back the way it had come. Waiting for a bit more distance to develop between them, Holk emerged from behind the tree and followed.

He kept just far enough behind to be able to see the creature moving through the forest. It headed farther up the slope toward the base of the cliff. Holk was pleased to note that as he drew closer to the fringe, the *things* were no longer present. He figured they must prefer the forest's interior.

As the Ti-Ock passed from the forest and continued climbing the slope toward what looked to be a sheer cliff face, Holk noticed that in its hand, the creature held a sack with a small bulge. *Perhaps it contains whatever had been dug out of the ground?*

Holk debated whether to keep following, or close the distance and dispatch the creature. Seeing as how Kiernan noted the two times the scribe encountered Ti-Ocks he had been immediately set upon, Holk held no qualms about taking the offensive. Surprise, after all, was the key to most engagements. His sole quandary was whether dispatching this solitary Ti-Ock was worth the possibility of alerting the others to his presence, or at least the presence of something hostile to them. He doubted if communication was an option. Any attempt on his part would more than likely provoke an attack. No, better to learn about your enemy. Only a fool fights in the dark.

The Ti-Ock reached where the hillside met the cliff face. It then turned southward and proceeded along the rock wall.

Holk kept to the protective shelter of the forest's fringe. Thus far, the creature seemed oblivious to his presence; its pace not having altered in any way. For a hundred feet, he kept it in sight. But when he had been forced to scramble around a tangled pile of vines having overgrown two fallen trees, the creature vanished.

His first impulse was to race up there and discover what had happened. But years of combat experience made him wary of such reckless behavior. Keeping behind the bole of a rather large tree, he searched the hillside for any sign of where the creature might have gone.

Minutes ticked by and still no egress or other methodology for the Ti-Ock's disappearance could be found. Unable to quell his rising curiosity, Holk cautiously emerged from behind the tree and quickly made his way to the Ti-Ock's last known position.

Hand gripping the hilt of his sword, Holk made ready to launch an attack should the creature reappear. As he drew nearer the cliff face, he saw the Ti-Ock's tracks in the dirt. In fact, the tracks were part of a well-trodden path. Seeing evidence of repeated Ti-Ock incursions, Holk knew he pressed his luck just by being there.

The path continued along the hillside for only a few feet before turning toward the rock wall. Holk grinned. There was a crevice, hardly noticeable unless one stood directly before it, through which the Ti-Ock path continued. Moving to the opening, Holk peered around the edge.

It proceeded straight for less than three strides before making a turn to the left. An animalistic odor wafted from the deeper recesses. Holk concluded that it must be the scent of a Ti-Ock.

Keeping still, he cocked his head to the side and listened. All he could hear was the faint sound of air passing through the opening, and of the forest behind him. There was nothing more that he wanted to do but to enter that opening, but knew that to do so could be a tactical disaster. First rule of combat, know your enemy.

Embarking on such an ill-conceived, stumbling-around-in-the-dark plan would assuredly be the height of stupidity. He didn't know where the crevice led, how many of the enemy he would encounter, or what defenses they may have in place. Better to wait until he knew more. He could always return.

After a quick scan to make sure the hillside remained deserted, he left the crevice and raced south toward the cave and the mirror that led to the Merchant via the Crystal room.

—**9**—

"What did you do to these mirrors?"

Upon his return to the Merchant's Room, the being appeared when Holk again approached the old wooden table. The Merchant's salutation had been cut short by Holk's demanding question.

Surprise cut a swath across its face. "You think *I* did something? How interesting. Could you perchance explain what it was that I did?"

Holk brought forth and held out the mirror which led to the Prison Room. "You know perfectly well what you did!" Moving his hand toward the mirror, he touched it as he said, "These no longer...."

As soon as his hand touched the mirrored surface, the Merchant vanished and was replaced by a wall with two barred windows overlooking a watery expanse. The mirror had worked. It had returned him to the Prison Room.

"Damn!"

Taking out the mirror that led to the room wherein lay Kiernan's remains, he activated its magical properties. After quickly passing through the series of wall-mounted mirrors that would take him back to the Merchant, he again stood in the increasingly familiar hallway. Anger filled him as he stomped down its length and rounded the corner to see the Merchant still hovering behind the old table.

"That wasn't funny!"

Its face registered surprise. "It wasn't? *What* wasn't? I had no intention of being funny. How could remaining in one spot be considered humorous? Your kind grows ever stranger with each new interaction."

The mirror remained firmly clutched in his hand. He held it out as he came to a stop before the table. "This mirror didn't work before. Now it does."

Gazing curiously at the mirror, the being shrugged. "I detect no alteration in either its power or its function."

"Look. When I was out in the forest on your wild goose chase, I tried to use this mirror to return. Only, it didn't work."

"Wild goose chase? I do not recall asking you to chase a wild goose. But that would be humorous though, yes? As to the mirror, your assumption about my having affected it in some manner was in error. I can fully understand, given your limited knowledge of just about everything, how you could come to that conclusion." His expression turning quizzical, the being asked, "Would this be considered amusing?"

Holk was anything but amused. "No, it would not."

"Ah, very well."

"What about the mirror?"

"The mirror? Oh, yes. It doesn't work outside you see, only within the confines of our little world here."

Holk gave the being a less than pleasant look. "You could have told me that?"

The Merchant returned a look full of hurt with a touch of indignation. "Did I know that you did not know? Am I to give full discourse upon every possible subject to every human I meet? Such would entail more time than your frail existence could sustain."

"Still…"

Acquiring a smile, the Merchant held forth its hands and the mirror pouch appeared upon the table. "Let us not forget why it is that you are here."

"But, I did not find the item you wanted."

"Oh, but you did. I appreciate your efforts very much. Without your intervention, I could never have reacquired it."

"There was nothing there."

"Hmmm. Once again, your scope of perception has fallen short I'm afraid. Many items of note are all around, yet humans are unable to see them. Yes, I do think that should satisfactorily explain things."

"No, it doesn't. What exactly was it that I was sent to retrieve?"

The Merchant paused a moment as it considered the question. "Such knowledge would hardly set well with you. No, I do not believe you really wish to know. Most humans are not happy about such things. Although, I suppose there is a possibility, albeit a small one, that you are the exception." It motioned to the pouch. "Feel free to take it. You have earned it."

Holk considered if he truly did wish to know, but figured it hardly mattered as long as he was out nothing further, and he still acquired the pouch for the mirrors. He hesitated only a moment while wondering if this would prove to be some kind of trick. Seeing no underlying chicanery evident in the being's expression, he took the pouch.

"As you can see, it is made of the finest leather and constructed by a master craftsman."

He did have to admit, the pouch was expertly made. The three mirrors that had until then been stashed away within his shirt, fit perfectly within the pouch's compartments. There was even a pair of loops sewn into the back which allowed it to be worn upon the belt. He soon had it in place on his right side.

The Merchant waited quietly and patiently during this, but grew excited when he saw red-capped mushrooms appear and placed upon the table. Once all fourteen of the afore-promised mushrooms had been laid out, the sunstone Holk had entered into trade for appeared beside them.

Holk picked up the 'stone while the Merchant happily gobbled the red-capped deliciousness. "So, you strike it against the ground?"

Shaking its head, the being quickly swallowed to clear its mouth. "Good gracious, no. That would be most inadvisable. Chips would fly and the 'stone would in short order be no more."

"Then how do you get it to…"

The being gestured to the tabletop. "Strike it against wood. Wood, after all, is not nearly as rare as the sunstone."

Holk brought the sunstone down hard. Upon impacting with the tabletop, the veins within the stone flared with light. Startled by the sudden brilliance, he dropped the sunstone upon the table.

"It is not hot," the Merchant stated. "If you wish a stone that would give heat, I could arrange for that, though it would entail a much greater recompense than the sunstone."

Holding his hand above the 'stone, he felt the lack of heat then picked it up again. For all intents and purposes, it felt just like a regular stone from off the ground. "How long will this last?"

"The size of the 'stone determines the light's longevity. For one this size, say an hour or two?"

Holk nodded appreciatively. "Is there a way to douse the light?"

"The light, no. But you can drop the sunstone in a bucket of water if you like. Though why you would wish to do so is beyond me. Perhaps this is one of your human oddities I fail to understand."

"No. I mean, can I make the light go away."

"Ah, I see. Now your statement makes a little more sense. To 'douse the light' is your way of asking how to make it vanish." When Holk nodded, the Merchant said, "No. Even if you smashed it into dust, it would still glow for some time afterward."

He slipped the stone into his pack. "I'll keep that in mind."

"Now, in what other manner may I be of service?"

There were many questions Holk greatly desired answers to. Mainly, how to get out of this place, *and* information about the Ti-Ocks. Recalling a passage in Kiernan's journal that intimated the Merchant became less social and communicative after Kiernan had asked about the Ti-Ocks, he kept those questions in check. Inquiring about the arch that the scribe thought may be the way out could have just as detrimental effect on Holk's future dealings with the Merchant, too.

"Right now, none. Just…"

"Yes?"

"If you see Streyan, mention to him that I would like to speak with him."

"Should I meet a human by that name, I will assuredly pass on your comment. This Streyan you wish to meet, he *is* human, is he not?"

Certainty gave way to doubt. *Is he?* "I think so."

"Very well."

Holk nodded. "I think that will be all for the moment."

Taking on a sad countenance, the Merchant said, "I shall wait with great anticipation until our next meeting," then he was gone.

Picking up his lantern, Holk spent a bit more time exploring the Merchant's room. But as before, found only the small wooden table and the lone torch burning above in a wall-mounted sconce.

There was still the other mirror yet to explore in the room filled with steam where the floor had been so very hot. Pulling out the mirror that would take him to Kiernan's Room, he translocated. Once there, he headed to the back of the cavern to the full-length, steel bordered mirror and traveled to the Steam Room.

From where he appeared, he moved quickly through the steam toward the far end and the two mirrors. The one on the right bore the two red stripes and would take him to the Merchant's Room. To his left sat the squarish mirror bearing a silver frame that he had yet to try. Its surface was heavily beaded with condensation.

No marking adorned the slick rock upon which the mirror was mounted. Good or bad, he had to try. Drawing his sword in case it took him to a place of Ti-Ocks, he pressed his hand against the reflective surface.

Instantly, the steam vanished only to be replaced with the cool air of another subterranean cavern. Similar to others he had encountered, it held stalactites and 'mites, and stretched for a goodly distance. His lantern's light revealed it to be deserted.

A brief search revealed but a single mirror. He gazed into its reflective surface for several moments; when no alteration of his reflection occurred, reached out and touched it.

The first inhalation in this new place told him he was not alone. An odor, animal in nature, permeated this cavern. It wasn't quite the same as what he had smelled emanating from the crevice in the cliff face wherein the Ti-Ock had vanished.

Panning his light around a cavern nearly identical to the one he had just left, he saw further evidence that something may inhabit this place. Bones lay strewn across the rocky floor. Lying against the base of one stalagmite sat a portion of a ribcage that looked all too much like a human's. A bit more searching revealed the skull that belonged to it. Definitely human.

Other than slight movements to pan the light, Holk remained immobile. He couldn't help but wonder if there was any real danger. For after all, Kiernan had to have come this way, and the scribe hadn't mentioned anything about a beast. Still, some creature could have made this place its lair after Kiernan had perished.

Off to the right came the sparkle of light being reflected. From the size and shape, it could only be a mirror. Before stepping toward it, he scanned the rest of the small cavern. The mirror was the only one. Keeping eyes and ears alert for the room's occupant, Holk kept to a slow, cautious pace as he crossed to the other side.

Small and round with a cracked and peeling wooded frame, the mirror beckoned. Having closed nearly a third of the distance, he was brought up short by a sound from off to his left. Turning the light, he panned it across the few stalagmites the room held.

Shadows played across the far wall as the light moved back and forth. Again the sound came, but what caused it continued to elude his search. When the noise sounded once more, Holk realized that it came not from before, but from above. Slowly, he angled the lantern so its light gradually illuminated the ceiling.

Sword poised to strike, his heart racing as it did at the onset of battle, Holk was set to defend himself from whatever carnivorous creature he may find. When the light revealed a fur covered appendage gripping the sides of a stalactite, he took a step backward.

The appendage belonged to a rather large fur-bearing, salamander-like creature that had wrapped itself around the descending stone projection. Easily four feet in length, its yellowish eyes gazed from behind a snout both long and wide. Never before had Holk seen a creature like this. When it opened its mouth, twin rows of teeth designed for ripping and tearing were revealed.

"You just stay there and we'll have no problems."

Eyes never leaving the creature, Holk continued to progress toward the mirror. At halfway, the creature shifted its position upon the stalactite to better keep him in view. He prayed there were no more. Every few steps, he briefly moved the light to illuminate nearby stalactites in search for other creatures that may be in the cavern. Assuming it to be alone could prove fatal.

The creature again shifted position. Now lower upon the stalactite, its head rose at an angle as a single eye watched Holk's movements.

The faint sound of a pebble being dislodged drew his attention to another of the creatures off to his right. Half hidden behind a stalagmite, it directed a pair of yellowish eyes toward that which had so foolishly entered its lair.

Returning the lantern's light to the one wrapped around the stalactite, his heart sank upon discovering it was no longer there. Shadowy movement along the cavernous ceiling was quickly revealed to be the creature scurrying amidst the hanging 'tites. It circled around Holk until directly opposite the other one.

Now flanked on both sides, Holk wished he had taken the regular lantern instead of the bull's-eye since it only directed light in a single direction. The sunstone sat in his pack. To access it, he would have to remove his pack and that might entangle his swordarm at a critical moment.

He debated racing forward to touch the mirror, but then remembered his hand-held mirrors in his newly acquired mirror-pack. He had put the one to the Prison Room in the first slot, the one that would take him to where Kiernan's remains lay in the second, and the unknown one found in the monolith back in the forest within the third.

Very carefully, he hooked the lantern's handle on the hilt of his knife, then reached down and pulled back the flap of the mirror-pack. Just as a guttural growl of yet a third creature sounded from behind him, he laid a finger against the mirror's surface in slot one and instantly translocated back to the Prison Room.

I could get to like this. Get in a tight spot, and return to safety.

But that still doesn't remedy the fact that at least three, maybe more, of those salamander-like creatures waited for him in that room. If he planned to use that room's mirror to further the search for the way out, he better think of a way to deal with them.

What about his third hand-held mirror, the one from the forest? He still had yet to discover where it led. *It might be a good idea to see where it goes before I take on the salamanders.* Where it led may just make the whole salamander problem moot.

First things first. He removed the sunstone from his pack and placed it in his pouch where he could access it on a moment's notice. Next, he went to the storeroom and took three torches from the stack of a dozen; two he placed within his pack, the third he stuffed in his belt. Deciding against swapping lanterns, he retained the bull's-eye. Should additional light be required, he could now use either the sunstone, or ignite the torch without undue trouble.

Ready, he closed and locked the storeroom's door. Drawing his sword, he slipped a finger into the third pocket of the mirror-pack and touched the surface of the hitherto unused hand-held found in the monolith's recess.

Cool dampness and the sound of water dripping in the distance filled the small, alcove-like cavern wherein he now found himself. Panning the lantern's light, he discovered one end opened onto a much larger, cavernous expanse.

The smaller cave in which he arrived overlooked the larger from a height of a hundred feet. For a subterranean cavern, it was enormous. As he played the light across the larger to reveal its shadowy secrets, Holk detected an underlying odor in the air, one that was unfamiliar. Foul and smelling somewhat like a charnel house, it set his hackles to standing on end.

It wasn't the scent of a Ti-Ock, of that he was certain. Continuing to pan the light, it soon fell upon a dark mass lying amidst the floor down below. Considering the distance from where he stood, it had to be quite large. The object was too far away for him to adequately make out, but he did notice that within the lower half of the dark shadowy mass, many objects sparkled in the lantern's light.

Jewels?

His first thought was treasure, but it could just have easily been an exposed vein of quartz. Only one way to find out; he had to get down there.

The edge of the small cave dropped sheer for twenty feet before turning into a gentler slope. As Holk sought a way down, he came to the conclusion that there had to be something interesting, possibly valuable, in this cave. For why else would anyone go to the trouble of constructing a mirror that led there?

He didn't relish the idea of attempting to climb down. Instead, he activated the mirror and returned to the Prison Room. Once there, he reclaimed his "strip-rope" from the storeroom, then touched the third mirror to return to the cave.

A jagged outcropping near the drop-off made a good anchor for the rope. After it was secured, he tossed the remainder of the rope over the edge. Slipping the lantern's handle over his knife's hilt, he took hold of the rope and descended.

The descent to where the incline angled less severely went without incident. He left the rope dangling against the wall as he once again took up the lantern and went forward to investigate.

The odor grew in intensity the closer to the dark mass he came. Features clarified. The surface was a strange texture, kind of like fish scales that glistened darkly in the light. Drawing closer, he discerned the fish scales had nothing to do with fish, instead being reptilian in nature.

When that realization hit, Holk came to an immediate halt. *A reptile?* If it was, it was the biggest one he had ever heard of. The body was huge, easily the size of a building. He saw where a serpentine neck emerged from the body, though the head was concealed as the neck curled around the creature's far side.

It had a tail. Like the neck and head, it curled around the far side. But perhaps the most curious aspect of the creature was the wings sprouting from its back. They were large, easily half again the size of the creature. Though he had never seen one, he was certain that what lay before him could be nothing other than a dragon.

Right out of some bard's tale, there before him was a dragon resting atop a pile of treasure. Holk couldn't believe what he was seeing. *There were no such things as dragons!* Of course, he had once thought there were no such things as magic mirrors that transported people from one place to another. Ever since his time in *The Devil's Kiln*, Holk had been forced to re-evaluate what he knew to be true time and again.

Dangerous creatures if the tales were true; temperamental too. Stealing from their hoard was said to bring swift and terrible retribution. At thought of the hoard, he directed the light to the treasure upon which the beast rested; gold, jewels, and many other items of worth such as statues, weapons, and anything else which could be considered valuable. This was perhaps the greatest concentration of wealth Holk had ever heard. Kings were paupers when compared to what lay before him.

Panning the light along the dragon's treasure-bed, it came to illuminate a cache comprising over a dozen diamonds of incredible size. They were not directly beneath the beast, rather they lay loose along the edge.

I might be able to pay the Merchant enough to leave this place.

Greed warred with common sense. He *did* have the mirrors. If the beast were to awaken, a quick touch would see him translocated to safety. Figuring this to be his best chance at freedom, he stepped toward the cache.

No heat radiated outward from the beast's scaly hide. Its sides rose and fell in a slow, rhythmic tempo. Most likely, the beast slept, or perhaps hibernated? Either way, Holk did not plan to remain long enough for it to awaken and discover that it was not alone.

Stepping quickly toward the cache of diamonds, he froze when the beast gave a snort. But when no further sound or movement followed, he continued forward. He came to stop at the fringe of the hoard. Mere feet separated him from the diamonds. Assuredly, these gems would be sufficient to cover the Merchant's price for freedom. Kneeling down, he gathered them one at a time.

As the eighth gem slipped into his pack, he came to the realization that the beast's sides no longer expanded in breath. The only warning he had the beast no longer slept was a twitching of the massive wing above his head. In a flash, the dragon rolled.

Holk leapt backward, barely avoiding being crushed beneath its bulk. Two red eyes stared at him from a reptilian head oddly devoid of horns. Catching his foot on a protruding outcropping of the cavern's floor, he stumbled backward with flailing arms to land on his back.

A deep roar shook the cavern.

His hands flew to his ears on their own accord in an attempt to block the painful sound. Seeing a taloned claw twice his size flying toward him, he rolled out of the way, but not quick enough. Talons brought pain as they pierced side, leg, shoulder and arm. The pain increased tenfold as the claw drew him from the cavern's floor, to a point before a maw filled with rows of dagger-like teeth.

Thief!

The maw opened and Holk knew his death was but moments away. Reaching toward the mirror-pack with his uninjured hand, he wormed a finger into the first pouch and touched the border of the mirror contained within. But when the claw flexed, tearing flesh, his body spasmed with excruciating pain and the hand slipped from the pouch.

Seconds passed in a blur of blood and pain. The next thing he knew, he lay within the creature's maw. In the faint light of the lantern that lay askew on the cavern floor below, he saw the silhouette of the teeth rising no more than a foot away. Terror filled him.

The beast's jaw moved and flung him against the fearful, flesh-tearing array. Knowing it was now or never, he put every ounce of will he had into bringing his hand toward the mirror pack. A finger wormed its way inside. From beneath him, a long tong pushed upward, raising him level with the tops of the teeth. As the tongue moved again, and sharp points pierced his body, his finger touched the mirror's surface.

Instantly, he lay upon the floor of the Prison Room. Pain wracked his body, his senses grew dull, yet he knew if he gave in to it, he was lost. His eyes fell upon the door to the storeroom; within lay a dozen of the red-capped mushrooms that contained healing properties. They were his only chance at survival.

Using his good arm, he dragged his body toward the door then somehow managed to extract its key from within his pouch. Pure agony assailed him as he worked to bring the key to the keyhole. It slipped inside, the key was turned.

The room spun and his vision grew ever more obscured. He managed to get the door open far enough for him to pass. Leaving a trail of blood like a slug depositing slime, he reached the far side and the shelf upon which the mushrooms sat. Reaching upward, he caught the edge of the shelf. In an attempt to rise, he put pressure on the shelf and...*crack...*the wood broke to drop a hail of items upon his already abused body. Some of those items were the mushrooms.

No more strength did he have. It was by sheer force of will that he managed to bring a mushroom to his mouth. He could feel his life quickly slipping away. Five more he managed to ingest before his arm would lift no more. He hoped six would be enough.

As consciousness at last drew to a close, motion in the room beyond caught his attention. A figure strode toward him; armored, helmed, and bore an unsheathed blade. The last thing Holk saw before slipping away altogether, was an armored foot coming to a stop in front of him.

—10—

Sunshine warmed his body. *Sunshine?* The fact that he lived was greeted with no small amount of surprise. He lay in a half-conscious state for some time before the snap-crackle of burning wood brought him the rest of the way to consciousness.

There was no pain. That fact in itself proved remarkable. The last moments before passing out were vague, but that he had been mortally wounded and in great pain remained vivid. He had entered the storeroom in search of mushrooms, but then… his memory grew obscure. Had there been someone else? Armor…sword…*feet?*

Opening his eyes, he raised his hand to shield them from the sunlight streaming through the barred windows of the Prison Room. From his left came heat from the fire; he turned his gaze toward it.

A lad sat upon a short stool beside a ring of stones in which the fire burned. Maybe eleven years old, he wore a ratty old cloak; the legs sticking out of it were barren of covering as were the dirt-stained feet. Unruly locks of blond hair cascaded to shoulder length.

On the ground next to the lad, a burlap sack that had seen better days leaned against the legs of the stool. Worn and frayed, the sack bulged, filled with items unknown. Through a ragged hole in the side, a metallic glimmer could be seen. Unfortunately, not enough of it was visible for him to discern what it could be.

A minute rolled by as Holk watched the lad do nothing but gaze into the fire. It was almost as if he was captivated by its brilliance. When he at last tried to adjust his position to one of greater comfort, it broke whatever spell had mesmerized the lad.

Hopping off the stool like a rabbit scared by a hound, the boy took three quick steps backward then came to a stop against the wall. In one hand he held a handheld mirror, the other remained poised above its reflective surface. Eyes locked on Holk, the lad appeared set to activate the mirror's power at the slightest provocation.

Forcing a grin, Holk nodded to the lad. "Hello."

Remaining stock-still, the boy did not answer.

"I'm not going to hurt you." When that declaration produced no affect, he added, "I promise."

The lad appeared unconvinced.

"You're the first person I've seen since coming here."

Facial muscles moved ever so slightly, but the lad kept his distance.

Holk pushed himself into a sitting position, then had to take several deep breaths to ward off passing out. He held head in hands until the spell passed, but kept one eye pointing in the general direction of the boy.

"Name's Holk."

Once the danger of being rendered unconscious passed, Holk raised his head. For the first time, he saw the mirror-pack strapped around the lad's waist. It was a match to the one he bore, but where his had but three mirrors, the lad's looked full.

Fearing his mirrors had been taken, he sought his pouch and sighed when he felt the three mirrors within. He pulled out the first and saw the twin lines drawn by Kiernan. They had not been replaced or stolen.

"What's your name?" When the lad didn't answer, he took a calculated guess and asked, "It wouldn't be Streyan, would it?"

Eyes widening in surprise, the lad nodded.

So, this was the Streyan Kiernan mentioned.

"Look, I won't hurt you. Why don't you return to your stool and we can talk?"

The hand moved away from the mirror as the boy relaxed a fraction. He remained where he stood.

Holk shrugged. "Suit yourself."

His clothes held numerous bloodstained puncture marks, the skin beneath showing pink and new. Flexing one limb at a time, he discovered tightness with only a minor accompaniment of pain when the muscles stretched too far. That dragon had sure done a number on him. He was lucky to be alive.

Streyan watched in immobile silence throughout Holk's self-inspection.

Once satisfied that all wounds appeared to have been healed, Holk again turned his attention to the boy. Gesturing to the stool, he assumed his most disarming look and said, "Come on. I won't harm you."

The boy failed to make any move to return.

Holk shrugged as if he didn't care, but he did. This was the first person he'd seen since coming to this place. Aside from the fact that it would be nice to talk with another, even if that other was a boy, he figured Streyan could be a great help in his bid for escape. "Suit yourself."

Slowly so as not to spook the lad, he rose to his feet, stretched, then walked over to the window. Outside, the sky was blue with a band of clouds high overhead leisurely making their way across the horizon. A gentle breeze carrying the ocean's scent blew in through the bars.

Glancing over to the boy, he found him still rooted in place. He turned to face him and held out his hand. "Thank you."

Streyan looked at the proffered hand as if it was a viper. He took one step back.

"Look, I am only trying to thank you for saving my life. Where I come from, a man that has his life saved by another is indebted to he who saved him." When his attempted show of gratefulness went unanswered, his ire rose slightly, but he quickly pushed it back down.

"It wasn't me."

The voice was soft, quiet, and took Holk completely by surprise. He recovered quickly. "You didn't save me?"

Streyan shook his head. "It was Kazzra."

"Kazzra?"

The boy nodded. "He came here to finish you off, but discovered you didn't bear the mark."

"Finish me...," then realization hit. "Are you talking about the dragon?"

Again Streyan nodded. "He was upset when you disturbed his lair. Stealing from his hoard called his wrath down upon you. It isn't wise to disturb Kazzra while he's sleeping. He gets cranky."

The gems! Before he even opened his pack, he knew they were gone. The dragon had retrieved them. A quick search revealed none of his other possessions had been taken. So much for buying his freedom.

Holk turned his gaze back upon the boy who had come a little bit closer. "Why didn't he just kill me?"

"Like I said, you don't bear the mark."

"What mark?"

"It's hard to explain. Everyone who enters this place is marked. You can't see it, but it's there."

"And I don't have this, uh, mark?"

Streyan shook his head. "When he realized you were not marked, he summoned me to care for you until you were better."

"But if I had this mark, he would have killed me?"

"Oh, definitely. It is the duty of everyone here to destroy those with the mark."

"Why?"

The boy paused for a moment before saying, "I don't know."

"But you know of this mark?"

"Yes."

"How?"

"Kazzra told me."

Holk thought about that. "Then, that would mean you do not bear this mark either."

"True. You are the only one I've encountered who did not bear the mark."

"Can you sense this mark?"

Streyan shook his head.

"What happens to those that have the mark?"

"Sooner or later, they die."

He turned his gaze to the watery expanse outside the window. Inside, he quietly debated the merits of trusting what the boy said. Finally, he decided to, but would proceed with caution.

When he turned back to Streyan, he found the boy seated on the stool staring at him.

"I don't suppose you could tell me how to get out of here?"

"No."

"Why?"

After a moment of quiet, the boy replied, "I am not allowed to."

"What do you mean, 'not allowed to'?"

Lowering his gaze to the floor, Streyan said, "I'm just not. Each must make their own way from this place without help from another." He raised his eyes to meet Holk's. "Or they aren't allowed to leave."

"Did Kazzra tell you that too?"

Streyan nodded.

"How do you know he's telling you the truth?"

"He is."

"But how do you know?"

"Because I trust him. He's been a friend for many years."

That took Holk aback. "How many years have been in this place?"

The boy shrugged. "Hard to tell. I was three when I arrived. Kazzra found me and took care of me."

"Judging by how old you look now, I'd say you've been here for at least eight years, maybe more."

"Could be."

"Haven't you ever wanted to leave?"

"No. Why should I?"

"Why should you?" Holk moved from the window and stepped toward the boy. "Because this place is a prison, a hole in the ground." He pointed toward the window. "There's a great big world out there waiting to be explored. There are wonders and joys to be found outside this place that you can only imagine."

The emotion that rose in Holk's voice as he spoke caused Streyan to rise from the stool and step back. The lad's hand hovered close to the mirror's surface. Bringing himself back under control, Holk calmed down and gave the lad a grin.

"Sorry about that."

Streyan made no reply.

"It's just that I want to get out of here very much. I miss my family."

The hand moved away from the mirror and the boy relaxed.

"If you can't help me to leave, can you at least answer a few questions?"

The boy nodded.

"Great."

Holk gestured to the stool and Streyan hesitantly took a step toward it. To encourage the lad, Holk backed several paces until ten feet separated him from the stool. At that point, Streyan returned and sat. When he once again looked comfortable and relaxed, Holk posed his first question.

"What can you tell me about the Ti-Ocks.?"

"Not much. I stay away from them. They're mean and will hurt you if they can."

"Do they know the way out?"

"Of course."

"So, in order for me to escape, I might have to traverse territory inhabited by them?"

"Probably. There are many ways out, none of which are without risk. All are guarded."

"Guarded?"

"In one manner or another."

"How so?"

"I don't know. That's just what Kazzra once said."

"Do you think Kazzra would help me to leave?"

Streyan shook his head. "He doesn't like you. You stole from him."

"But yet he saved my life?"

The lad merely shrugged.

Beginning to pace, Holk considered the incongruity that was the dragon Kazzra. Ready to put forth his next question, he was forestalled when Streyan abruptly leapt to his feet.

Snatching his pack from off the floor, the boy turned fearful eyes toward him. "They know you're here!"

"Who…?" But the boy placed hand to mirror and vanished. A moment later, three Ti-Ocks appeared in the room

Three sets of boar-ish eyes turned toward where Holk stood. One gave out with a squeal reminiscent of a pig and pulled its curve-bladed axe from off its back; the other two followed suit.

Shrugging off his initial shock, Holk drew his sword. Ever since leaving the *Kiln*, he had felt like a fish out of water, completely out of his element. But with sword in hand and an opponent before him, all that faded away. He was no stranger to battle. Even though the odds were three-to-one and they were armored where he was not, he welcomed it. The rush of battle was a familiar friend.

The first Ti-Ock swung its axe with more enthusiasm than skill. Holk easily knocked it aside. Then after a quick sidestep to avoid the attacks of the other two, he returned with a slice that created a line of sparks as the first creature's armor warded off the attack.

Spying an axe blade descending in an overhand hack, he dodged to the side. As the haft of the axe passed harmlessly by, he brought his sword up against the wooden handle. The snap and crack as the wood parted produced a cry of success. A metallic *clang* rang out when the axe head hit the ground.

Roaring, the creature lurched forward, but Holk kicked out. Slamming his foot in its breastplate, he knocked the creature back into its fellows. Holk didn't give them a chance to recover. Rushing forward, he caught the one whose weapon he broke with a downward thrust right where the breastplate met the creature's neck. Bones and sinews parted as it sank with deadly accuracy.

One out of commission, he pulled forth his sword and backed up. The other two had recovered and moved to flank him. A series of grunts and squeals were exchanged by the pair.

Not giving them the opportunity to get into place, he charged the one on his right. Shouting, Holk shot forward, parried a sideways slice of the axe, then twirled sharply and caught the creature in the side of its head with his elbow. The impact sent the creature stumbling backward into the wall.

The third Ti-Ock gave out with an ear-piercing, high pitched squeal, then charged with axe raised at a forty-five degree angle.

Holk feinted a move to the right. When the axe shot forward, he dodged back to the left.

Not connecting as it thought it would caused the Ti-Ock to momentarily lose its balance. Even such a small span of time was enough for Holk to exploit. With precision honed through numerous battles, he thrust his blade into the gap just under the armpit, seven inches of steel pierced flesh to sever an artery. As the blade pulled free, blood gushed forth. A kick sent it off to the side as the final Ti-Ock moved to engage.

This time, the creature came at him a bit more cautiously. Axe held before it, he slowly circled to the left as Holk matched it pace for pace. Neither made a move to engage.

Realizing the beast didn't plan to attack, Holk feinted with a thrust. Axe came down to ward off the blow. At the last second, Holk changed the trajectory and ran the edge of the blade along the underside of the wrist holding the axe.

Though the creature roared in pain, it didn't relinquish its hold.

Holk stepped back and grinned. He saw blood welling from the wound and drip to the floor. "Had enough?" The lack of response came as no surprise. "Then let's finish this before more of you arrive."

As if the creature understood what had been said, it squealed and charged. Its axe came forward in a two-handed overhand hack designed to split Holk in twain.

There was little skill in the attack and Holk's sword readily knocked it downward to the side. A fist struck the now exposed Ti-Ock face, sending it stumbling to the side. Holk lashed out and drove the point of his sword into its exposed side. As the creature fell, the blade came free in a spray of blood. The battle was over.

"Streyan?" No reply, the lad was gone.

His first encounter with the creatures had showed them to possess minimal skill when it came to melee combat. This boded well for his chances should further meetings prove unavoidable. Though if there had been more than just the three, the outcome may have been quite different. Using a somewhat clean section of the Ti-Ock's garment, he removed the gore from his sword before resheathing it.

The armor worn by the creatures was decent, if not superbly crafted; merely bands of iron interwoven with cloth which gave it some strength. One breastplate proved to be of a size he could don. Not a perfect fit by any means, but it allowed his sword arm to move freely and didn't encumber him overmuch. A helm was found to fit, though the foul stench coming from within needed to be removed before he could wear it.

Each Ti-Ock carried a belt pouch that had been irrevocably fouled with gobs of rank meat. He tossed them out the window. Further searches revealed nothing of interest, not even a mirror which surprised him. How had they come to be here? And how had they planned to return?

As he gazed upon the dead Ti-Ocks, he considered what he should do next. They had known he was in this room, or so Streyan suggested before vanishing. And that was another thing, how had the boy known they were coming? Thinking back on just before their arrival, he couldn't recall anything that might have heralded their appearance. Somehow though, the boy had known. If he could figure out how to do it, such a skill might prove handy.

But that was neither here nor there. He needed to do something with the bodies. Already, their foul stench was filling the room, and it would only grow worse as time wore on. After a few moments' consideration, he decided to transfer them to the room in which rested Kiernan's remains. He doubted if the scribe would mind.

One by one, he took each Ti-Ock by the hand and used the handheld mirror to translocate to the cavern. Once there, he dragged the corpses to a corner as far removed as possible.

After the creatures had been transferred to their new resting place, he went to the Lake Room and washed thoroughly both himself and the two pieces of armor he had taken for his own.

Clean, and with armor in place, Holk felt like a new man. His recent encounter with the Ti-Ocks had revealed they possessed hardly any skill with their axes. The fear he had felt ever since seeing Kiernan's drawing was no more. He could take them so long as they didn't come at him in any great numbers.

"Streyan?"

Hollering again for the lad failed to produce any better results. There were many other questions he would have liked to pose, but until he came across the boy again, they would have to wait.

The Prison Room could no longer be thought of as safe. Ti-Ocks had come and it would be foolish to assume it was an isolated incident that would not be repeated. From this point on, he needed to exercise caution.

He locked the door to the storeroom, then used the mirror and appeared in the room full of mushrooms. There, he consumed quite a few of the edible ones, then gathered fifteen of the red-capped ones with the healing properties of which three he stashed away in his pouch. Using the hand-held, he returned to the Prison Room where the remaining dozen red-caps went into the storeroom for safe keeping. There might be another incident like what he had experienced with Kazzra, for in a place like this, one never knew.

By this time, it had grown dark and the exertions of the day were finally taking their toll. Despite the threat that Ti-Ocks might return, he remained in the Prison Room to sleep. The benefit of fresh air and a small amount of light from outside outweighed the risk. Settling within the shadows of the darkest corner, he laid his sword on the ground next to him. It took some time, but sleep finally came.

A grunt brought him immediately awake. Two shadows moved in the room not far from where he sat. That they were Ti-Ocks was unmistakable. When one turned, the faint moonlight coming in through the windows revealed its pair of tusks.

Holk remained absolutely motionless as he slowly brought his hand to rest upon the pommel of his sword.

The Ti-Ocks snorted quietly to one another as they stood upon the floor where their brethren had fallen. A *crack* sounded and light flared to life. One of the creatures held a sunstone.

Should he dispatch them? He could readily do so, but such an action might provoke further complications when more of the creatures came in search of these. Keeping still with only his eyes in motion, he tracked the movements of the two creatures.

The light emitted by the sunstone was enough to push back the shadows and reveal him in his corner. If they but glanced his way, the point of whether he should fight would be moot. Fortunately, their attention was being directed down toward the bloodstained stones of the room's floor.

Further grunts and squeals came from the pair. One gesticulated wildly to the other as it gave the longest series of "Ti-Ock speech" sounds that Holk had yet heard. When it concluded, the other gave a short burst of varying-pitch squeals. A moment later, the pair vanished.

Holk couldn't believe they simply left. They hadn't even searched the room. Merely came, looked at the place where the others had fallen, then departed. The more he learned of these creatures, the less he understood them.

The rest of the night passed in uneasy restlessness. Every noise from the world outside caused him to start awake, each time fully expecting the Ti-Ocks to have returned to extract their vengeance, but they never did.

—11—

The morning sun streaming through the windows brought him back to the world of wakefulness. Last night, during periods when sleep eluded him, he considered what to do next. He toyed with the idea of trying to sneak in and make off with more of Kazzra's hoard, but memory of his nearly fatal attempt quickly put that thought to rest.

He could attempt to make his way through the forest. Though the chances were slim, a way to avoid the *things* might be found. Or perhaps sneaking through the crevice located within the walls of the valley wherein the Ti-Ock had gone. It could be that the arch to which Kiernan had made mention might be found therein.

The last course available to him, returning to the cavern with the giant salamanders, seemed the most prudent or at least the least dangerous. Those creatures were a definite hazard to be sure, but nothing compared to a company of Ti-Ocks or a giant tapestry of *things*.

Coming to his feet, he resigned himself to facing the salamanders. Before doing so, he collected four torches from the storeroom. He also took the remaining lantern since the bulls-eye lantern currently rested in Kazzra's cave. Locking the storeroom door, he used the mirror that would take him to Kiernan's Room, then walked to the mirror leading to the Steam Room.

He paused briefly before the mirror to light the four torches, then touched the mirror's reflective surface. Once in the Steam Room, he hurried through the hot mist to the squarish mirror with the silver frame.

Holding the four torches in one hand, he drew his sword with the other then touched the mirror. Instantly, the mist was gone and he stood once more in a room with many stalactites and 'mites…and the salamanders. He tossed the torches in an arc before him across the cavern floor, then set the lantern on the ground behind him. The darkness rolled back as light filled the cavern.

From the far side of the room, the mirror he needed to reach glistened tantalizingly in the torchlight. First things first, he would deal with these creatures. .

He found one among the 'tites hanging from the ceiling. Motion from off to his right drew his attention to where two more lurked. Their yellowish eyes gazed upon him.

Brandishing his sword, Holk gave the pair a come-hither motion with his hand then said, "Come on. Let's do this." But the creatures kept their positions. A fourth off to his left made itself known. After a full minute of each side staring at the other, Holk began thinking the creatures would not attack after all.

Perhaps it's the armor. Could they think I am a Ti-Ock? He was, after all, wearing bits of their armor. He grinned at the thought.

When another minute came and went with no advancement by the salamanders, Holk slowly bent over to pick up the lantern; the torches he left lying in place. Attention roving between the salamander in the 'tites above, the two on his left and the one on his right, he made his way slowly across the cavern floor.

Once passed the ring of torches, he thought an attack might manifest if the creatures had been held at bay by the fire. But no, they retained their positions, content to merely watch his progress.

He kept his pace slow, but steady. The urge to hurry was countered by the knowledge that sudden movements inevitably provoked animals to attack. But would that be a bad thing? If he had occasion to pass this way again, would they remain as docile as they were now? Would additional salamanders be present next time? Now that he was halfway to the mirror, he figured to worry about that should the need arise.

Three-quarters of the way across, the one above left its perch. It traveled along the ceiling to another stalactite closer to Holk. The movement caused him to tense believing an attack was imminent. It was all he could do to keep from quickening his pace. Once at its new perch, the creature seemed content to merely watch Holk's progress. His heart rate didn't return to normal until he stood before the small, round mirror whose wooden frame was cracked and peeling.

The salamanders continued to merely watch, none making so much as a step toward him. Perhaps they were not dangerous after all? One opened its maw to reveal the deadly, flesh-ripping teeth within and such thoughts were quickly dispelled.

Reaching out, he touched the mirror.

Light blinded him, assailing him from all sides. Using his swordarm to shield his eyes, he took a step backward. A second step brought him into contact with something smooth and solid. Whirling around, he squinted against the brightness and saw that he had backed against a mirror. It reflected the light from his lantern back to him. In fact, the entire room was composed of mirrors.

Scores covered the floor, walls and ceiling. Small and large, square and not, it was a patchwork with a uniform six inches of distance separating one from the next. When he realized his feet were in contact with two mirror's reflective surfaces, he quickly moved them to the rocky space between.

It took a moment for his eyes to adjust to the heightened illumination caused by so many mirrors reflecting, and re-reflecting the torchlight. When the glare no longer caused discomfort, he made out markings that had been painted next to each mirror. A few had but one marking, while others held up to five. The first thing he noticed about each mirror's markings was that they had been drawn in a vertical column.

The first marking of each mirror was a single line that had been crossed out. Some only had the crossed out single line. The second symbol on many was a "T". The rest of the symbols were wavy lines, vertical lines, circles, and half a dozen other notations. Apparently, Kiernan had been busy in this room.

Taking out the scribe's journal, Holk flipped through the pages in hopes of finding an explanation of the symbols. As he feared, there wasn't one. Looking at the scores of mirrors before him, Holk felt daunted by the task of searching each one in turn. *This could take months!*

But then he remembered something the scribe had said in his journal, that he had searched every room until the only way remaining was through the arch. Holk didn't have to search these, *Kiernan already had*! All he had to do was figure out the scribe's methodology, and he would know where to go.

The "T" was easy to figure out. That had to indicate a Ti-Ock presence. Also, since every mirror had a single line that had been crossed out, it would stand to reason that Kiernan used the single line to indicate which mirror he was currently investigating. That way, if he ran into trouble and had to use a handheld to escape, upon his return to this room, he would know which mirror he had used last. When the scribe completed the investigation of a mirror and went on to investigate the next mirror, he would cross through the line so as not to get confused. All Holk had to do was find a mirror with a single line that was not crossed through. That would indicate the last mirror Kiernan had used.

A quick visual search proved little help in discovering Kiernan's final mirror. It did however reveal the presence of six crates, sitting in three adjacent stacks off to the side. Holk went to see what they might contain only to find them empty.

Resigned to a slow and methodical search, he moved to the edge of the room and began moving through the array of mirrors across the floor. Each held a crossed out single line along with other, incomprehensible markings descending in a column beneath. Holk would truly love to figure out what they meant. If he couldn't find a mirror with a single, uncrossed out line, he might just get the chance.

When the mirrors upon the floor proved to be a bust, he turned his attention to the wall. Taking his time, he made his way slowly around the room from one crossed-out line to another. Coming full circle, he turned his gaze to the ceiling that rose a good six feet above his head. There were markings alongside those mirrors as well.

How did he...? **The crates!** Kiernan must have used the crates to reach the mirrors on the ceiling. Six crates positioned in three stacks, the first stack with a single crate, the second with two, and the last, three. The scribe had positioned them like steps. And if the scribe had used them to access the final mirror...

Hurrying back to where the crates lay, Holk gazed up to the mirrors overhead and saw where a triangular mirror with a chalky white border had but a single line. It had not been crossed out.

"Yes!" He had found it.

Returning the crates to their original position beneath the mirror, Holk then used the two shorter stacks to climb onto the stack of three. The mirror was now within easy reach. His hand paused before its reflective surface just as he recalled a fragment of Kiernan's journal.

...Had to sneak through a Ti-Ock mine in order to reach the mirror that sent me to the arch. Appeared twenty feet in front of it and was immediately set upon by six Ti-Ocks...

Somewhere on the other side of this mirror had to lay the mine mentioned in the journal. If he appeared in the middle of it, things could turn bad, fast.

Before activating the mirror, he turned the lantern down until only a small flame burned. Drawing his sword, he braced himself for whatever may follow, then reached for the last mirror Kiernan had passed through.

Thunderous sound reverberated throughout this new place. Off to his left, a cascade of water dropped fifteen feet along a three-tiered falls. From there, it formed a river which cut through this bedrock of this long, narrow subterranean space and vanished through an opening far to his right.

Holk stood upon a shelf barely ten feet wide that ran the length of his side of the river. Another semi-level area ran the river's length along the far side as well.

Realizing that he was alone, he sheathed his sword then turned the screw on the lantern to provide more illumination. Once the flame burned brightly, he held the lantern aloft in order to better investigate this new place.

Upon the wall across the swift-flowing river glittered a mirror. *Of course, couldn't be on this side could it?* There was no bridge or other method in place to cross the river. That didn't bother him too much since

Kiernan had to have come this way, which meant the scribe must have discovered a way across. Turning his gaze to the waterfall, Holk decided to begin his search there.

Algae grew in great proliferation across the surface of the shelf. Stepping out, his foot slipped upon a slick patch, nearly causing a loss of balance. But a few moments of undignified wind -milling of arms quickly regained balance.

The thundering of the water as it cascaded down the tri-tiered fall reverberated deep within him. In another time and place, he would have reveled in the feeling of its power. But now, all he could concentrate on was getting across the water to reach the mirror.

Where the falls emerged into this ancient, natural waterway, the walls were steep and slick. There was no evidence that Kiernan had crossed at this end. Moving away to follow the river, Holk held the lantern aloft as he sought the scribe's method of fording the torrent.

From the falls to the outflow, he scanned the rocky ground meticulously. Any unusual irregularity prompted a short pause and a stint of close scrutiny. Each time proved an exercise in futility. Upon arriving at the river's outflow, he still hadn't discovered how Kiernan crossed.

Thinking that the scribe might have somehow scaled the walls, he checked for a navigable route along the rock wall above where the river flowed from the area. A good climber might have made it, but he doubted whether his abilities were up to the task. If Kiernan had gone this route, he was much more accomplished than Holk would have thought. No, there had to be another way.

Holk gazed across the flowing water to the mirror. It seemed to mock him with its inaccessibility. Why put a mirror on the other side of a flow of water no one could cross? Swift, deep and spanning a distance of over twenty-five feet, the water posed a nearly impassable barrier. Perhaps if he entered the river near the falls, he might manage to cross before the current carried him away to parts unknown. Striped down to his smalls, maybe. But to continue on without his sword, armor, and other essentials, unthinkable.

As he continued to ponder the situation before him, his gaze fell upon the outflow. The upper portion of its inner surface was not smooth as one would think after years of continual erosion by the water. Spying irregularities in the rock large enough to afford hand and foot holds, another possibility occurred to him. He went closer to inspect the viability of making his way along the inner walls of the outflow channel. When he saw the single red line painted upon an outcropping two feet within the tunnel, Holk knew that Kiernan had gone this route.

The rock wall above the tumultuous underground river continued to offer numerous projections of rock. Hooking the lantern over his sword hilt, Holk nodded to the red line and said, "Lead on, Kiernan."

He took hold of protruding nodule and once it proved stable, sought another for his foot. Very carefully, he left the relative safety of the shelf and entered the tunnel.

Taking it one handhold and foothold at a time, he pressed forward into the tunnel. Less than two feet separated his feet from the rush of water below. He knew that should a misstep cause him to fall, the current would drag him quickly away. Fortunately, the imperfections in the rock were many and allowed his progress into the tunnel to proceed at a good pace.

Behind him, the roar of the falls gradually diminished as he pushed deeper into the tunnel. How far he went he couldn't be certain, but the sound from the falls had grown quite distant when a dark opening loomed in the rock wall ahead.

It turned out to be a channel through which water flowed to join the larger river. Pausing at the opening, he took the lantern and held it aloft to see how far this other channel went. It extended past the reach of the light. About to hook the lantern back to his sword hilt, he caught sight of another line of red some two feet within the channel. Kiernan had gone this way.

"Okay, scribe. I'm still with you."

Hooking the lantern once again on his sword hilt, he very carefully made his way into the narrower channel. It was sufficiently narrow that he found it easier to brace his feet on either side with the flow of water running beneath him than to continue making his way along a single wall.

The channel gradually narrowed the farther into it he went. Following gentle, serpentine switchbacks, Holk soon grew aware of a scent permeating the air. Familiar in its unpleasantness, he knew it to be the same odor encountered coming from within the crevice the Ti-Ock had disappeared into back in the valley. Realizing he could very well be approaching an area inhabited by the beasts, he paused a moment to reduce the wick on his lantern until it exuded just enough light for him to see his immediate surroundings.

From that point on, he would progress a ways, then pause to listen. Upon failing to hear any indication others were near, he pressed onward. And so he continued until coming to where the narrow channel opened onto a large underground lake; the scent of Ti-Ocks was strong.

The walls bordering the lake were steep, but not high. They came to an end ten feet above. Holk paused at the end of the channel to inspect the walls rising to either side. The one on his left looked to have the most protrusions and imperfections. After a short pause to scout a suitable route, he climbed to the top.

The top as it turned out was a wide area of semi-uniform evenness that completely encircled the small lake. Radiating outward from the lake's edge, the area came to an end at more steep walls.

Holk paused to take in this new area and give his fatigued arms and legs a rest. It wasn't long before he noticed signs of Ti-Ock occupation.

On the nearest wall sat an empty torch sconce. Shrouded in cobwebs, it had the look of long disuse. Not far from there were remains of several crates haphazardly piled against the wall. What he saw at the light's fringe prompted him to his feet to investigate.

It was a rope and pulley mechanism with a series of attached buckets. Descending to the lake, it could have only been used to bring water up from the pool below. It too had the look of disuse with cracked buckets and frayed ropes. From the looks of things, Holk doubted if the Ti-Ocks had been in this area for quite some time.

He spied a wooden ladder lying against the wall. Investigating, he discovered it to be in sad shape; several of the rungs being either broken or missing altogether. It appeared less than trustworthy to see him to the top. Perhaps there was another way?

A search of the current level on which he stood revealed the ladder to be the only means whereby he could reach the top of the wall and whatever lay beyond without scaling the wall. The marks at the head of the small channel which led him there indicated Kiernan had come this way. Perhaps the scribe *had* used the ladder? He inspected the area along the lip bordering the pool below and sure enough, he found tracks, most likely Kiernan's, that led away.

From the way the tracks went all over, the scribe had searched the area just as Holk had. Where the ladder lay was the greatest concentration of footprints. Holk figured the ladder to be his best bet. As he set the ladder up against the wall, he couldn't help but wonder why the ladder lay on the ground, instead of resting against the wall. If Kiernan had used it...

Knowing the answer would most likely forever elude him, Holk set foot against the second rung, it being the lowest one still remaining intact; the first one lacked half its center. Finding that it supported his weight, he climbed.

Only one rung gave way beneath his weight before reaching the top. There, he found a vast cavern stretching out before him. More discarded remnants of Ti-Ock occupation were evident. In the immediate area, more discarded crates, barrels, and tools. The tools were indicative of mining; shovels and pickaxes.

The cast offs before him held scant interest compared to the trio of torches burning in the distance. Not only that, but the movement of figures could be seen. Ti-Ocks! The rest of the cavern remained dark.

Extinguishing the light from his lantern so as not to give away his position, Holk finished his ascent and stood upon the cavern floor. *What would Kiernan have done in this situation?* Gazing to the light, Holk reasoned that the scribe would have gone to investigate…and so would he.

Making his way carefully, he left the pit and the pool far below. His eyes scanned not only the area illuminated by the torches, but the neighboring darkness as well. As he drew closer to the burning torches, he discovered a trio of tunnel entrances, the openings of each being lit by one of the torches.

The left-hand tunnel looked to be the main tunnel as the opening stood twice as high and a third again as wide as the other two. Ti-Ocks would emerge from this tunnel and proceed to the other two, and vice versa.

A pair of railcart tracks extended from the main tunnel, one going to each of the two smaller entrances. Ti-Ocks would push carts loaded with rock, what Holk took to be mined ore, from the smaller tunnels and return with empty ones. This must be the mine that Kiernan mentioned in his journal, the one through which he traversed in order to reach the mirror that took him to the arch. Taking in the three tunnels, Holk wondered which one he would have to enter. He fervently hoped that Kiernan had made his marks there as well. The thought of exploring tunnels filled with Ti-Ocks left him ill at ease. One or two he could handle, but this many may push providence a touch too far.

Coming as close as he dared, he found a position against the cavern wall from which he could observe the Ti-Ocks while remaining within the sheltering darkness. Though he had no experience with mining operations, he did know that every business had a period of either inactivity, or reduced productivity. It was merely a matter of when it would occur. Making himself comfortable, he took a mushroom and nibbled at it while watching the Ti-Ocks go about their business.

—12—

The comings and goings of the Ti-Ocks continued unabated for quite some time. At one point, a solitary creature emerged from the main tunnel beside which loped a beast about the size of a large dog. From his vantage point, all Holk could tell was that the beast had a coat of long fur and a short, stubby tail. He watched the pair until they disappeared into the first of the smaller tunnels.

Would the beast have the same senses as his hounds back home? If so, he could soon be in for a world of hurt. He took some comfort in the fact that the beast had taken no notice of him during its initial pass through the cavern. With any luck, it never would.

Holk watched for more of the dog-like creatures, but none appeared. A short time later, the Ti-Ock and beast reappeared from the smaller tunnel and returned into the larger. Less than ten heart-beats afterward, a mass migration of Ti-Ocks emerged from out of the smaller tunnels. Minutes later, the last creature passed into the main tunnel.

The cavern grew eerily quiet.

Could this be his chance? Were they gone for the night...or day as the case may be? There was no way to tell.

Holk remained still and quiet where he sat against the cavern wall deep within the shadows. When after a span of time passed during which no Ti-Ock returned, he climbed to his feet.

The lantern he hooked over his sword hilt. Slowly, and with every sensory faculty straining to catch any foreshadowing of a Ti-Ock's return, he made his way toward the main tunnel.

Several carts stood off the track, parked as it were in a haphazard fashion along the cavern wall near the entrance. One had a broken wheel while the top third of another's side was missing. It looked as if the wood had been bashed away by a massive hammer. Intrigued as to what could have caused such a hole, Holk took in other mining carts that showed similar damage.

Pondering the imponderable would get him nowhere. Reining in his curiosity, he brought his attention back to the mouth of the main tunnel. Flickering torchlight glowed from within.

Moving along the wall, Holk approached. Upon coming to within a foot of the entrance, he paused to listen. There was only silence. Taking it slow, he took the last step and peered around the corner.

The tunnel continued for well over a hundred feet before curving to the left. Torches in wall sconces burned every twenty feet, maintaining uninterrupted illumination throughout its length. Should he risk exploring where it led, there would be no way to remain unobserved should a Ti-Ock appear.

"Okay Scribe," he quietly whispered, "did you go in there?" Turning his attention from the tunnel to the cavern rock comprising its mouth, he sought Kiernan's tell-tale red marks.

After searching the rock wall beside which he lurked a foot in either direction and all the way from the ground to as high as he could see, he failed to discover any indication of the scribe coming this way.

A quick glance to ensure the tunnel remained empty and then he crossed to the opposite side. There he searched the rocky surface. It wasn't until he knelt on hands and knees to inspect near the bottom that he saw the single red line. It had been marked through. There was another symbol next to it, one that he had yet to see; two diagonal, wavy lines encompassed by a circle. Considering the enigmatic symbol briefly, Holk failed to fathom its meaning.

He felt relief to know that the main passage was not the way to the arch. Coming back to his feet, he glanced to the other two tunnels farther down along the cavern wall. One of them had to be the one.

The first tunnel proved to be a narrow passage dug deep into the rock with a single railcart-track running along its center. One torch burned in lonely isolation far down in its nether recesses. Searching the rock along the tunnel entrance for Kiernan's marks, he again discovered it close to the ground. Unlike the main tunnel, this one only had a single, crossed-out line. The circle with two wavy lines was not present.

"That leaves one more," Holk mumbled to the darkness. Moving to the second of the smaller tunnels, he searched for the mark even though he knew this had to be the one. There could be another marking present that might indicate danger. He was surprised to find only a single, marked-out line near the bottom of the rock wall.

"Not this way either?"

Surprised, Holk wondered if perhaps this was not the mine Kiernan had spoken of in his journal. *Could the scribe have been referring to another?* Moving to stand just within the tunnel, Holk took Kiernan's journal from out of his pack. Using the light from the torch burning above, he sought the reference to the mine. It failed to enlighten him any further as to how, or where, Kiernan had reached the mine. All it said was,

*Had to sneak through a Ti-Ock mine in order to
reach the mirror that sent me to the arch.*

That was it. Flipping through the pages failed to reveal anything more.

Slipping the journal back into his pack, Holk considered the situation; three tunnels, all apparently having been crossed off by Kiernan as not being the way. So, if these three mining tunnels were not the avenue by which Kiernan had reached the mirror through which the arch lay, could there be yet another? The journal only said that the scribe had snuck through the mine, not that the way lay through a tunnel. Further searching was in order.

Moving out of the torch light illuminating the tunnel entrance, Holk kept near the wall as he began a circumnavigation of the cavern. Once back in the concealing safety of the shadows, he walked slowly, all the while running his hand along the rock wall to maintain contact. Fifty feet from the tunnel, his foot hit an obstruction rising from the ground. If not for the steadying presence of the cavern wall, he would assuredly have fallen.

The obstruction turned out to be one of the railcart rails. Squatting next to it, he ran his hand along its surface. An attempt to move it proved the rail to be fixed firmly in place. A glance deeper within the cavern revealed the shadowy presence of another. *Perhaps the remnants of an abandoned spur?* The spur was by no means intact, for the one before him lacked neighbors on either side. But where there had been a spur, there could be another tunnel.

Excited by the prospect, Holk came to his feet and after a glance back at the trio of tunnels behind him to ensure he remained alone, followed the intermittent rails to their destination.

A rail here, two rails there, the abandoned patchwork led him on. At one point the shadows melded into complete darkness and he was forced to utilize some source of light in order to continue. Pulling forth his sunstone, he smacked it against the outer leather of his scabbard.

Light blossomed forth; not nearly as bright as what his lantern would emit, but more than adequate to follow the rails. He cupped the sunstone in his hands, leaving the barest of openings to allow a small glow to light the way.

Continuing deeper within the cavern, the rails grew more infrequent. Another cart materialized out of the darkness. It lay on its side. Nothing appeared to be wrong with it other than having been tipped over. Holk gave it a cursory inspection that revealed little before continuing on.

The rails finally turned from running parallel to the cavern wall, to heading straight for it. They ended at what must have once been a tunnel entrance, but now stood clogged with rubble consisting of stones the size of pebbles to that of large boulders too large for him to move. Holk figured the tunnel must have suffered a cave-in.

Panning the sunstone's light to inspect the area, he discovered Kiernan's red line high on the wall near a gap at the top. It had not been marked through. *This was the way!*

Climbing the rubble pile proved easy enough and at the opening, Holk allowed the sunstone's light to shine within. A narrow crawlspace extended through the pile for several yards to where the rubble came to an end.

With the 'stone in one hand, he entered the opening and made his way through to the far side. There, the rubble petered out until the tunnel once again ran clear and unobstructed. As he descended the pile, a protrusion beneath the rocks at the bottom caught his eye. A closer examination revealed it to be a boney, skeletal leg. The cave-in must have caught one of the miners. But why hadn't the body been recovered? Assuredly other Ti-Ocks must have known it was in there. Did they care so little about their dead?

No longer having to worry about giving away his presence, Holk returned the sunstone to his pack and relit the lantern. Rails ran in perfect, uninterrupted alignment along the center of the tunnel. Not far from the blockage, a cart filled with ore sat tilted to the right. It had come to rest at a ninety degree angle where its right side leaned against the wall.

Curious as to what the Ti-Ocks mined, Holk paused and inspected a chunk of ore. Veins of silver coursed through the rock. "So, this is a silver mine," he mumbled. The combined amount of silver embedded within the rocks filling the cart would be worth a fortune if he could but get them back home. Sighing, he tossed the silver-laced rock back into the cart and continued on.

Signs of abandonment greeted him around every turn of this serpentine-like tunnel; carts on their sides lying broken, tools stacked against the rocky walls as if waiting for the miners' return, along with a myriad of other equipment.

It seemed strange to Holk that those who ran the mine would leave behind equipment of obvious value. Even the broken carts could have been repaired in lieu of purchasing replacements. Of course, it was also possible that everything had been intentionally left behind after the cave-in, but that made little economical sense. Wouldn't it have proven profitable to spend a small amount of time to recover their equipment? Certainly the ore in the cart near the cave-in would have made the effort worthwhile. Ti-Ocks, Holk came to believe, had absolutely no sense about such things.

Pressing deeper into the tunnel, Holk reached a "Y." The railcart tracks continued down the left-hand branch, while the tunnel curving off to the right was but bare earth. A search revealed Kiernan's red line just within the right-hand tunnel. The one to the left had one that was crossed through. Holk entered the passage to the right.

After a short distance, the tunnel grew more natural in appearance. Where the tunnel with the track had been carved by Ti-Ocks, this one showed very few signs that tools had been used. The walls grew rougher and the smoothness of the passage took on the undulating aspect of natural formation.

Holk pressed forward through a trio of smaller caverns, each being hardly more than a widening of the tunnel. There were no stalactites or 'mites. Instead, he encountered ribbons of rock forming irregular, and at times thin columns that climbed from floor to ceiling. Two in particular caught his eye.

Each couldn't have been wider than the width of his palm. One rose nearly vertically while the other made its way in a less than symmetrical spiral around the first. Together, they formed perhaps the most unique configuration nature had to offer.

Past the trio of caverns, the tunnel began angling downward. Gradual at first, it soon grew quite severe. Holk was forced to make use of protruding rocks and other rocky imperfections along the walls to keep from falling. The downward slope lasted for what seemed like forever before reaching where the slope went completely vertical. The tunnel, or perhaps the more accurate term to use at this point would be shaft, continued down into darkness.

Holk discovered two somewhat flat, rocky protrusions upon which to place his feet while he considered whether or not to continue.

The sides of the shaft were far from smooth. Rocky outcroppings and fissures would provide ample places for feet and hands. How far into the earth would he have to go? Had Kiernan in fact gone this way? The line at the beginning of the tunnel indicated he had. There was nothing for it. Holk had to try.

Descending through the shaft proved easier than originally anticipated. His only concern was the climb back out. It wouldn't be nearly as easy.

A fissure for a foothold here, a protruding rocky nodule for a handhold there, and down into the bowels of the earth he went. His every move caused the lantern hooked over his sword hilt to swing and bang into his leg causing shadows to dance in a spectral-like ballet.

How long he descended before becoming aware of the breeze, he couldn't be certain. It wafted upward through the shaft. Not long after, he came to a wide, vertical fissure twice the length of a man. The breeze came from within.

Drawing abreast of the opening, Holk saw the scribe's red line. It had not been marked through. Encouraged by this affirmation that he was on the right track, Holk unhooked the lantern from his sword hilt and passed it through the opening to see what lay on the other side. To his amazement, it was a room.

Not a large room to be sure, it had been constructed in similar fashion as the Prison Room and the large room wherein he had encountered the Merchant. The wall separating the shaft from the room had worn away over the years and collapsed. There were no doors or windows; the fissure through which he gazed was the only way out.

Eager to leave the shaft behind, Holk stepped through and into the room. Once within the room, he saw the mirror on the wall to his right. It was framed in a thick border of solid gold bedecked with emeralds the size of his thumb. The gems caught the lantern's light and created a halo-like aura, wreathing the mirror. On the wall next to it were three of Kiernan's symbols.

The top one was the line. Next came a "T" that Holk understood to mean a Ti-Ock presence would be encountered wherever the mirror took him. Beneath the "T" was an arch. Holk had found the mirror!

Excitement warred with caution as he approached the site of Kiernan's last translocation. According to the journal, once he activated the mirror's latent power, he would be set upon by Ti-Ocks. The scribe stated six of the creatures had attacked him as soon as he appeared.

Holk paused before touching the reflective surface. First, he extinguished the lantern causing the room to plunge into total darkness. Next he drew his sword. If a similar fate awaited him, he planned to be ready. With sword ready, he reached out with his other hand…and paused.

From out of the corner of his eye, a faint sliver of light broke the darkness. As he turned his gaze upon it, the light vanished. Figuring it to be nothing more than his eyes playing tricks, Holk reached out for the mirror. Again, the light appeared in his peripheral vision.

This time he kept his gaze directed forward. In the half-sight one has when transitioning from day-vision to night-vision, the light was only apparent out of the corner of his eye. It vanished whenever he gazed directly toward it.

Rising from the floor, the ribbon of light ascended in a perfect vertical line to a height of six feet. Holk kept his gaze averted so as to keep it in his peripheral sight and side-stepped toward the light. Either it gained clarity with closer proximity, or his eyes were adjusting to the stygian blackness for when he came to within arm's reach, the light remained visible even with his gaze turned full upon it.

The breeze felt back in the shaft had its origins on the other side of this ribbon of light. He could feel its coolness upon his skin as it passed through. Intrigued, he momentarily put aside his plan to follow Kiernan's route via the mirror, and lit the lantern.

Naught but a stone-formed wall greeted him when the lantern blossomed into life. However, the blocks of stones that formed the wall were set in a slightly different pattern than the rest of the room. He never would have noticed it had the ribbon of light not caught his eye.

Holk was mighty curious as to what lay on the other side of this wall. A breeze, not to mention a light source, indicated another way from this room other than the mirror, and the fissure leading to the shaft.

Setting the mirror upon the floor, Holk placed both hands against the wall. Thinking there may be a secret door concealed within the stone wall, he shoved. The wall didn't so much as budge. He tried leaping at the wall and striking it full-on with his shoulder. All that action accomplished was to cause his shoulder to ache.

Rubbing where it throbbed, Holk stepped back and considered the wall. He knew a noble that had a secret passage running from his bedchamber to that of a guest room to enable discreet midnight rendezvous. The end at the bed chamber was accessed by moving a picture on the wall that caused a hidden door to slide open.

Starting with the blocks running along either side of where the ribbon of light had been, he tried moving, pushing, and even striking each of them with the pommel of his sword. After testing them all, he still had not opened the way.

Past experiences aided him not at all in this endeavor. Other than the one instance with the noble, Holk had no other wells of information from which to draw. After all, how often does one find themselves in such a situation? Tavern tales and barrack's gossip offered little help since soldiers were more interested in brave, heroic deeds than skulking about in the dark along hidden passageways.

The other end of the noble's secret route had a latch keeping it secure which could only be manipulated from within the passage. It occurred to Holk that perhaps something similar was at work now.

The blade of the sword acquired from the Merchant was narrow, narrow enough in fact to slip within the crack. It was a tight fit, but he managed to insert it four inches before the blade grew too thick.

Ever so carefully, he slid it upward within the crack until reaching a point at eye level. When he failed to encounter any resistance, Holk brought the blade downward. It continued its descent within the crack before encountering something that brought it to a halt.

Encouraged, he pressed downward on whatever it was that barred the blade's way. When that failed to produce a result, he withdrew the sword and re-inserted it a foot beneath the obstruction. Moving it upward, he took it slowly until the blade once again was brought to a halt.

This time when he increased the pressure, the resistance lasted less than three heartbeats before giving way. A muffled "click" was heard.

"Yes!"

Pulling the sword free, Holk gave the wall a nudge with his shoulder resulting in only a slight movement. Increasing his effort failed to force the wall open any farther. Thinking it must swing inward, he slipped the tip of his sword into the crack and began to pry.

Not hard for fear of damaging the blade, he used the blade like a crowbar, and soon, hinges squealed as the wall opened a fraction. Further repetitions of insertions and pryings saw the wall swing ever farther into the room.

The door, for door its dimensions said it had to be, reached a point where its edge had completely entered the room. Sheathing his sword, Holk took hold of the edge and opened it the rest of the way.

A narrow, ascending stairwell led up to a landing some thirty feet beyond. Burning merrily in a sconce, a torch illuminated the area above.

Torch? A burning torch meant the presence of someone, or something, with intelligence. Sniffing the air failed to reveal Ti-Ock scent. *Who could it be? Streyan perhaps?* Drawing his sword, Holk grabbed the lantern and proceeded to climb the steps. Exercising great caution, he approached the landing.

—13—

Every sense alert for the slightest sound or scent that would indicate the presence of another, Holk climbed the steps. The torch burning in the sconce drew his attention. Its flame flickered in the breeze coming from beyond the top of the landing, giving off a smoky offering that could possibly mask other, subtler, odors.

The cold steel of his sword gave comfort as he paused upon the third step from the top. A passageway moved off to the right. Hearing nothing, Holk took the final two steps quickly and peered around the corner.

No more than six paces away, the passageway ended at another door. It stood ajar. No light came from the other side, the opening remained as black as pitch. Coming off the steps, Holk stepped lightly toward the door and peered into the darkness beyond.

What little light passed through from the torch burning at the landing revealed the beginnings of a wall that continued forward on his right. To the left, the area beyond the door opened up. About to enter, he detected an odor that was all too familiar to one seasoned in battle. It was the odor of death.

Holk took hold of the door and readied his sword. After a steady inhalation then slow release to banish feelings of unease, drew open the door. He was ready for almost anything but what he saw. A small room lay beyond the door. Clothes that were more rags than suitable attire lay strewn about the room. The remains of several crates that had been fashioned into crude tables sat near a cot whereupon a mound of the rags was piled haphazardly.

He took his sunstone and gently whacked it against the wall. The resulting light gave further detail to the wadded clothes upon the cot. It was from the clothes that the odor of death came. Entering the room, he advanced to the cot.

Using the tip of his sword, he carefully hooked it on a brownish-red, frayed section of cloth lying atop the pile at one end and moved it aside to expose the cadaverous face of a long-dead human. Quickly removing the rest of the rags, the corpse was soon exposed.

From the breastplate it wore, Holk knew this had been a soldier of some kind. The coat-of-arms embossed upon the left breast was that of a serpent coiled to strike on a field of red. Twin, parallel lines ran diagonally from upper right to lower left. It was an insignia unfamiliar to him.

The state of decomposition seemed to indicate the man had perished over a month ago, possibly longer. There didn't appear any signs the man had died as result of wounds such as those that had done in Kiernan.

Natural causes, poison, or had he simply given up? Holk didn't know, but vowed not to meet the same fate. Hoping to find something that would aid him in his bid for freedom, Holk lit the lantern and set about taking stock of the items in the room. The first thing he noticed was the walls lacked mirrors. This was the first room other than the Merchant's that didn't have one.

Turning his attention to the clutter atop the makeshift table next to the bed, he moved aside several broken pieces of wood and exposed the wooden edge of a handheld mirror frame. Excited at finding another of the handhelds, Holk pulled it out only to discover the mirror had been shattered. Moving aside the rest of the clutter revealed the missing pieces. Lying intermixed with the broken remains of the first, lay what used to be the frame of a second. Each broken into multiple sections, the wooden pieces held but jagged fragments of the mirror's reflective surface.

Tentatively, Holk touched one of the broken fragments, half expecting to be transported elsewhere. But apparently the magic of the mirrors ceased to work once broken for he failed to translocate.

He cast a curious glance to the corpse on the bed. *Why would you smash the mirrors?* Such an action made no sense.

From the crate-box table, he turned his attention to a heap on the floor against the wall consisting of bones, irregular snatches of dried hides, and what looked to be bits of leather. The leather piqued his attention, but a more thorough examination revealed them to not belong to one of those *things* from the forest. Rather, they were the remains of some critter the now-dead occupant of this room had most likely eaten.

Two crates with broken slats sat against the wall on the other side of the room. Holk smashed them open with his foot and discovered a curious, dodecahedral item barely large enough to fit in the palm of his hand. It was wrapped in a purple, velveteen cloth and weighed more than it should.

Formed of a dark rock, each of its twelve, pentagonal sides were inlaid with a silver, runic figure. One face bore a rearing horse, on the side directly opposite was that of a sword. The rest of the faces held naught but indecipherable squiggles.

He was careful to not touch the item except at the vertices where the pentagonal faces met. One never knew what magic might be lurking within such an item. He slipped it into his pouch and continued his search. Other than a variety of ill-used clothes in varying sizes, nothing else that could be thought of as useful or interesting was found.

The breeze which had fluttered the torch burning at the top of the steps came from a narrow crack in the ceiling not far from the foot of the dead man's bed. An inch at the widest, it meandered its way in a natural progression for over three hand-spans before coming to an end. The air issuing forth smelled of earth and long-buried subterranean worlds forever cut off from the green life of the surface.

Casting one last look around this small room, his gaze settled once again upon the face of the dead man. "What happened to you? Did you just give up?" Shaking his head, he turned toward the door. Making his way from the room, Holk hurried down the steps and came to stand before the mirror. His eyes fell upon the symbol painted in red upon the wall.

"This better be the way out."

After extinguishing the lantern and placing the sunstone in his pouch so its light would be concealed, Holk drew his sword and reached for the mirror, beyond which the scribe's journal had indicated Kiernan had been immediately set upon by Ti-Ocks. In absolute darkness, his fingertips brushed against the reflective surface.

Ti-Ock stink assaulted his nose. That and the fact that his fingers no longer touched the mirror were the only indications that he no longer remained in the room at the base of the concealed steps. The air of this new place felt stagnant and rank.

Holk remained motionless. The only sound to break the stillness was the beating of his heart. Each lub-dub resounded like a cacophony that would assuredly attract anyone or anything that happened to be nearby.

There's no one here.

Seconds ticked by as the silence remained unbroken. He cocked his head first to one side then another in an attempt to detect some faint indication that he was not alone. After nearly a full minute of such activity, he concluded that he was alone and opened the pouch wherein laid the sunstone. When the pouch's mouth parted, light blossomed forth. The sunstone continued exuding light. He immediately closed the pouch until only a miniscule opening remained to allow light to pass.

The light pushed back only a small portion of the darkness. It was as if he stood in a bubble of light within a sea of darkness. He tried discerning his surroundings, but dared not risk announcing his presence with greater illumination. According to Kiernan's journal, the arch had been twenty feet from where the scribe appeared. Stepping forward cautiously, four paces brought him to the point where the light coming from out of the pouch fell upon the arch.

It was as portrayed in the journal. In the stone above the arch's apex, a starburst had been engraved. Great artistry had been used in its design.

Assuredly, this could not have been the work of Ti-Ocks. The beasts thus far encountered had not seemed capable of such fine and delicate craftsmanship. Beyond the arch lay naught but darkness.

Pausing two paces before the arch, Holk once again strained to detect the sound of another's presence. When it failed to materialize, he moved to pass through the arch. Just before reaching the arch, the toe of his boot sent a bit of metal clanking across the stone floor to a point beyond the arch. The suddenness and unexpectedness of the jarring sound froze him in place. When the object came to rest, he again sought signs that his presence had been discovered. Relief filled him when the silence continued unabated.

He pulled forth the sunstone to provide better illumination. If the clattering, skittering of the metallic object, which the increase in light revealed to be a knife's broken blade, hadn't produced a curious Ti-Ock, then most likely there were none in the area.

Its light pushed back the darkness to fully reveal the arch and his immediate surroundings. Surveying the room in which he had appeared revealed that the arch to be but one of two ways from the room. Behind him and to his right, a flight of steps climbed toward a platform before another archway some fifteen feet above. This second archway was constructed of plain, unadorned stone giving the aspect of little importance.

Returning his attention to the starburst above what he thought of as Kiernan's Arch, Holk saw how the light from the sunstone sparkled along the rays shooting out from the starburst's center. The effect was subtle, but there.

Beyond the arch lay another passageway. The light failed to penetrate far, though it did extend far enough to reveal a trio of columns made from the same stone that comprised the walls, floor and ceiling. Ten paces from the arch, the columns stood as silent sentinels that waited with eternal patience for what this human would do next.

Always leery of the unknown, Holk stepped forward until less than a foot separated him from the space within the arch. *Would it be safe to go through? Dare he?* After another wary glance to the sparkling rays of the starburst, he made to pass through.

"I wouldn't do that if I were you."

Spinning about, Holk glanced up to the platform before the other arch and found the boy Streyan sitting at the edge, legs kicking back and forth as a child was want to do. A myriad of questions raced though his mind in the ensuing moment of silence. *How did the boy get there? Was Streyan following him? And what did he mean by that statement?*

"Why?"

The boy shrugged. "Not sure."

"Are there Ti-Ocks on the other side?"

"I can't be certain, but I would think it likely." Gesturing to the room, the arch looming behind him, and the arch through which Holk had been about to enter, he added, "This area is claimed by them and they are not welcoming hosts."

Holk pondered that for a moment then gestured to the Arch. "Is the way out through there?"

The lad nodded. "One of them."

"How do you know? Kazzra?"

Again the boy nodded.

Realizing his sword was held at the ready between them, he sheathed it. "What did Kazzra say?"

"He only mentioned it once. Claimed that the Starburst Gate would alter the rules for those who passed though."

"Alter?"

"So Kazzra said."

"In what way?"

"That I don't know. He failed to go into any great details about it. Simply forbade me from ever passing through them."

Holk arched an eyebrow. "Them? There are more than one?"

"Yep. This is one of four that I have encountered. The strange thing is that they are all in Ti-Ock territory."

"Why would that be strange?"

The boy shrugged. "I don't know. Don't you think it to be strange?"

"Maybe." He eyed the lad for the span of two heartbeats before asking, "Have you been following me?"

"Not intentionally. I just happened by when I saw the light from your sunstone and thought to take a look. Those sent to this place quite often end up before this particular Arch and I was curious who it might be."

"You've seen others who have tried to pass through this Arch?"

Sadness came to his face and he nodded his head.

"What happened to them?"

"They died."

"From passing through the Arch?"

The boy shrugged. "I don't know. I've known seventeen who tried. Sixteen came up dead within two days."

"And the seventeenth?"

"I never saw him again."

So one made it out. There was a glimmer of hope that things might work out after all. But then he thought of the dead man in the room atop the hidden stairs. "Did the seventeenth man have an insignia on his chest?" He touched the area above his right breast. "Right here that was of a striking serpent upon a red field with twin lines running through it?"

Streyan shook his head. "No. The one of whom you speak was the last of the sixteen."

"How about the scribe, Kiernan? Did he pass through?"

Shrugging, the boy replied, "Maybe. I do not know for certain if he did or did not."

Holk considered that for a moment. "Would you mind answering another question?"

"If I can."

Reaching into his pouch, he removed the dodecahedral object discovered in the hidden room and held it up for the boy to see. "Any idea what this is?"

Streyan eyed the object and shook his head. "Nope. Probably important though. Things like that are all over the place. If you know where to look that is. Kazzra said it was best to leave them alone."

"Why?"

"He didn't say."

"That dragon doesn't tell you much, does he?"

Grinning, the boy shrugged. "He tells me what I need to know."

Holk doubted that, but kept such thoughts to himself. Moving toward the beginning of the steps leading to the platform whereupon Streyan sat, Holk quickly stopped when the smile vanished from Streyan's eyes and the lad came to his feet and back-stepped two paces toward the arch. Apparently the boy's affability would only be present when sufficient space remained between them. Even after Holk realized his error and returned to his former position before Kiernan's Arch, the boy remained on his feet.

"You should leave this place."

"I've been *trying* to." The words came out a bit more forcefully than Holk had intended.

"No." Streyan made a gesturing encompassing the room. "I mean, from here. They'll be here soon."

"Ti-Ocks?"

The boy nodded. "Lots of them." He then leaned back so his head passed through the archway and looked toward some distant point to his right before returning his attention to Holk.

Holk searched the boy's face for signs of deception, but only found honesty. "How soon?"

"Not long." Again he glanced through the archway and to his right.

Seeing the boy move his hand to the pack holding his bounty of mirrors, Holk held up his own hand. "Wait!"

Streyan's hand paused.

Holk pointed through the opening of Kiernan's Arch. "What will I find?"

"The way out? Death? I really don't know." With that, he slipped a finger within his mirror-pack and was gone.

"Damn!"

The way out? Death? Streyan's words haunted him as he turned to face the Arch. There was nothing out of the ordinary about it other than the way the sunstone's light played along the beams radiating outward from the center of the starburst. The area beyond the arch looked innocent enough.

...dead within two days. The fate of those who had gone before made him wary. *But one made it!* From out of the archway at the top of the steps wherein Streyan had stood but moments before came the unmistakable sound of approaching footsteps intermingled with guttural Ti-Ock speech. *Dare the Arch, remain to face the Ti-Ocks, or flee?* He'd be damned if he would ever take flight again. Drawing his sword, he turned his back on the approaching creatures, and stepped through the Arch.

Half anticipating to experience some sort of transition as he passed through, he was surprised at experiencing nothing. But that didn't mean nothing had changed. The lad said that the rules would be altered for him, not that *he* would be altered. *Would he even know the difference? Did it matter?*

The trio of columns evenly dissected a short, wide hallway. A door stood ajar at the other end. He could hear Ti-Ocks descending the steps from the platform before the other archway. Cupping the sunstone so as to restrict its illumination to the area just before him, he skirted around the leftmost column and raced for the door. Pulling it open, he darted through to another passage running perpendicular to the one he just exited.

He shut the door, and when the means to secure the door remained indecipherable, quickly glanced down the passage to his right and left. Light could be seen to the right; the left lay shrouded in shadows. A search of the walls adjacent to the door revealed none of the scribe's markings. If Kiernan had made it this far, he hadn't taken the time to mark his route. Figuring shadows were preferable to a revealing light source, he quick-timed it down to the left.

A dozen paces later, the light of the sunstone abruptly vanished. Tapping it against the wall caused the light to renew. He continued for a short distance before being brought to a halt by the sudden manifestation of guttural voices from behind. He pressed his back against the wall and held the sunstone tightly against his chest to contain its light. From the shadowy darkness, he watched as a group of Ti-Ocks emerged through the doorway he had so recently vacated and turned to make their way toward the light source at the opposite end of the passageway. At least two-score of the creatures appeared, each thankfully oblivious to his presence. Holk held his position until the last creature disappeared in the distance before resuming the exploration of the shadowy tunnel before him.

He kept the sword at the ready. His left hand clutched the sunstone, allowing the barest hint of light to escape between his fingers. This enabled him to barely make out the walls on either side as well as the passageway floor. Though nothing more than paler shadows in a world of shadow, they provided guidance.

The thought that this might not be the way leading to the exit from this place nagged at the back of his mind. It could very well have been toward the lit section, the way the Ti-Ocks had gone, that would prove to be the road home. But since this was the way least likely to incur Ti-Ock attention, it was as good a place to start as the other. He could always go back.

Minutes ticked by as Holk delved farther down what quickly turned out to be a forlorn and deserted section of Ti-Ock habitation. The walls continued unbroken with neither door nor opening. A few remnants telling of previous occupation were found; items such as broken planks of wood, empty torch sconces, and scraps of cloth. It looked as if no one had been down there for years. He continued on.

Finally, the aspect of the tunnel...changed. Where the walls reached the ceiling remained the same. Where they met the floor, however, grew narrower. It was as if the bottom section of the walls gradually moved closer together. This continued for a good hundred feet until the space between the lower half of the walls was half that of the upper. Curious and slightly off-balanced by such an incongruous construction, Holk pressed forward.

Not far beyond where the lower end of the walls ceased their inward progression and continued the unusual aspect, a gate appeared. Narrow bars set two hand-spans apart with a thick chain binding closed the section that swung open created a very effective barrier. No locking mechanism was attached to the chain. Instead, it bound the gate closed in perfect, unbroken-linked unity. It was as if the chain had been fashioned in place leaving neither a beginning nor an end.

Holk pondered the enigma of a gate that could not be opened. The bars were firm and lacked any sign of aging. It was as if he had come upon the gate but hours after its construction; which of course was impossible. Attempts at yanking and pushing only served to prove its formidable nature.

Irritation and no small amount of anger bubbled to the surface at his inability to continue. Beyond the gate, darkness beckoned teasingly, as if mocking him. Such an obstruction assuredly had to mean that his chance for escaping this prison was somewhere ahead. Gripping the gate in both hands, he shook the iron violently. It didn't budge.

Anger came over him. Unwilling to give up and turn around, he took three steps backward, glared at the point where the chain held closed the gate and gave out with a cry. Racing forward, he slammed the bottom of his boot against the chain with all his might. To his amazement, the blow wrenched the gate's upper section away from the ceiling and brought it crashing down against the floor with a very loud and resounding boom.

"Yes!"

Holes gaped in the ceiling where the rods of the gate had been attached. Chips of stone lay scattered across the floor. He glanced to the gate where it lay prone upon the floor and chuckled. "Well, I guess you weren't as strong as you thought." Patting himself on the back for a job well done, Holk stepped upon the bars of the gate and with great satisfaction, disdainly ground his heel against the metal. "Nothing is going to stand in my way," As he moved off the gate and continued down the passageway, he again exclaimed, "Nothing!"

Fifty feet beyond the gate, the passageway reached a dead end without door or other avenue to continue. *Why would they put a gate before a dead end?* It was inconceivable. The thought that perhaps a secret way may be concealed spurred a lengthy search of the stone walls and floor. Not finding any hidden catch or pressure plate, he slowly worked his way back down the tunnel.

It didn't take long before he noticed the gate had returned to its former position blocking the passageway. Standing motionless in shock, it took a moment for his brain to come to grips with what he saw. The gaping holes in the ceiling where the bars had earlier come free were gone. It was as if the felling of the gate had never happened. Yet he knew that it had.

Figuring that a well-placed kick had worked before, he backed several feet away, raced forward, leapt, and hit the gate with his foot. Every spec of power he could muster went into that kick. The resulting impact sent waves of pain up his leg. The gate refused to budge even when his knee buckled and the rest of his body crashed into the iron bars.

Holk sagged to the floor. An inspection of his foot revealed it wasn't broken, sprained perhaps. A few of the healing mushrooms later and the pain had subsided to a dull throb. He came to his feet and stood before the chain holding the gate closed. Raising his sword high, he considered attempting to shear the chain in two, but feared the possibility of being rendered weaponless in such a hostile environment should the links prove the hardier. Instead, he sheathed the sword then reached for his mirror-pack.

The thought of using the mirror and return to the Prison Room, *and then* having to go back over the route that had brought him to the Arch, was not a pleasant prospect. Although, after another hour of searching for a secret way and working again to overcome the gate, he gave in to the inevitable.

Pulling forth the mirror with the red mark that would take him to the Prison Room, he touched the surface.

—14—

Twin beams of moonlight through a pair of barred windows announced his arrival in the Prison Room. "What a stupid trap." Most denizens of this place more than likely possessed at least one of the handhelds and would be able to readily escape. Holk himself had spent relatively little time in the trap before making his escape. He couldn't help but laugh.

After slipping the mirror back into its pack with the other two, he crossed over to the nearest window and gazed out at the expanse of moon-dazzled water. The trek back to the Starburst Arch would take some doing, and with night having arrived Holk thought it best to sleep until morning before attempting the return trip. He was always at his best after a full night's sleep.

Far off in the distance, a light moved upon the water. Thoughts of trying to signal the ship, if ship it be, passed quickly. He did not wish a repeat performance with the giant birds. The two his earlier attempt attracted had nearly cost him his life.

He remained at the window until the faraway light faded into the night.

Long after the moon had set and naught but starlight streamed in between the bars, another light came into being. A small light to be sure, hardly more than the glimmer of a lightning bug being reflected off the surface of some high mountain tarn. But as in all things small, it eventually grew.

A man lay next to the light, oblivious in his slumber. As the light grew to illuminate the corner in which the man slept, the man stirred only to have sleep's unavoidable grasp pull him back to its nether reaches. And still the light grew in luminosity. It continued to grow until shadows that once filled half the room were laid waste.

An avian denizen of the night marveled at this unusual happenstance from its perch upon the window ledge. It cocked an eye at the source of the light, curious as to what it could be. Being of medium stature, the bird easily slipped in through the bars and hopped to the ground.

It kept an eye on the sleeping man as it carefully made its way closer to the ever brightening object. The light came from within something lying next to the man. Even with the glow now quite bright, the bird couldn't make it out. Curiosity drove it forward.

The light gave off no heat, which was in itself an odd thing. The bird simply didn't know what to make of it. Reaching out with its bill, it snapped at the light and darted back. When its action provoked no response, it moved closer still. About to snap at it a second time, the bird danced backward when the object that was the source of the light... moved. Subtle, yet unmistakable, it looked as if something on the inside had pushed outward on the material. Poised to take flight, the bird watched.

Dreams of better days were brought to a halt when an incredibly loud squawk pierced the night. Wrenched from deep within sleep's realm, Holk came awake and instinctively drew his sword.

Light filled the room. The last vestiges of sleep fell away when realization hit that the light came not from the morn, but from a point only a few paces away. To make the scene even more surreal, a bird flapped erratically along the floor next to the light's source.

It took him but a moment to realize the light came from within his mirror-pack. As the bird thrashed and cried in fear, the pack moved in matching fashion, almost as if it and the bird were connected in some way.

Unseen at first, it took a moment for his eyes to register a strand of light no bigger than a finger in width. It extended from the pack and had twined itself about the bird.

As the bird thrashed, the band wrapped ever tighter around the bird. Holk watched as its end encircled the bird's neck. A few moment's later, the bird ceased thrashing and lay still.

The bird and band of light remained motionless upon the ground for a few moments; then, the band uncoiled and slowly withdrew back into the pack. Once it had completely re-entered the pack, the light went out.

Holk tried to fathom what he had witnessed. With the light gone, the room had plunged back into deep shadows that were only broken by the faint gleam of starlight coming in through the windows. He took out his sunstone and struck it.

The mirror-pack looked benign. Lying upon the floor as it was, the only evidence that anything untoward had happened was the lifeless bird next to it. Holk gazed at the pack. With sunstone gleaming, he cautiously nudged the leather side with the tip of his sword.

When nothing happened, he moved the sword's tip to the flap and flipped it up so the pack lay fully opened. There was no light; not even the tiniest glimmer could be seen within any of the pouch's pockets. The edges of the three mirrors were visible, but he couldn't see anything different about them.

Holk took a step back and considered the situation. Something had come out of the pack. Even if he thought he may have been hallucinating or had dreamt it, the dead bird dispelled any such notion. Eyes never leaving the inner pockets of the pouch, he came closer and again poked the side of the pack with his sword; nothing happened.

Hooking the bottom of the pack with his sword, he gently upended it allowing the three handheld mirrors within to slide out.

They looked unchanged. The red dot Kiernan had used to designate the one leading to the Prison Room remained unaltered. One by one, he used the tip of his sword to spread them apart until each lay flat upon the floor. Their reflective surfaces looked the same. He even tried moving the sunstone back and forth to see if there might be hidden imperfections that might be revealed. But there were none.

*The light **had** killed the bird. It **had** vanished back into the pack.*

Now that the mirrors were safely out, he hooked the pack by inserting his sword within an end pouch. He then lifted it off the floor, allowing the pack to fully open so he could inspect each of the eight pouches. When nothing unusual was found, Holk lowered his sword and allowed the pack to fall to the floor.

If not the pack...

His attention turned to the three mirrors lying upon the floor. They appeared as they always had; still, dark, and unremarkable. As far as he could see, there was nothing unusual about either their aspect or composition.

Using the tip of his sword, he nudged the closest of the three then pulled back quickly. When nothing happened, he did the same to the next mirror. The third mirror, the one with the red dot designating it as the one that would return him to the Prison Room, proved just as unresponsive when it came its turn to be nudged.

Holk sheathed his sword. Kneeling next to the pack, he picked it up with two fingers, ready to drop it at the slightest hint of light. The pack remained dark. He then set about gathering the mirrors.

Treating each with great care, Holk gingerly reached out for the one closest to him. It was the one which would take him to Kazzra's cave. He laid a finger upon the frame and when nothing happened, pulled it close. Before lifting it from the floor, he moved the sunstone behind his back to shield its light so he could inspect the reflective surface for any emission of light. Not finding any, he carefully picked up the mirror and slid it into the pack.

The next was the one that would take him to the cave wherein laid the body of Kiernan. It, too, he treated with great care and after a close inspection, inserted it into the pack.

As he reached for the third and final mirror, the one bearing the red dot, small points of light flared in each corner of its reflective surface. Jerking back his hand, Holk watched as each of the four dots elongated and stretched toward the mirror's center. It took but seconds for the four bands of light to meet and erupt in a small, brilliant burst. As the light subsided, a worm-like appendage of pure light now protruded from the mirror's center.

Holk scrambled backward, sword leaping to hand.

The light-worm grew with every beat of his heart. It moved back and forth as would a stalk of wheat blown by the wind. Upon reaching a foot in length, the light-worm's end ceased its back and forth motion, and bent to touch the stone floor adjacent to the mirror.

It didn't move quickly; merely bobbed from one place to the next. For several minutes the light-worm continued as if inspecting its immediate surroundings. When it extended in Holk's direction, its movement slowed and the end bobbed several times.

He took another step backward, fearing that at any moment the light would leap forward as would a hound with a nose full of scent. But, the light merely bobbed for several heart-stopping moments before returning to its inspection of the area around the mirror. After another minute, the light-worm shrank back into the mirror and vanished.

The mirror lay dark upon the floor. When a hesitant step forward failed to cause the light-worm to reappear, Holk took a second. Stretching forth his swordarm to its full length, he took small steps until the sword's point came into contact with the mirror's frame. A single nudge caused it to slide ever so slightly across the floor; but again, the light-worm failed to rematerialize.

Keeping his distance from the mirror, Holk retrieved the pack holding the other two from where it sat upon the floor. He held it as he contemplated the mirror upon the floor.

Should I leave it there? Dare I risk taking it with me? In a quandary as to what to do, he decided to see if the light-worm would reappear a second time before committing to any course of action. It could have been a singular happenstance.

A full three paces from the mirror, he knelt to one knee and reached out his hand. Inch by inch he scooted ever nearer, poised to dart backward should the light reappear. At two paces away, the light had yet to return. When his hand came to within a foot and a half, the corners of the mirror flared with dots of light. They once again elongated to meet in the middle to form the light-worm.

Holk scrambled backward until a solid six paces separated him from the mirror. Just as before, the light-worm sniffed the air then proceeded to inspect the stone floor surrounding it. Minutes ticked by as it made a thorough search; then receded back into the mirror.

Once the mirror had gone dark, Holk moved closer and stretched his swordarm to its fullest until the sword tip touched the border near the red dot. The mirror remained unresponsive.

It doesn't appear for my sword. The two times it had emerged was when I reached for it with my hand. Glancing to the dead bird, he came to the conclusion that the light-worm came out for living flesh, not dead, cold steel.

His attention moved from the bird to the mirror. *But why that mirror and not the ones in the pack? And why now and not before?* The mirror had been in his possession for some time and the light-worm never before materialized. Then something Streyan had said flittered across his thoughts:

...the Starburst Gate would alter the rules for those who passed though...

"Is that what happened to you?" he asked the mirror. "I went through the Arch and now you are altered?" He thought about that and nodded. It had to be the answer. "You aren't much good to me now, are you? I can't even touch you without causing that light-worm thing to come." Hating to do it but seeing no alternative, he raised his sword high, set to strike the mirror and shatter it into many pieces.

Before the blow fell, the shattered mirrors from the hidden room came to mind. A dead man had lain upon the bed next to them. With sword poised to strike, the thought came to mind that perhaps the man may have died *because* he broke the mirrors. If he broke the mirror, would the light-worm be released? The only way to prove his theory was to smash the mirror. But if he was right, then he'd be dead, too. Afraid to find out, he sheathed his sword.

He'll regret losing the convenience of being able to return to the Prison Room whenever he wished, but he couldn't afford to take the mirror. Without it, he would have to access the Prison Room via the network of mirrors from the room wherein Kiernan's body lay.

What about his two remaining mirrors? Will they, too, be infected by the light-worm? And if so, would he discover that fact too late?

Had his need to use the mirrors in the event a quick getaway not been so great, he would have left all three on the floor of the Prison Room. But they had already proven their worth, primarily during his encounter with Kazzra the dragon. Escaping from a dragon's mouth in mid-chomp couldn't have been possible without them.

He took a moment to gaze into the pouch and inspect the mirrors. Both remained dark and unresponsive to his presence. Good. Perhaps the Prison Room mirror would be the only one infected. Pulling out the one leading to

Kiernan's Room, or perhaps a more apt term would be Kiernan's Tomb, he pressed his thumb against the reflective surface and translocated.

After slipping the mirror back into the pouch, he made his way to the wall-mounted mirror that led to the room full of steam. From there, he began the arduous journey through the series of rooms that would return him to the Ti-Ock mine; Steam Room to Salamander Room, then Salamander Room to Mirror Room.

Scrambling up the three boxes to touch the mirror attached to the ceiling, he appeared at the underground river. An extended stint of shelf-scooting brought him to the crevice which took him to the Ti-Ock mine. A short nap and three hours later, the Ti-Ocks once again departed en masse and he could safely make his way to the abandoned mine area beyond the cave-in.

During his trek through the abandoned area he utilized his sunstone to light his way. It was just prior to reaching where the tunnel began its downward descent that he noticed the illumination in the tunnel grow brighter. It took him but a moment to discover the change in light was due to a glow coming from out of his mirror-pack.

Undoing his belt, he quickly removed the pack and flung it to the side. The top fell open and the light-worm emerged. Just as it had twice before, the light-worm inspected its surroundings before withdrawing back into the pack.

Curses reverberated throughout the tunnel as Holk vented his anger and frustration. He couldn't take the mirrors with him. Whatever had happened to the first mirror had now affected a second, or perhaps the third as well? He wasn't about to find out.

Once his vitriolic tirade came to an end, the reality of the situation hit home. *There was no going back!* Without the mirrors, he could never return to the Prison Room, Kiernan's Room, or any of the other places in the chain of mirrors prior to the River Room. There was but one mirror within the River Room and it lay across a wide, torrential flood of water. He couldn't even reach the Merchant to see about bartering for another mirror.

A dozen of the healing mushrooms rested in his pouch. Without the ability to return and gather more, he had best insure the ones he had were used with great care. Holk thought about Streyan and how the boy had warned him about going through the Arch. Had the lad known this would happen? He would sure love to find out.

Giving out with a kick, he sent the mirror-pack skittering back down the passageway. As he turned to continue along the path toward the Arch, light grew behind him as once again, the light-worm made its appearance.

It didn't take long before the loss of the mirrors no longer bothered him. After all, weren't strength, wits and steel everything a soldier needed to prevail? Such had been hammered into him long ago when he was naught but a green recruit.

Strength to persevere
Wits to overcome.
Steel to prevail.

Holk couldn't help but crack a smile at memories of times long gone. His drill master had been as nasty a piece of work as anything that walked on two legs. But he had forged a ten-thumbed layabout into a skilled fighter. Better to rely on one's abilities, than those of magic.

Whistling a merry tune, he continued on his way.

The room with the Arch was as devoid of life as it had been the previous time. As he stood before the Arch, his confidence began to wane. *What if going through a second time altered things yet again? Dare he chance it? Dare he not?*

Glancing toward the steps leading to the landing upon which Streyan had sat gave him pause. In the back of his mind, he wondered what the lad had been doing up there. *Hadn't the boy said he had been merely "passing by" when he saw the light from the sunstone? Passing by to where?* Curiosity got the better of him and he walked over to the steps.

A search of the walls adjacent to the stairway failed to uncover any of the scribe's markings. He looked up to the landing and the walls to either side. No marks were found there either. Could it be that this might be a way Kiernan had not explored?

In his journal, the scribe claimed to have explored every avenue except what lay beyond the Arch. But the same passage also claimed that he was immediately beset by Ti-Ocks. The thought occurred to Holk that perhaps the scribe hadn't the chance to notice the steps before beating a hasty retreat. If that were the case... Better not to risk further complications with a second trip through the Arch; at least not until all other alternatives were exhausted. He ascended the steps.

At the top he found a hallway running perpendicular to the landing. On the wall directly opposite sat an empty torch sconce. Previously, the Ti-Ocks had come from the right. Peering cautiously around the corner, Holk discovered a dark corridor that extended without door or branching passageway into the shadows. To the left he discerned a second torch sconce just prior to the passageway vanishing into darkness. Since the Ti-Ocks had come from the right, Holk opted for the left. He could always come back and explore the right.

His hand clutched the sunstone tightly to his chest, allowing only a faint glow to illuminate the walls to either side. Once past the torch sconce, he discovered a scrap of purplish cloth, wadded upon the floor lying against the wall. He prodded it with the tip of his sword and discovered it to have been torn from a larger swath. Further inspection revealed it to be rather plain, but large enough to cover him from neck to waist and shoulder to shoulder. Thinking it might prove useful, he tucked it into his pack.

Twenty paces later, a distant greenish glow appeared in the corridor ahead. A moment's pause showed that the glow remained constant. Interest piqued, Holk took tentative steps forward.

Neither sound nor odor could be detected coming from the corridor ahead. As he drew closer, the glow grew in brilliance. It was not a cheery green such as might be associated with the Spring Festival back home, rather it glowed a darker, more ominous shade; a shade that generated feelings of apprehension. Holk clutched his sword all the tighter and continued forward, intent on discovering the truth behind this radiance.

Another thirty paces and the fact that the glow came from within a room became clear. Ten more and he could readily determine that the glow came from something, something several feet off the ground.

By this time, the light from the sunstone was no longer needed. Holk slipped it back into his belt pouch.

At first he thought the glowing object rested upon some kind of truncated column, or perhaps a table. But when he drew near the end of the hallway, could tell that the object hovered unsupported three and a half feet from the floor. His feelings of apprehension were quickly turning into dread. Upon reaching where the hallway opened into the room, Holk came to a stop in order to give the room a quick once-over before entering.

The object looked spherical and roughly the size of a small pumpkin. The light bathed the room with a sickly green hue. To his right sat an ornately carved table upon which rested three bowls. Two were the size of cups and flanked a much larger one. The larger bowl was completely filled with a shimmering, green opalescence. The sight caused his gorge to rise. Swallowing hard, he ripped his eyes away and his stomach calmed.

A door loomed in the wall to his left. Arcane symbols covered its surface, the greatest density of symbols being in the vicinity of the ringed handle. The way the light was being refracted by the handle, Holk figured it to be constructed of some kind of crystal. What may have lain on the far side of the room remained shielded by the glow of the object. Only indistinct shadows of the room's farthest reaches could be discerned.

From the corner of his eye he caught sight of the shaking of his blade and realized he quaked in fear like one new to the blade before his first battle. He turned his back on the room and allowed his gaze to take in the darkness of the corridor. Now no longer looking at the glow, his fear gradually subsided to a more manageable level.

If Streyan had in fact been passing by the landing as claimed, then that would mean he had been either coming from this room, or to it. There had been no branching passageways or doors through which the lad could have gone.

Holk had half a mind to turn around and leave this room alone. Past experiences had developed a trust in his innate senses, and the fear the green glow generated clearly stated that he should give it a wide berth. Yet the question remained, what had Streyan been doing there?

Fear or no fear, he had to see where that door leading from the room went. If a mere lad could make it through unscathed, should not a seasoned fighter? Steeling his courage, he turned back to face the glow. It remained just as strong and fearful as before. Holk gripped his sword hilt firmly and stepped into the room.

His fear increased two-fold and sweat broke out upon his brow. Stepping quickly, he skirted the edge of the room and made his way to the door. There, he gripped the crystal ring and found it cool to the touch. The door swung open easily on well-greased hinges to reveal another hallway leading away from the room.

Once in the passageway, he closed the door and the glow vanished. He leaned against it as a sigh of relief escaped him; his fear and dread dissipated rapidly. But then his fear spiked anew upon noticing that the blade of his sword held a subtle, green glow. Sheathing the blade did much to quell the rising fear, however, portions of the hilt held the greenish glow as well.

The glow came from the pommel and the crossguard. The section where his fingers had held it glowed not at all. It was as if whatever portion of the blade that had been exposed to the greenish glow, now exuded the same greenish luminescence. Holk didn't know what this meant, but didn't think it would improve his situation. Allowing his gaze to linger where the steel glowed green, he failed to feel the fear rising within him as it had earlier. Since he could discern no ill effects, and wasn't about to cast off his weapon, he kept the sword sheathed and continued on his way.

—15—

Striking the sunstone to once again produce its light, he left behind the room with the green, glowing object. Holk had followed the passageway only a short ways before noticing a rise in temperature. Subtle at first, the air in the tunnel grew warmer the farther he went.

The corridor curved to the right, grew narrower, and when it once again proceeded in a straight line, light appeared in the distance. Not the greenish light as encountered in the previous room, but rather the normal light such as a torch or lantern might emit. Comforted by the normalcy, Holk hurried on.

The light grew in brilliance as he drew near where the corridor opened upon a large cavern. The temperature increased rapidly during the last twenty paces of the corridor. Pausing just before the entrance, Holk took in the odd sight before him.

Six large, rough-hewn monoliths rose in a somewhat circular pattern from the cavern floor two-score paces away. Within the ring formed by the six, a seventh laid skewed on its side. Holk couldn't see most of it as one of the six constructing the circle obscured his view. The monoliths were the source of the heat.

Upon the ground near one of the stone spire's base sat a lantern which turned out to be the source of the light. A closer inspection of the area surrounding the lantern revealed an over-stuffed mirror-pack that looked rather familiar.

Streyan.

Though the cavern appeared deserted, Holk figured the boy couldn't be far; not if the lad's mirror-pack was there. After another quick scan of the cavern, he moved as quickly and silently as he dared toward the pack. He was ready for some answers and this time wasn't about to allow the boy a chance to get away.

Ten paces in, he found the boy. As he neared the ring of stone monoliths, more of the seventh came into view. Streyan lay upon its stony surface, stretched out on his back and looking to be asleep. Holk grinned to himself.

Another ten paces and the lad had yet to realize he was not alone. Holk quickened his pace and inadvertently kicked a loose stone across the ground toward the nearest monolith. Its impact against the stone spire resounded throughout the cavern and the boy sprang to a sitting position.

"No!" Hopping off the fallen spire, Streyan raced to beat Holk to the pack.

The boy sped faster toward the pack than Holk thought possible. Streyan closed the distance and amazingly, was going to beat Holk to it.

Holk refused to allow the boy to gain access to the mirrors. Drawing his sword and leaping at the same time, his body crashed into the boy's not two feet from the pack. The collision knocked Streyan off his feet and sent him sailing through the air to land with an "oomph" upon the ground between two of the upright monoliths. In a flash, the boy was back on his feet.

Standing astride the pack, Holk menaced him with the point of his blade. "Not this time, boy."

Streyan looked at the sword, then at the pack, then assumed a petulant look as he returned his gaze to Holk. "But that's mine."

"I'm not taking it." Thinking of the light-worms that had emerged from his mirrors, Holk used his foot to shove the pack several feet across the floor behind him. When Streyan tried racing around a monolith to circumvent him and reach the pack, Holk matched his movement and foiled the attempt.

The boy moved back within the circle of monoliths and stood next to the fallen one; his gaze never once straying from Holk. When Holk moved to enter the ring, an alarmed expression came over the lad.

"St…stay where you are."

Holk shook his head and continued advancing. "No, son. *You* stay where *you* are."

Spinning about, Streyan shot toward the gap between two monoliths directly opposite where Holk was about to enter. "Don't!"

Holk rushed after. He wasn't about to let the boy get away; there were too many questions that needed answering. As he passed through the monolithic ring and entered its interior, green tendrils of glowing radiance lanced outward from his sword blade.

The sheer unexpectedness of their appearance brought him up short. A moment after they connected with the monoliths, Holk was knocked from his feet by some unseen force. Before hitting the ground, another blow reeled him into the side of the fallen monolith.

Green haze swirled like a rapidly growing vortex in and around the ring of upright monoliths. None of the haze held presence within the spired circle.

Holk managed to gain his feet only to be thrust upward four feet off the floor. The unseen force held him in place for the span of two heartbeats before throwing him back to the ground. Just prior to hitting, the force changed direction and back into the air he went.

"What...?" he began, but a blow to his diaphragm knocked the air from his lungs.

The swirling haze intensified its rotation. Though buffeted from side to side like a rag doll in a restless child's hands, Holk heard not a sound to indicate who, or what, was doing this to him.

After being slammed against the side of the fallen spire, Holk had a moment's respite. He spied Streyan through the haze to where the lad stood several feet beyond the ring of monoliths. The boy bore a sad expression. His lips moved as if attempting to communicate, but his words couldn't penetrate the swirling, green haze.

Using his left hand as support against the fallen spire, Holk regained an upright position. A glance upward revealed that the spinning haze extended to the farthest reaches of the cavern. He returned his gaze to Streyan, but the boy no longer sought to communicate. The lad had retrieved his mirror-pack and now stood with hand raised in farewell.

"Wait!" Holk yelled as Streyan's other hand moved toward the mirror-pack's opening. Before another word could be uttered, the air turned viscous. The space around him appeared unchanged, yet over the span of several heartbeats, movement became all but impossible.

The swirling of the green haze increased in speed. The thickening of the air inhibited movement almost completely. For the first time since boyhood, Holk knew true panic.

He turned eyes wild with fear toward Streyan. His plea for help stillborn; it was all he could do to merely separate his lips to breathe. Inhalation grew labored as his chest worked against the restriction imposed by the thickening of the air around him.

The boy's lips worked again, and though Holk could not hear the word, knew it to be "Goodbye." With that, Streyan slipped a finger within the mirror-pack and vanished.

Constriction increased and Holk could no longer extend his diaphragm to draw in breath. Pressure built evenly across the entire surface of his body as the air grew ever more rigid. Discomfort quickly grew into throbbing; throbbing into pain.

Asphyxiated induced dots danced before his eyes. The beating of his heart could be felt throughout his body as blood sought to continue along its lifelong route. Vision blurred, darkened, then he knew no more.

At some point, consciousness returned; and so too did pain. From the tips of his toes all the way to the top of his head, his body throbbed most unpleasantly. He cracked open an eye and quickly shut it again as the contents of his stomach sought to surge forth.

It wasn't the pain that had caused him to react so, but the world around him. A mist enveloped him, one that was neither wet nor cold. In fact, he couldn't feel it at all, nor smell it for that matter. A dark purple in color, the mere sight of it had triggered the nauseating reaction. Taking a few breaths to calm his stomach, he steeled himself and opened his eyes.

He barely had time to shift onto his side before a spasm deep within his stomach sent its contents up and out. Closing his eyes did much to quiet his belly. Once the spell ended, he rolled onto his back and kept his eyes shut tight.

The possibility of having struck his head came to mind. Pain and nausea were common to soldiers after receiving a blow to the head. A brief examination revealed neither an enlarged bump, nor an area tenderer than another. Still, that didn't mean it hadn't happened.

Recalling recent events did little to convince him he hadn't struck his head. Vague memories of Streyan, stone spires, and being tossed around like so much chaff in the wind did more to convince him of serious head trauma than anything else. If he had, his situation had just grown direr.

Lying still as the minutes passed failed to ease the feeling of unease which had steadily grown upon him. It came not so much from the possibility of injury, but from another source; one he could not quite put his finger on.

Opening his eyes in order to discover the source of his unease caused bile to rise in the back of his throat. He quickly discarded the thought. If visual inspection of his surroundings was out of the question, then perhaps a tactile one might prove beneficial. With that thought in mind, he turned his attention to the floor upon which he lay.

To his utter amazement, neither stone nor wood comprised the surface beneath him. In fact, there *was* no surface at all. Holk extended his arm to its fullest reach and still encountered naught but empty air. Panic took over and forced his eyes open causing an intense spell of nausea. By sheer strength of will, he snapped his eyes closed once again.

No floor, no walls, no ceiling; it made no sense. He didn't feel as if he was falling. There was no sense of motion. In fact, there was little in the way of sensation of any kind. Inhaling brought no scent, not even that of his stomach's contents that had recently been expelled. He felt neither hot nor cold. Had he been falling, there would be a rush of wind; instead there was complete and utter stillness. Truly, he must be mad.

In his right hand, he could still feel the heft and weight of his sword, though it felt a bit odd. There was something… then it hit him. The sword was not being pulled toward the ground, merely retaining its current position all by itself. He could move it to and fro, up and down. But when he brought the sword to a halt, it remained still.

About to give in to the belief that his mind had finally been overcome, Holk felt the presence of another. Power, ageless and terrible, washed over him stealing what wits he had left. Gibbering in fear, he sensed that the presence was aware of him.

Human.

More a thought than voice, the single word coursed through him like a jagged knife, leaving behind a swath of pain and agony.

You have not that which we desire.

Each word increased his pain and terror. Screams, uncontrollable and filled with madness, filled his ears. Somewhere in the nether recesses of his mind, he realized they were his own. A moment later the intensity of the presence increased and left his mind bereft of all reason. Before Holk slipped into blissful unconsciousness, a thought penetrated the dark halls of madness.

Perhaps another might find you of use.

Consciousness returned, not by the slow steps of normal human recovery, but in an abrupt manner such as might occur after one was doused with a bucket of water fresh from a snow-bound mountaintop.

A single scream erupted from a deep primordial place. Using the full measure of his lung capacity, the cry wrenched him from madness and returned him to reality.

He was not where he had been. The surface beneath where he lay felt smooth as glass and cool to the touch. Cracking open an eye revealed a sky, ruby in color with wisps of what he would think of as clouds if they had been white instead of a deep orange.

Turning his head to the side brought a field of silver into view. The silvery "ground" upon which he lay extended to the limit of his vision in absolute flatness without hill, tree, or any other obstruction marring its smooth perfection.   Though unnaturally smooth, the surface had a grittiness that Holk found disturbing.

Fear still held sway within him, although its mastery diminished with each passing heartbeat. A shaky hand settled upon the hilt of his sword. The cold steel gave comfort and aided the return of his courage.

Dizziness assailed him as he sat to get a better look at his surroundings. The landscape looked nothing like anything he had ever seen before. Ruby-red sky, orange clouds and silvery ground; truly, he must have lost his mind.

Recent memories sought to return, but with them came fear. Feeling his fleeting courage waning beneath this renewed onslaught, Holk fought to banish the memories. *Home; mother; father;* upon these he concentrated until the burgeoning terror had at last been vanquished.

Once able to calm his mind and turn it to the problem at hand, he climbed to his feet and took in the featureless landscape.

Where am I?

It was clear he was no longer in the subterranean complex of mirrors and caverns. Where he was exactly...well...that escaped him at the moment. But with everything that he had recently experienced, he wasn't nearly as overwhelmed as he once would have been.

The orange clouds above floated by on an unfelt current. The air around Holk remained static; just one more incongruity of this strange, alien land.

Figuring the answer to his whereabouts and how to depart from this place would not be found by remaining where he was, Holk once again scanned the horizon. Every direction looked the same with nothing but unremitting, silvery flatness. Unnerved to say the least, he set out across this foreign landscape.

Two steps into his trek, a dark object appeared on the horizon. It appeared to be an upright, rectangular construction; what exactly it was couldn't be determined from such a far distance. Intrigued, Holk set out toward it.

Each step brought him closer to the object than a man's stride should have been able to accomplish. Half a dozen paces covered a distance three times that and it soon became apparent that what Holk was heading toward was a cage.

Narrow bars set close together formed a prison of sorts. It measured roughly four feet by five and rose to a height over an arm-span taller than Holk. The most curious aspect of the cage, aside from the fact that it had no door, was the lack of any seam. It appeared as if it had been constructed all of one piece.

Within the bars sat an armored man slumped against the side of the cage. At first, Holk believed the man may yet live, but upon drawing nearer to the cage, realized life no longer remained. The eyes were sunken and its skin had drawn tightly against the bones beneath.

Light from the red sky overhead reflected off an impeccably polished breastplate and shield. Both bore a yellow sun on a golden field. Bony fingers still gripped the hilt of a longsword that made his sword look like a pig-sticker.

The weapon looked to be made of steel, but bore an unusual sheen that Holk was at a loss to identify. It gave the weapon a slight shimmering appearance. A red stone the size of an egg had been set into the crossbar of the hilt; it may have been a ruby though he couldn't be certain. The overall appearance of the weapon was that of master craftsmanship.

Holk wanted that sword. He felt that with it in his possession, his ability to survive whatever trials lay ahead would be increased dramatically. Reaching through the bars, he dislodged the sword from the skeletal grip and pulled it from the cage.

The balance was perfect and weighed only half that of his. Being of comparable size, it slid easily within his scabbard. He laid his old sword next to the dead man in the cage. Not the most equitable of trades, but he figured no one would complain.

Drawing his new blade, Holk made several passes through the air. The weapon moved effortlessly and took relatively little strength to wield. He gave the unusual sheen a closer inspection but failed to discern anything about it other than it made the surface of the blade shimmer, similar in nature to heat radiating off a heated surface; only there was no heat. All in all, a most curious weapon. Sheathing it once again, he returned his attention to the cage.

How had the man come to be within if there was no seam or point of entry?

Holk tried rattling the cage in an attempt to unveil the cage's secrets, but it failed to give them up. Finally realizing his energy could be better spent, such as working on getting him back home, Holk returned his attention to the unnatural landscape.

Silvery, unchanging desolation stretched from one horizon to another. The only aspect of this entire place that varied from one moment to the next were the orange clouds high overhead. Drifting along in the upper atmosphere, they at least provided some point of reference; "upstream" and "downstream." Turning toward the point where the clouds originated, Holk decided to follow the clouds "upstream."

As he moved from the corpse in the cage, he kept his eyes peeled for any sign of other breaks in the monotony of this silvery land. Ten steps into his upstream trek, he glanced over his shoulder and was surprised to find the cage now to be a far distance away.

Holk didn't like this place and wanted nothing more than to leave it behind. Continuing upstream, another five paces brought an object into view. As fast as he had left the cage behind, he proceeded to advance on what quickly proved to be another cage identical to the first; complete with a slumped over, armored individual wearing the exact same style of armor. Only this time, there was no sword gripped in its skeletal hand. Instead, the sword remained sheathed.

Again, the cage proved to be seamless and without point of entry. If not for his inability to open the dead man's prison, Holk would have availed himself of the armor; for the dead man looked to be roughly his size. Armor of such superior craftsmanship would assuredly prove to be vital. Sighing, he moved off from the cage and continued his trek.

Another cage came into view some distance farther upstream and to his right. Before closing half the distance, another appeared on the horizon to his left. Holk continued to the one on his right. When it proved to be identical as the first two, seamless and with a dead man slumped against the side wearing armor of the same design, he made for the one on the left.

Three more dark silhouettes appeared farther upstream before he reached the third cage. After a cursory glance at the long-deceased, armored individual caged within, Holk continued toward the fourth, then to the fifth.

With each cage visited, more dark silhouettes came into view farther ahead. As he went, the number of cages appearing on the horizon increased. Soon, there were over a dozen within his field of vision. Each held an armored, dead man.

Why would anyone spend time to construct individual cages? Wouldn't it have been better to create a single large one? Holk merely shook his head as he progressed into an ever growing forest of cages.

Another incongruous aspect was that the cages were spaced some distance apart. None were less than ten paces from their neighbors. Pausing next to one while pondering that fact, his attention was drawn to movement off on the horizon.

It moved laterally at the limit of his field of vision for several heartbeats, during which time, he saw similar motion to his left and right. Glancing behind him through the bars of the cage, he saw movement out that way as well. They were too far away for him to make out clearly, but whatever they were, they had him surrounded. Drawing his newly acquired sword, he put his back to the cage and waited to see if they would be friend or foe.

Minutes passed and the dark shapes appeared content to maintain their current position. Moving back and forth, they reminded Holk of soldiers on guard duty. That thought gave him little comfort for what kind of soldiers would there be in a place like this? *Were they comrades of those within the cages? Or were they the ones who put them there?*

When it appeared they did not mean to approach, Holk figured he'd best try to beat a hasty retreat. Planning a route through an area containing the most cages, he made for the mid-point of a gap between the two most downstream of his position.

He took one step away from the side of the cage and...

Wham!

Faster than an eagle in flight, all four objects that had been moving along the horizon shot toward him and came together in a resounding clash. The objects had been quarter-sections of a cage, a cage in which he now found himself.

The construction was seamless and resisted his every attempt to bend, hack and smash his way through. He was trapped!

—16—

Time couldn't be measured when nothing changed. In the silvery land with the red sky, night never came. The only way in which Holk could gauge the passage of time was his growing hunger and thirst. What few healing mushrooms were left in his pack he conserved like a miser would a hoard of coins.

Thrice he had fallen asleep. Each time upon awakening he would consume only a single mushroom. They did much to revitalize him and ease the ache of hunger, but their effects didn't last long. Hunger would quickly return.

With naught else to do, his attention inevitably turned toward the nearby cage and the dead man within. Being of average height and bearing what at one time must have been fair looks, the man would have passed unnoticed on the streets of Holk's hometown. In this alien landscape, the dead man's normalcy felt wrong though Holk couldn't explain why.

Sometime after his third sleep period, motion from off in the distance drew his attention. At first he thought it might be more of the cage sections moving about, but that notion was soon dispelled as a mass of gigantic proportions gradually made its way through the forest of cages toward him. Drawing his sword, Holk came to his feet and watched.

It would pause at cages, though not all of them. Remaining motionless for several minutes before each, once as long as ten, it would then move on to the next.

As it drew nearer to the cage containing Holk, its features failed to become clearer. Translucent and bulbous, its shape was in a constant state of flux. Perhaps the most unnerving aspect was how there was little transition from one shape to another. It would go from being very tall and towering over the cages to squat and bulging like a short, fat man.

Whatever this was, it had no discernible appendages, head or anything else one would think to find on a living creature such as eyes, nose or mouth. It slithered…though slithered would not be an entirely accurate way to explain its mode of locomotion. Slithering would indicate a gliding and undulation along the ground. This had none of that. Its lower end did not appear to move, yet it did.

During its pause at a cage forty paces away, Holk noticed something within the creature. Though unclear from such a distance, it grew to clarity when the creature continued its movement through the forest of cages and drew closer. It was a landscape.

Stunted trees and misshapen buildings of an unnatural construction could be seen within the creature. But as the creature moved, so too did the scene within it change. It wasn't until the creature paused at the cage next to his that he realized what he saw could not be within the creature.

When the creature moved, the scene failed to move in sync with the creature, yet still changed as would a coastal scene viewed through the porthole of a ship traveling upon the ocean; the body of the creature being the porthole.

Holk didn't have time to ponder this new revelation. The creature had moved from the cage and was coming toward him. Fear welled and he held his new-found sword between them.

"Back!"

The creature failed to respond and continued its ponderous approach.

Thrusting the blade through the bars of his cage, Holk again cried, "Back! Come no closer."

Either unaware or unconcerned with Holk's warning, the creature pressed forward. It came to within several feet from the tip of the sword before coming to a halt.

The scene within the creature was now in stark clarity. Beings half the size of humans bearing a dog-like bestiality moved among house-like structures situated among hills and trees. Despite the proximity of such a massive creature, Holk couldn't help but have his attention drawn to the scene playing out within its bulbous mass.

The beings wore clothes, walked on two legs, and smaller versions of the dog-like beings raced as if in play among the buildings.

Houses? Could they be houses? Had they been humans, he would have thought the scene portrayed the humble life of a small village.

A ripple coursing through the bulbous creature ended his contemplation of the village. Though there were no eyes gazing upon him, Holk knew that the creature was aware of him. Backing to the rear of the cage, he held his sword at the ready and waited.

The creature approached until it practically touched the bars of the cage. Suddenly, red light flared from the gem in the sword's crossbar. Bright, warm and comforting, the radiance instantly dispelled his fear and renewed his courage.

The moment the light sprang to life, the creature vanished only to reappear twenty feet away. So quick had been the transition that Holk almost hadn't seen it happen. He grinned at the creature, brandished his sword and stepped forward until the glowing gem had passed through the bars and shone unobstructed upon the creature.

"You don't like this, do you?"

Time passed as the glow radiated forth. The body of the creature continued changing from one aspect to another, all the while as a whole seeming to remain motionless. After an unknown number of heartbeats, the creature moved off toward a nearby cage and the glow faded to nothingness. Holk watched as the creature wended its way through the cages. When it finally passed out of sight back the way from which it came, he turned his attention to the sword and the gem it held.

Whatever power the gem held, it kept the creature from him when active. The hope that he may make it from this place blossomed anew until his gaze fell upon the skeletal warrior within the cage nearest his and the sword identical to his that was gripped in its bony hand. Obviously, the power of the sword would not affect his escape from this cage, since those who met their doom throughout this land had been unable to do so. Still, he could keep the creature at bay and that was something.

Settling down with back leaned against the bars, Holk glanced periodically toward the horizon into which the creature disappeared. *Had it been his captor? Or could it have merely been an inhabitant of this land that just happened by?*

The way the creature had paused near the cages unsettled him. *What could it have been doing?* He had felt nothing when the creature stopped before his cage. It could have been that the power of the sword prevented the creature from causing him harm. Of course, the creature could have been nothing more than a visitor similar to those that would frequent *Killery's Menagerie of Fantastic Creatures* that came to his hometown when he was a boy. He, too, would stop before different cages to view odd and fascinating animals.

But perhaps the most perplexing aspect of the creature had been the scene of a town peopled with beast-like humanoids. The creature hadn't been large enough to have an entire village within its body. Holk couldn't rationalize the inconsistencies and so after a while, believed that he had imagined that part of the encounter.

He had plenty of time to contemplate the creature. Six sleep periods passed before a dark shape moved once more upon the horizon. Just as before, the large bulbous creature worked its way among the forest of cages, pausing at some while bypassing others.

Holk came to his feet and drew his sword. He watched as the creature drew ever closer. In every way save one, this creature was identical to the one that had come visiting earlier. The difference was in its hue, it was somewhat bluer than its predecessor. The reason for the color disparity became clear when the creature paused at a nearby cage.

Instead of a village scene with beast-like humanoids, this creature held a scene of radiant, blue water surrounded by beige sand. A strong breeze blew through tall, thin trees growing along what Holk took to be a desert oasis. When the creature moved in his direction, he could almost feel the heat radiating from the sand.

Again, the light sprang forth from the gem and forced the creature back. This visitor remained motionless nearly twice as long as the previous one had before moving off to wend its way through the cages before once again vanishing from whence it came.

Holk had much to contemplate during the time between his next three rest periods. First and foremost were the creatures and the way their skins appeared transparent to reveal a world apart. Or at least that was how he thought of it for there simply was no other explanation that made sense.

The other item was the sword with the gem that sprang to life whenever the creatures came close. Did it react to the creature, or perhaps it reacted to the threat posed to the one wielding it? Either way, it had definitely saved him twice now.

True, it *had* saved him. But to what end? There were plenty of men wielding similar weapons scattered throughout this silvery landscape. Each had a sword of similar design so it would follow that they, too, had been safe from those massive, shape-changing creatures. Yet they had died.

A way needed to be divined that would enable him to break free from the cage holding him. Though the sword may keep the creature at bay, it would not fill his stomach or quench the nagging thirst plaguing him. Without food and water, he would soon die.

Two mushrooms remained. He planned to consume half of one after his next sleep period in order to make them last. If he hadn't figured a way out by the time the last one was gone... Shaking his head, he banished such thoughts; they would only sap what courage and strength was left to him.

A way must be found!

Another creature reappeared after his next sleep period. This one held a scene depicting a dead landscape. Holes of perfect circular symmetry dotted a land barren and lifeless. Most of the depressions ranged from small craters to ones that could consume an entire house. Others were so large that they themselves were dotted with collections of the smaller variety.

Again the sword kept the creature at bay and it eventually continued on. Holk leaned against the bars of his cage as the creature disappeared into the horizon. His strength was waning; eating half a mushroom was not nearly as affective as a whole one. The duration before fatigue set in was greatly diminished. Twice more he slept and twice more he ate half a mushroom.

"Looks like this is the end."

Staring through the bars to his nearest neighbor, Holk chuckled sadly. "After all I've been through, I never thought the end would come in such a way."

The skeletal visage of the warrior stared silently back.

Sighing, he looked down to where his last remaining mushroom-half rested in his palm. He contemplated eating it and be done with it, but instead slipped it back into his pouch.

His stomach cramped and his throat was parched to such an extent that his voice cracked when he spoke. Despite such discomfort, he would wait until after awakening one more time before eating it; if his will remained strong, perhaps he would wait until the one after that.

"You know, I've been through quite a bit these last few weeks."

Attention again returning to the dead warrior, Holk paused and after a few moments of silence, realized he had been expecting a response. Laughter tinged with a touch of madness boiled forth. He raised his sword in a salute.

"At least we can keep the creature away until the end comes, right?" Again he laughed. When the laughter drew to a close, he lowered his sword.

"But what good does it do to keep it away if you are going to die anyway? Allow yourself to endure a few more days of starvation and thirst? Better to die quickly than to wither away like that."

Empty sockets in a face withered and drawn failed to deliver a response.

"Did I tell you how I came to be here? You might not believe it, but I was in an area where magical mirrors would transport you from one place to another. Hard to swallow, I know. But it's the gods' own truth."

He retrieved his mushroom half and showed it to his skeletal neighbor. "Got this from there; a whole subterranean cavern was full of these. What I would give to be there now."

Again he contemplated eating it, but instead returned it to his pouch. "I think I'll save this for tomorrow."

Several moments passed while he rested quietly against the side of the cage.

"Any idea what those creatures are that come through here? You might think I'm crazy, but it looks like they have worlds within them."

He looked questioningly at his neighbor.

"Wouldn't it be funny if this silvery land was inside one of those creatures? Maybe someone else in another cage in another place will see us sitting here having this talk. Wonder what he would make of it? Probably think he'd lost his mind.

"I have to admit, I've considered the fact that my mind has been lost and that this is merely a madman's delirium." Patting the ground, Holk shook his head. "But I think not. It seems all too real."

"So, where are you from? Some place around here? Judging by the number of your fellows that have been entrapped here, my guess would be that you are not, but do know how to get here.

"And that leads me to my next question. *Why* are you here? War? That would make sense seeing as how each and every one of you are armed and armored. Could it be that you are trying to kill those translucent, world-encasing creatures? They don't appear to like the glow put out by the gem in your swords."

Glancing to the sword lying next to him, he added, "It would be interesting to know how it does that." He returned his attention to his neighbor. "I don't suppose you could tell me?"

The skeletal gaze offered little explanation.

Holk sighed. "I didn't think so, 'twas but a thought."

He sat talking to his neighbor, not an entirely sane activity, but it helped to while away the time. Beginning with the time just prior to the ill-fated attack that resulted in the annihilation of his fellow soldiers, Holk chronicled for his neighbor the series of events which culminated with his current predicament. By the time the full telling had been accomplished, his eyelids were heavy and he pardoned himself of his neighbor explaining that he must put aside the conversation in favor of sleep.

"We'll continue our conversation when I wake." *If I do.* In his present state, he felt that to be a very real possibility but was far too weary to care.

Dreams of home, silvery lands, and skeletal warriors came to an end and consciousness returned. Cracking open his eyelids, his tenuous state of consciousness solidified in a flash when he spied one of the massive, translucent creatures standing at the bars of his cage.

In the moment following recognition, Holk took in the pastoral scene of wild horses racing across a meadow beneath a blazing sun in a clear-blue sky unfolding within the central body of the creature.

Horror filled him upon realizing that a portion of the creature had oozed between the bars and was slowly engulfing his boots. An attempt to pull his feet free proved futile, they were stuck fast like a fly that had landed on a dollop of honey.

Casting about for his sword, he discovered it lying on the ground next to him. As soon as his hand gripped the hilt, the gem burst forth in an amber starburst.

A fleeting disorientation followed and he was outside the cage; his feet still entrapped within the creature. He scarcely had time for this new development to register before experiencing another bout of disorientation.

The glow continued unabated as he was hit with two more times of momentary disorientation. After the last, his feet were no longer mired within the creature. It had let him go and now stood twenty feet away. Holk felt as if the creature was watching him. But since the creature had no eyes or any other semblance to human sensory equipment, it was hard to tell for sure. Then it hit him:

He was out!

Being in contact with the creature when it translocated away from the red glow must have caused him to accompany it. Coming to his feet, Holk felt renewed hope of survival bolster his strength. He grinned at the creature.

"My thanks for freeing me."

They faced off with the glowing red sword between them for a short time before the creature moved off. Holk lowered the sword and didn't sheathe it until the creature moved off and the gem's glow had vanished.

Turning to glance behind him revealed that the creature had brought him quite a ways from his former prison. He could see where it now sat empty. Now he knew how to escape the cages should he again be ensnared. Worried that another of the cages may appear, he searched the horizons but could not see the tell-tale shadows that had preceded the earlier one's appearance.

He did, however, discover a brightening of the landscape off to his right. Figuring any sort of change to be a chance at freedom, he made toward it with all speed.

It hadn't taken long before his newfound strength waned and he was forced to consume the last mushroom portion. The small remnant filled him with vigor and enabled him to quicken his pace even more.

The brightening soon clarified into what looked like a bubble rising from the landscape. It was reminiscent of the way bubbles formed on the surface of water during a downpour. Twice as bright as the land surrounding it, the bubble rose to a height greater than that of King Redstorm's castle back home. At the base where the bubble met the land, periodic perturbations formed cave-like openings. Holk made for the largest one.

At the edge of the opening, he paused and peered carefully within. The interior was not hollow as one would expect of an actual bubble. Instead, it was solid and formed of the same silvery substance that made the landscape. A tunnel of sorts extended some distance deeper within the bubble until curving out of sight to the left.

Holk felt rather relieved upon leaving the exposed surface of the silvery land and entering an area where there were but two avenues from which an attack could be launched; ahead in the tunnel and behind.

Moving forward cautiously, he set out to see where this would lead.

—17—

As bright as the bubble's outer shell had been, the interior proved to be contrastingly dark. Not a complete dark to be sure; the walls did radiate a small amount of light allowing him to make out the contours of the tunnel.

Once he moved beyond where the passage curved to the left, the illumination dimmed even further as the light entering from the tunnel mouth no longer contributed its brilliance.

Holk stepped quickly as he followed the tunnel. It retained a uniform size as it progressed deeper within the bubble. At one point, he came to realize the tunnel slanted downward, and that he was gradually descending into the bowels of the silvery land.

Time seemed to pass slowly. The tunnel extended on and on, never changing and always continuing its downward slope. It didn't take long before the effects of the mushroom wore off and the onset of fatigue once more became a real concern. When the burden of fatigue grew too great, he would pause and sit with back against the wall to recoup his strength. After a small measure had been recovered, he would return to his feet and continue.

Twice he rested, each time taking more willpower to resume his trek through this endless passageway. Not long after his second rest break, he saw motion in the dim light of the tunnel ahead. Holk came to a stop and pressed against the passage wall.

He was ready for a fight, but feared what may be encountered in this strange place. An adrenalin rush foreshadowing combat refreshed his weary body. From past experiences, he knew this state of vigor would not last. Once it faded, he would be worse off than before. Best to take advantage of his returned strength while he could. Moving ahead, he quick-timed it down the tunnel. Twelve paces brought him close enough to determine that the motion belonged to another of those large, translucent creatures that had visited him during his recent incarceration.

It moved deeper into the tunnel, and for the time being, appeared oblivious to Holk's presence. He came to within twenty paces then slowed and paced the creature as it continued progressing down the tunnel. If it knew it was not alone in the tunnel, it gave no sign.

Holk's hand repeatedly crept toward the hilt of his sword, but always stopped short from touching it. This close to the creature, the gem's red glow would surely shine forth and announce his presence. Curious as to where it went, he maintained his distance and followed.

At this distance, he couldn't quite see the scene playing out within its massive bulk. As he followed, his eyes were drawn to the shadows and intermittent pockets of light coursing through its bulk. When blue light appeared on the far left side of the scene, curiosity inadvertently caused him to quicken his pace.

In the blink of an eye, the creature went from twenty paces away to less than a foot. Putting it into full reverse, he leapt backward in shocked surprise. As he did so, a trio of bulges exuded outward from the creature; one at eye level, another bulged toward his chest, and the third approached his knees.

Fearing to be entrapped within it as had his boots during an earlier encounter, Holk clasped the hilt of his sword and drew it forth. Immediately, the gem's glow flared with blinding brilliance and the creature vanished only to reappear farther down the tunnel.

"Not this time!" Waving the sword, he gave chase.

As he closed the distance, it blinked out of sight only to reappear farther down the tunnel. Holk raced after.

Maybe it was the thrill of the chase, or perhaps some inherent property within the ruby glow of the gem, but instead of waning, his strength waxed. Laughing with giddy euphoria as his fatigue melted away, he pursued the fleeing creature.

Popping in and out, each time farther down the tunnel, the creature sought to escape the ruby glow. Holk didn't understand his need to catch the creature. After all, it was three times his size and had indicated a desire to consume him. But, he had a sword in his hand, his enemy was in flight, and this was something he could understand. The need to catch and vanquish this creature drove him onward.

A junction appeared in the tunnel ahead. The creature appeared down the right-hand fork. Holk followed.

Other openings came into view, some on the left, others on the right. The first seven the creature ignored. When it appeared near the eighth, it vanished again and failed to re-materialize once more within the main body of the passageway. Holk raced past the opening before realizing the creature had gone inside. Backing up, he peered within, saw the creature and the chase resumed.

This new passage was narrower and barely had the height to accommodate its massive bulk. For Holk it mattered not. Anywhere his prey could go, he would follow.

The chase led to a short, wider expanse of the narrow passageway. Upon entering, Holk felt an immediate dampening of his enthusiasm, and lethargy filled his limbs. Once past and back into the narrow tunnel, his vigor returned.

Passing into a second widening, this one much larger than the first, nearly took his breath away. Dread washed over him. Stumbling from the unexpected onslaught, Holk kept from falling and continued the chase. Before exiting this widened area of the passage, he noticed veins of a dark, reddish substance marring the tunnel's silvery perfection. Once past, his vigor again returned as the feeling of dread melted away.

Little time was given to ponder what had happened before another widening appeared in the gem's glow. This one was twice the size of the previous and reddish veins created a patchwork consisting of scores; some were as thick as his arm.

The previous two areas where the passageway had widened came with a sense of dread, the previous one nearly overpowering. Trepidation about continuing brought him to a halt just before where the veins of red began.

In the first area, there had been a sense of dread. The second such area had been larger and the dread had been much more potent; having nearly overwhelmed him. *Did he dare continue into this larger area? And just what was the source of this dread?* His eyes turned to where the veins began not two feet away and were forced to turn away when the dread intensified. *Has to be.*

Twenty paces into the widening of the passage, the translucent creature stood as if waiting for him to continue. Daring him?

"Fear is a soldier's true enemy."

Words of Sergeant Wilkers, his squad commander during his time as a green recruit, returned to him.

"It will rob you of your will and take the heart right out of you."

"What can we do?" another of Wilkers' men had asked.

"Focus on the task at hand. If in battle, think of nothing but your opponent and how to overcome him. If not, concentrate on the feel and heft of your sword, the ground beneath your feet, your comrades, anything but the fear that would seek to overthrow your will. Once it has a foothold, fear will destroy you."

Holk stared at the creature. In his hand the metal of the sword felt cool; the ground beneath his feet firm and unyielding. All thoughts of fear and dread were banished to the nether reaches of his mind. Keeping his attention focused on those two things and the creature before him, he took a step forward; then another.

When the dread hit, it was unlike anything he had ever felt before. It sapped his will and turned his knees to jelly.

… cool steel… solid ground… creature… cool steel… solid ground… creature…

His mantra steadied his nerve, returned strength to his knees, and enabled him to take another step. Each step was an eternity. Fear and dread assailed his fortress of will, seeking to bring it down. Another two steps and the mantra continued bolstering his courage.

Ten steps and the creature vanished only to reappear farther down the widened passageway. Holk couldn't help but force a grin. Nothing was going to stop him from reaching that creature. *Nothing!*

Upon reaching where the passageway returned once more to its narrow state, the dread vanished. Sighing in relief, he leaned against the tunnel wall and wiped the sweat from his brow. The creature was moving away slowly down the tunnel.

"Thought you had me there, didn't you?"

Pushing away from the wall, he set out after the creature.

Fortunately, there were no further encounters with the veined, wide passageway sections. Not far after leaving the last one, the passageway came to an end. There was no doorway, opening, or other egress from the tunnel. The creature was trapped.

It continued until coming into contact with the end of the passageway, then stopped.

Holk paused thirty paces from the creature. Now that he had caught it, he wasn't sure what to do with it. Taking a cautionary step forward, he halfway expected the creature to vanish and appear on the other side of the wall; but it didn't. He continued forward with the sword and its glow-emitting gem held before him.

When the distance between them had been reduced to fifteen paces, the surface of the creature began vibrating ever so slightly. At twelve paces, the vibrating intensified.

A high-pitched keening split the air when only eight paces remained between them. Though barely audible, the sound cut through him like a sword. At seven, the keening intensified and he was forced to stop.

"Gah!" he exclaimed as he put hands to ears in an attempt to shut out the noise.

The vibrating of the creature was now quite pronounced.

Somehow, he summoned the wherewithal to take one more step forward. The keening raised an octave and his pain increased tenfold.

Crying out, he dropped to his knees.

"You're…not…going…to…stop me!"

Lurching forward, he stretched forth his hand and brought the sword to within a single pace of the creature. For a moment, the keening increased to a point where he could no longer hear it. The pain increased still further and if he hadn't already been lying prone upon the floor, he would assuredly have collapsed.

Spots danced before his eyes, blood trickled from his nose, and throughout his body muscles spasmed. Just when he thought he may have pressed this too far, the pain vanished.

In that moment of euphoric relief, he heard what sounded like the compacting of snow beneath the tread of a man. Looking up, he saw the creature vibrated no longer and had turned opaque. As the sound of compacting snow continued, the creature grew darker until finally turning a steelish-blue color. Once the color was uniform throughout its body, the sound stopped.

Holk slowly came to his feet. Never taking his eyes from the still form of the creature, he stretched his sword toward it. As it came close, the glow from the gem suddenly winked out leaving him with only the dim light emitted by the walls of the passageway for illumination. The sudden disappearance of the gem's glow caused him to dart backward three steps in startlement.

The creature remained motionless. It was eerie in its motionless; to Holk it felt as if a snake was coiled and ready to spring. Moments passed and the feared attack failed to materialize.

Taking a tentative step forward, he again reached out his sword to the creature, this time bringing the sword's tip into contact with its midsection. It was solid and hard. Whatever the creature had been, it was now somehow changed. Holk lowered his sword but did not resheathe it.

The creature's surface was smooth. He brought his hand up to touch it but paused before his fingers touched the surface. There was something that didn't feel right. Something… Bringing his hand back, he considered what next he should do.

Was it the glow of the gem that had transformed the creature? Or could it have been something else? No way to know for certain.

In the dim light exuded by the walls, he couldn't get an adequate look at the creature. Taking out his sunstone, he struck it against the pommel of his sword. An explosion of kaleidoscopic light filled the end of the passageway.

The sunstone's light was being refracted by the creature as would a prism. It not only took the light and changed it to a multi-colored display, but amplified it as well, producing a greater intensity than the light from the sunstone alone could achieve.

Passing the sunstone back and forth before him, he watched in wonder as the lights changed and moved to match that of the 'stone. Unable to resist the temptation, he brought his hand up close to the glass-like surface of the creature and ran his fingers across its hard exterior.

Pungent steam assailed him as he found himself no longer at the end of the passageway. The creature remained before him, but they were now in a cavern; stalagmites and 'tites abounded. To his left came the splashing of water where it fell from somewhere in the cavernous reaches above to a small pool below. Off to his right, similar splashes indicated other falls of water freefalling into their own pools.

Glancing to the nearest, he saw where its overflow ran into a steam-issuing fissure in the floor. Taking a step toward the fissure, he felt the heat of the steam being exuded. The steam from the fissures held no odor; this was not where the pungent smell originated. He had encountered this odor before. It took him but a moment to recall from where. It was the odor of Ti-Ocks. He was back.

The creature had acted like one of the magical mirrors. It had brought him to this cavern. *Could it be that the creatures were in some way similar to the translocating mirrors?* An intriguing thought and the logic seemed sound. *But why had the creature brought him to this specific cavern? Was there a reason, or just happenstance?*

Though the odor of Ti-Ocks filled the cavern, none could be seen in the area not obscured by the cloud of steam. He cocked his head to the side and listened for any tell-tale signs of their presence; there were none.

He'd worry about Ti-Ocks when he encountered them. Until then, he needed to take care of business; namely slaking his thirst and attending to his gnawing hunger. After that, he intended to find a certain lad and this time, there would be no mistakes.

Kneeling next to the pool, he cupped his hands and drank. The water was warm, but not uncomfortably so. His knees grew hot as he knelt, indicating the presence of a subterranean heat source, likely volcanic in nature. Though with everything that has happened since the *Kiln*, he would be a fool to make any sort of assumptions.

The water did much to revitalize him. Now that his thirst was slaked, it was time to deal with his hunger. If he could find a cavern full of mushrooms, he'd be set. He glanced around.

The mist filling the cavern obscured much of it. Not far off, he made out a rock wall riddled with natural imperfections. Starting there, he set out to see what there was to discover. The grumbling of his stomach said it hoped he'd find food.

Not two paces into his exploration, he came to a stop upon hearing the unmistakable sound of footsteps approaching. Dousing the sunstone by placing it within his pocket, he remained still and quiet. It soon became clear that there were two, maybe three, individuals. Considering the cavern was filled with their stink, it could only be Ti-Ocks.

That suited him just fine. He was ready for a fight.

Light appeared in the direction of the footsteps. Two torches illuminated a trio of Ti-Ocks. Slung across the backs of each were the deadly looking, curved-headed axes that seemed to be the Ti-Ock's weapon of choice. They were coming his way.

Strike first and strike fast.

Spurred on by more of Sergeant Wilkers' sage advice, Holk quietly drew his sword and moved to intercept the three. When they saw him, they reached for their axes; the two Ti-Ocks bearing torches moved to flank him on either side while the third advanced straight toward him. Ti-Ock guttural speech passed between the beasts.

Three to one? The odds didn't matter to him. For far too long had he been out of his element. Now with steel in hand and opponents to overcome, all worries vanished.

They closed rapidly. Holk sidestepped toward the one on his right so as not to be outflanked. About to launch an attack, the Ti-Ocks suddenly slowed, then came to a stop. Their attention was momentarily directed to a point in the cavern behind him. The one in the middle grunted to the other two and they re-slung their axes across their backs. It then reached into its jerkin and pulled forth a small sack. The creature said something to Holk, then tossed him the sack.

Holk instinctively caught it and felt the weighty contents within. A tear along the side revealed the glimmer of.... *Gold? They gave me gold?* The unexpectedness of this action preempted his attack. He kept his sword at the ready as the now non-threatening Ti-Ocks moved past and toward the massive, glass-hardened creature he had chased through the passageways of the bubble.

One of the torch-bearing Ti-Ocks produced a small, black object and placed it against the hardened side of the creature, held it there for several moments then removed it. After handing its torch to the other torch-bearer, it and the third Ti-Ock rocked the creature on its side and lifted it from the floor. As they carried it back the way from whence they had come, the Ti-Ock now bearing two torches glanced his way and said something in Ti-Ock speak, then moved to follow his fellows.

Holk contemplated attacking them anyway, but had never been one to attack just for the sake of bloodshed. Besides which, his interest was piqued as to what the Ti-Ocks planned on doing next.

After allowing the trio of Ti-Ocks to move off until their torches were but indistinct blurs in the mist, he moved to follow. Keeping the light in sight proved relatively easy, and the mist filling the cavern provided ample cover to keep his presence from being discovered.

The Ti-Ocks wended through a forest of stalagmites and 'tites before the mist thinned and the cavern grew brighter.

Once he could distinctly discern each individual Ti-Ock, Holk slowed to allow more space between them. Towering 'mites provided additional cover as he continued trailing the beasts.

They came to, and entered, a naturally-formed archway that opened onto what looked like the bed of a now dried-up underground river. The tunnel was somewhat rounded, and other than the floor, rough. Torches burned in wall sconces approximately every twenty feet.

At this point, the mist had all but dissipated; and with the torches burning at even intervals, following the Ti-Ocks would prove nearly impossible without being detected. Holk didn't care. If they discovered him and battle ensued, so be it. Resting a hand on the hilt of his sword, he paused a moment to allow still greater space to develop between him and the beasts, then entered the tunnel and continued to follow.

—18—

Holk hid within a naturally-formed recess in the passageway wall. Through an archway directly across and down a bit, Ti-Ocks busily worked. The trio of Ti-Ocks had delivered their burden to this room where half a dozen Ti-Ocks wearing purple robes took charge of the now-solidified creature. After that, the trio departed and continued down the passageway to parts unknown.

The cloth with which the robes of these new Ti-Ocks had been crafted was identical to the piece Holk discovered during an earlier exploration that even now rested within his pack. But it was not the similarity of the cloth that intrigued him and kept him secreted in his stony nook. Rather, his interest had been piqued by the way the purple robed Ti-Ocks had begun a systematical sectioning of the creature.

Two placed the creature upon an elongated wooden table. While they held it in place, another used a thin tool the length of a man's arm to slowly slice off sections. After a dozen or so pieces, each the width of a knife's blade had been removed, two of the remaining Ti-Ocks removed them to a place deeper within the room and out of Holk's line of sight.

He had a pretty good idea what they did with them, for not long after the first batch had been removed, a Ti-Ock reappeared with a mirror in its hand. The creature, now transformed into a crystal-like substance, was being used to create mirrors, mirrors Holk felt certain were identical in nature to those encountered throughout this underground complex.

Four times batches of creature-slices were carried off. Each time Ti-Ocks would reappear with mirrors and place them in a growing pile along one side of the room. The number of mirrors was less than half that of the sections taken back. Holk concluded that not all sections survived whatever process they used to transform them into mirrors.

Just like those previously encountered, each bore a different border that varied in width, thickness and color. Some mirrors were rather large, larger in fact than the sections being removed. Others were of the hand-held variety; those having the same wooden borders as the three he had possessed earlier. Holk would give his right arm to know how they did that. For if they could create mirrors that transported a person from one room to another, then certainly one could be made to take him home?

Despite the nagging hunger and the return of nearly overpowering fatigue, Holk hunkered down in his crevice and waited.

The creature had been reduced to half its former size when, as if on some unseen signal, the Ti-Ocks left the room en masse and departed down the corridor just as the trio had earlier.

Holk waited until they vanished from view then emerged from his nook and crossed to the room's entrance. There he peered around the corner and saw that the room was larger by half than he had first guessed.

In the rear of the room where the Ti-Ocks had taken the sliced-off sections, laid two blocks of stone, each long enough for him and another man to stretch head to toe and still not be able to touch the ends. Three bowls sat upon each; one large and two small. The sight filled Holk with trepidation and dread. It didn't take him long to realize they were very similar to those encountered in the room with the greenish glow.

Four sections of the creature laid upon the block on the right. Three were stacked in a haphazard pile to the side while the fourth had been placed prominently upon the block. The larger bowl sat just above its top and the two smaller ones had been placed to either side.

Keeping his eyes averted from the bowls and the feelings of dread they elicited, Holk entered the room. He first went to the remaining chunk of the creature resting upon the table. Next to it laid the long, thin tool that had been used to remove sections. He passed it by and went to view the pile of mirrors.

Now that he was within the room, he saw how the mirrors formed two separate piles. One held the large mirrors; next to it had been stacked the hand-helds. Visions of light-worms kept him from coming too close to the hand-helds.

Bracing himself, he crossed to the twin blocks of stone and moved to stand before the one with the sections ready to be transformed into mirrors. Dread filled him, but he fought it back and continued forward. Not looking directly at the bowls helped reduce their affect.

As he approached, he noticed something that had escaped his attention before. In a small pile next to the three haphazardly stacked mirrors were four black, dodecahedral objects. Each of their twelve faces held runic markings.

Holk's hand went to his pouch and felt the object resting within. It too was black, dodecahedral and bore runic markings. *Could it have come from here? What was its purpose?* Always more questions with little in the way of answers.

With their placement on the block in such close proximity to the bowls and creature-sections, it was a certainty that they were somehow involved with the mirror creation process. The how of it remained elusive. He needed answers and there was only one person from whom he might acquire them. *Streyan.*

Somehow, he had to find that boy, but how? His eyes returned to the stack of finished mirrors lying near the wall...

...for some, if you stare into them long enough, it will give you a foreshadowing of what you will find on the other side...

...with Kiernan's words playing across his mind, Holk made his way to the stack of mirrors, giving the hand-helds a wide birth.

A rectangular one rested on top, its width measured an arm span across while its length was that and half again. Bordering the reflective surface ran a narrow strip of red that sparkled at the corners.

"Now, let's see what we can find."

Focusing upon the mirror, he stared at it for several minutes with no results, then removed it from the stack and set it aside.

The next was a third smaller, circular, and had what appeared to be a knot-filled, oak border. He again gazed into its reflective surface in the hopes of discovering a way to find the boy. With the growling of his stomach and the incessant ache of starvation, he added a room filled with mushrooms to what he hoped to find.

As the moments passed, a vision within its reflective surface grew to clarity. Flames, bursts of flame shooting upward dotted the image. They came from fissures marring a cavern floor. Armed Ti-Ocks could be seen passing along a trail that wended its way through the flames. Holk set this mirror aside.

The third mirror held no image, nor did the fourth. Picking up the fifth that was twice the size of a hand-held and boasted a border of pearly magnificence, he soon saw a pool filled by a cascade of falling water.

Several large boulders bordered the pool. To one side he saw the unmistakable caps of mushrooms. His stomach cramped; hunger increasing tenfold at the sight of sustenance. Setting the mirror to the side, but not with the previously discarded ones, he vowed that if his quest to find Streyan in these mirrors failed, he would use it.

The following mirrors held little in the way of help. Some led to caverns, others rivers, and a few to places that produced feelings of trepidation. One had him sweating and contemplating flight after but a few moments of observation had passed.

None proved helpful in locating Streyan. He'd known it to be a long shot when he began. After the last mirror held nothing but a vision of water cascading down a nearly vertical shaft, he sighed and returned the stack back to as close to its former state as he could recall before setting the mirror with the border of pearly magnificence upon the top.

He gazed into it once more in the hopes of gleaning any further bits of information about where he was about to go before moving his hand forward and touching the reflective surface. Instantly, he was engulfed in darkness.

A whack to his sunstone brought illumination to dispel the dark and reveal his surroundings. He stood between the boulders at the pond's edge. Cool droplets splashed him from the nearby cascading stream of water. Despite their coolness, he knelt at the pool's edge and drank deeply.

To his right grew the patch of mushrooms foretold by the earlier vision in the mirror. They ranged from the size of a gold coin to that of the palm of his hand. The smaller ones were identical to those he had eaten before. Taking one, he bit into its firm flesh. Nothing had ever tasted so good.

The first one went fast, as did the dozen that followed. By his fifteenth, he began slowing as his hunger had been well satisfied. Another twenty went into the pouch at his waist.

After a second long drink at the pool, he moved beyond the boulders to a dry section of cavern floor near the wall beyond the reach of the falling droplets. Now that his thirst had been quenched and he had a full belly, Holk's fatigue returned with a vengeance. Setting the sunstone on the cavern floor next to him, he leaned his head against the wall and sleep quickly followed.

He awoke to darkness and hunger. Smacking the sunstone against a nearby rock outcropping, he returned to the mushrooms to again eat his fill. Fatigue still demanded his obedience, so after his hunger had been quieted, he once again settled against the wall of the cave to surrender to its will.

Upon waking the second time, he discovered the cavern to no longer be the pitch blackness it had been upon his earlier awakening. In his sleepy state, he thought this might be the product of the sunstone. But as consciousness took a greater foothold, he realized that the sunstone could not produce such an amount of light. With that realization, the final vestiges of sleep fell away.

The light came from the pool area. Holk couldn't tell exactly where as several of the boulders bordering the water's edge were obscuring his view. About to rise and investigate, he stopped when there came the sound of splashing.

Someone was in the pool.

Moving slowly so as to not alert the swimmer, he moved along the cavern floor in an attempt to spy who it was through the gaps between the boulders.

The first thing he saw was a rather familiar looking lantern. Moving a little farther brought a fully-filled mirror-pack into view. *Streyan!* Fortune must have given him her favor for the lad to be delivered unto him with such ease. Saying a silent "Thank you" to the Capricious Lady, he moved to the nearest boulder and peered around the edge.

A pile of well-worn clothes laid at the pool's edge. The surface of the water rippled from recent movement yet the lad was nowhere to be seen. Holk had only a moment to wonder where the boy was before Streyan's head broke the surface of the water. Giggling, the boy settled onto his back, swam a short distance, then turned and dove beneath the surface once again. His bare bottom revealed whose clothes sat at the water's edge.

As soon as Streyan vanished beneath the water, Holk moved to take possession of both the boy's clothes and the mirror pack. The pack he lifted with the tip of his sword; and while keeping it at arm's length to avoid the emergence of any light-worms, placed it out of sight behind a boulder. He then tossed the boy's clothes atop the pack then went to stand before the pond.

This time, Streyan did not emerge giggling and splashing. Instead, he surfaced slowly with a less-than-happy gaze directed at Holk.

"Well, well, well," Holk said. "Didn't think to see me again, did you?"

The boy merely treaded water as he glanced to and fro about the pond's edge.

"Looking for your pack and clothes?" Holk nodded to the boulder hiding them. "I put them over here for you." He gave the boy a smirk. "Wouldn't want them getting wet now, would we?"

Streyan's gaze settled upon the boulder for a moment before returning to Holk. "I want them back."

"In a bit. If you're a good boy."

"They are mine," Streyan said with no small amount of irritation. "You have no right to take them."

"Look, all I want is some answers and to get out of here. You help me, and I'll give them back. If not..." His sword arm rose above where the mirror-pack sat.

The lad's eyes widened; whether from the threat to his collection of mirrors, or the sudden realization that the man before him held a new weapon was unclear. Either way, the boy grimaced, then nodded. "If I can."

"That's what I wanted to hear."

Moving his sword down to the boy's clothes, he hooked them on the blade and tossed them over to the water's edge. "Get dressed."

Streyan swam to the edge, but before climbing out he said, "Turn your back."

Holk laughed. "I don't think so. Get dressed or stay in the water. It makes no difference to me."

Modesty had the boy returning to the center of the pool.

"Now, the first thing I'd like to know is where I went."

Streyan frowned. "What do you mean?"

"I mean, the last time we saw one another was at that ring of stones. It sent me somewhere and I want to know where."

The boy shrugged. "I don't know. Kazzra never said where it went, only that no one ever returned."

"I don't think he can say that anymore, for here I am."

Treading water, Streyan failed to comment.

Holk remained silent for a moment then said, "I know that it is the Ti-Ocks that make the mirrors."

Streyan didn't even flinch.

"I saw where they made them."

"That's interesting."

Nodding, Holk said, "Yes, very."

When he didn't say anything further, the boy asked, "And?"

"You knew that, didn't you?"

"Kazzra did mention it some time ago."

"Did he mention how they do it?"

Streyan shook his head. "No."

"Do you think he knows?"

"Probably. He knows everything."

Holk seriously doubted that but kept such thoughts to himself.

"I'd like to talk to him."

"That wouldn't be a good idea."

"Why?"

"Kazzra is the sort that it is unwise to bother." Streyan assumed a curious look. "Why do you want to talk with him?"

"To see about making a mirror."

That got a reaction. "A mirror?"

Holk nodded. "One that will take me home, or at least away from this place."

"I doubt if he would help you."

"True. But he would help you, wouldn't he?"

"If I asked."

"Could you ask for me?"

Streyan shook his head. "I don't think so."

"Why not?"

"Because the answer would be no. It is not for him to make the mirrors, or to interfere with what the Ti-Ocks are doing. He might get into trouble."

"What kind of trouble can a dragon get into? And who would he get into trouble with?"

Streyan just shrugged.

"You had to have said that for a reason."

"It's complicated."

Holk leaned against a boulder and assumed a relaxed demeanor. "I got the time."

The boy treaded water and remained silent.

"Are you going to explain?"

Streyan shook his head.

"Hmmm. It seems we are at an impasse. But then, you are a naked little boy and I am an armed man prone to violence."

He hooked the tip of his sword into the belt of Streyan's mirror-pack and set it on top of the boulder. Glancing to the boy, he saw trepidation in the lad's eyes.

"Those are mine."

"Yes, you've said that before."

Sliding the blade beneath the leather thong holding the pack closed, he sliced it in two. Then with a flick of his wrist, he flipped the flap open to expose the mirrors within.

"Stop."

Holk glanced to the boy. "Are you going to help me?"

"I can't."

Ever so gently, he moved the tip of his sword to the end of the pack, and with brief nudges, edged the endmost mirror halfway from within its pocket.

"You don't know what you are doing."

With one final swift motion, Holk thrust the mirror out of the pack and down the side of the boulder where it shattered on the floor.

"No!"

Holk returned the tip of his sword to the pack and began nudging the next mirror outward. Pausing when but a third of the hand-held was free, he arched an eyebrow questioningly at the boy. When no answer was forthcoming, the mirror joined the first with a clatter. As it came to rest, a long crack dissected its reflective surface.

Retuning the blade to start on a third, he heard Streyan say, "Wait."

"Why? You're not going to help me and these mirrors are now useless to me. What do I care if they get broken?" As if to prove his point, he thrust the third from the pack and sent it to shatter on the remains of the first two.

"Kazzra will be angry with you when he learns of what you've done."

Holk shrugged. "Again, I don't care. I'm trapped here, not likely to get out alive. What matter the manner in which I die? Either from starvation or being mauled by a dragon, dead is dead and I'm tired of playing these games." A fourth mirror shattered on the cavern floor.

When the sword returned for the fifth one, Streyan shouted, "Not that one!"

Glancing to the boy, Holk asked, "Why?"

"If you break that one, we'll never get to Kazzra."

"We?"

Defeat was clearly written on Streyan's face when he nodded.

Holk moved his sword away from the mirror-pack. "So you plan to help me?"

"If you promise not to break anymore of my mirrors."

"How do I know I can trust you?"

"You can."

Swimming, the lad left the center of the pool and came nearer to the edge. "I will help you reach Kazzra and ask him to help you, if you promise to not break anymore of my mirrors."

There was sincerity in the lad's eyes, but even still, Holk wondered how far coerced cooperation would go. "And you further promise not to play any tricks on me?"

"Yes. Can I have my clothes now?"

Holk gestured to the pile near the edge of the pool with the end of his sword. "Go ahead."

"Turn around."

"Fine."

Turning around, he hooked the end of his sword in the mirror-pack and held it so he was between the pack and the pool. He only trusted the boy so far.

The sound of the boy leaving the pool was followed by that of him donning his clothes. When Streyan said, "Okay," Holk turned around and motioned the boy to approach.

On his way, Streyan grabbed the lantern.

Keeping his body between the boy and the mirror-pack, Holk waited for Streyan to come close then grabbed him by the collar. He felt the boy tense.

"Don't worry, I'll not hurt you. Not unless you try to do me wrong."

With Streyan grasped in a hold from which the lad was unlikely to escape, Holk brought the mirror-pack to just within arm's reach of the boy. As Streyan reached for the pack, Holk tightened his grip.

"If we end up anywhere but Kazzra's cave, you die."

The boy nodded and reached for the pack. One of his fingers slipped into the pocket holding the mirror Holk had been about to smash, and they vanished.

—19—

Kazzra lay asleep, curled upon his massive hoard. The mirror had not delivered them to the small cave high above where the dragon slept. Instead, they appeared less than ten feet from the great beast's head.

An eye cracked open.

"So, you have returned, human."

Streyan immediately tried to break free of Holk's grasp as he cried out, "Help me!" but was held too tightly.

The great head raised from a mound of golden disks, each the size of a turtle's shell. One disk adhered to the underside of the jaw for a moment before dropping to clatter among its fellows.

Holk flung the mirror-pack to the side with a flick of his sword, grasped the boy in a firm embrace with his free arm and brought the blade to within a hair's breadth of the lad's throat.

The proximity of the blade quieted his struggles. "He broke my mirrors!"

Kazzra opened his mouth, revealing teeth designed to rip and tear. There was malice in the eyes. "So, this is how you repay my kindness?"

"I have not hurt the boy, merely used him to get to you."

From deep within the dragon's throat came a rumble, the sound of which shot tendrils of fear through Holk, but he steeled his nerve and continued.

"I know the Ti-Ocks are the ones who make the mirrors. I also know where it is they create them."

"What does this have to do with me?" In the shadows behind Kazzra, his great tail moved to and fro.

"I don't think there is any way for me to get out of this place. Even Streyan has said that no one ever escapes."

"I did not!"

The great beast's head rose to tower above him. "It is true that very few of those that find their way here manage to win their freedom. However, are you so sure that incurring my wrath will win you that freedom?"

"If I believed there to be any other way, I would not have chosen this route. As it is, I figure the Ti-Ocks will be out of material for their mirrors soon. If I don't act now, the opportunity will be lost." Which was true, the creature from which the Ti-Ocks were removing sections for their mirrors had little over half of its bulk remaining.

The great head turned its eye upon the boy. "Are you hurt?"

Streyan shook his head. "No, but he broke four of my mirrors."

"Only to impress upon him the seriousness of my need to meet with you. From what he has told me, you may know the manner in which the mirrors are crafted. And if so, I would ask that you impart that knowledge to me."

When the eye directed its gaze full upon him, Holk felt as if his soul lay exposed, such was the intensity of that scrutiny.

"It wouldn't do you any good, human. There are certain components that you must have. Without them, the mirrors will not work; or will work imperfectly."

Holk didn't like the thought of trying to pass through a mirror that wasn't working properly. Scenes of a grisly demise made him swallow.

"Are you referring to a twelve-sided object of the deepest black, inscribed with runes upon all sides?"

"That is but one of six."

"Six? I'm assuming the section removed from the creature is number two of the six components. And upon the table where the Ti-Ocks worked, were three bowls." He glanced into the eye. "Perhaps they are numbers three, four and five?"

Kazzra did not answer.

"I'm right, aren't I?"

"You intrigue me, human. None have been so bold as to try and coerce me into helping them. I sense that you truly do not wish to hurt the boy, and that may just stave off your death...for now."

"If I let the boy go, will you help me and not kill me?"

The great head tilted downward so the dragon's gaze fell upon the boy.

"Please, Kazzra," Streyan begged. "I don't want him to hurt me."

"Worry not, little one. He shall not harm you."

"Then we have a deal?"

"If you let the boy go, I promise that I shall allow you to live for a day. After that, I will hunt you down and kill you."

Holk laughed. "What kind of deal is that?"

"However, should you manage to gain your freedom from this place in that time, I will not."

He considered it for a moment. "And you'll instruct me in the method for creating the mirrors?"

Lips curling into what Holk took for a dragon's grin, Kazzra replied, "Of course. Streyan will also take you to a location from which you can reach the room wherein the mirrors are crafted."

"I will not! He broke my mirrors!"

A growl came from deep within the beast's throat and Holk felt the boy shiver. "You will do as you are told. Worry not, we will replace the mirrors this human has destroyed."

The boy's head lifted ever so slightly. "Even one that will take me to Shigraz?"

"Yes. Even one to Shigraz."

The boy turned his head to glance up at Holk and gave him a grin. "So, what are we waiting for?"

Holk wondered what this Shigraz was, but as long as it brought him one step closer to his goal, he didn't really care. About to release the boy, he considered for a moment the ease at which Kazzra had acquiesced to his request. *Did Streyan truly mean that much to the beast? Or was he being deceived?* Figuring that he'd gone too far down this road to turn back, he lowered his sword and released his grip on the boy. To his surprise, Streyan only took two steps forward before coming to a halt.

The dragon's head rose as if to strike and for a moment, Holk thought his end had come. But instead, the dragon paused only a moment before lowering his head to a point just before and little above his own.

"You are correct in your assumption that the bowls contain components three, four and five. And yes, the material from the creature constituted number two as does the black object being number one. But it is the last component that you may have the hardest time in acquiring."

Fearing some ploy of the beast, Holk asked, "Why?"

"For in order to have the mirror deliver you to a specific destination, something from that destination must be used in the mirror's construction."

"What do you mean?"

"I mean..." the dragon lowered his head until he was at eye level. "You need an item that is native to where you wish to go. Most often rock is used. For you see, in order for the object to be effectively incorporated as part of the mirror's creation, it needs to be ground into a fine powder." Kazzra chuckled. "You have a day to acquire it; then I hunt."

"But how can I get something from my home when I don't have a way to get there?"

Kazzra laughed. "Not my problem. Our deal is struck." He made to return to his resting place upon his hoard.

"Wait!"

"Yes?"

"How do I put the components together once I get them?"

"Do you really think you will?"

Weren't the clothes on his back from home? Perhaps they could be used. "How? You said you would tell me."

The head swiveled back toward him. "So I did." Kazzra then instructed him in the proper sequence of actions in order to imbue a mirror with translocation properties.

Once Holk had repeated the process back correctly, Kazzra turned to Streyan. "Take him to the Grotto and then show him the way to the Cave of Winds." To Holk he said, "From there you proceed alone."

"Not a problem."

Kazzra's head reared back and laughter rolled forth. "See you in a day, human. Be sure to provide me with excellent sport."

About to respond, he felt Streyan's hand slip into his and they were no longer in Kazzra's cave.

Streyan let go his hand. "This is the Grotto."

They stood on the banks of a small stream running through a narrow cavern. On either side grew a variety of plants as well as several trees. Through an opening over a hundred feet in length in the cavern's ceiling above, Holk was surprised to discover starlight.

"Can we get out through that?"

The boy shrugged. "Maybe. I've never tried." Turning to head downstream, he indicated for Holk to follow. "The Cave of Winds is this way."

"Right."

Moving to follow, Holk kept glancing to the stars above and wondered what may lie beyond that opening. One thing he knew for certain, home did not lay that way.

"How far is it to the Cave?"

"Not far."

"Where do I go from there?"

Streyan kept his head down as he replied, "Can't tell you. Have to show you."

"Why?"

"Just do."

They reached where the stream cascaded down a gentle slope. Streyan followed it. Beyond the slope, the streambed deepened until they walked upon a shelf some three feet above the flowing water.

About this time, the stench of Ti-Ocks became noticeable.

"We need to be quiet. If they hear us, you'll never reach your destination."

Holk nodded and rested a hand on his sword hilt.

Streyan soon left the side of the stream and led them to a cavernous opening that was easily three times taller than Holk and two-thirds that wide. Ti-Ock stink was much more pronounced. The boy brought them to a halt.

Motioning for Holk to lean toward him, he whispered, "The Cave of Winds is not far. But to get to it, we must pass through Ti-Ock territory. Stay close and whatever you do, make no noise."

"Don't worry. I shall be as quiet as the dead."

"If they hear us, that's exactly what you will be."

Holk could tell the boy was not trying to be funny but believed exactly what he said.

The tunnel beyond the cavernous opening ran unusually straight for a naturally formed passage. Holk didn't think it had been dug out by the Ti-Ocks as the walls were rough, irregular, and lacked any markings that would have been left behind by tools.

They hadn't gone far before light came into view farther down. As they drew closer, silhouettes of Ti-Ocks could be seen moving about. Streyan slowed his pace and kept to the right side of the passage. Holk followed suit.

Armored Ti-Ocks there were aplenty, but also females and their young emerging and then vanishing in what quickly became clear as a network of tunnel openings.

"Their city," was all the explanation Streyan gave. When the boy made to continue forward, he was stopped by a hand on his shoulder.

"We aren't going through there, are we?" Holk couldn't see any way they would remain unnoticed if they did.

Streyan shook his head. "No." He then pointed toward a narrow opening this side of the first set of Ti-Ock tunnels. "There."

Holk was none too sure they could even make that without being discovered. But when Streyan started forward once again, he followed along behind.

Of storefronts and homes, there was no sign. The tunnel they traversed simply held a honeycomb of openings that extended down either side. It must be a major thoroughfare of some sort.

As the narrow opening drew closer, Streyan hunkered down more and practically plastered himself against the tunnel wall. Edging forward, he would pause when a Ti-Ock happened to glance their way. Once the creature turned away, he would proceed a little farther.

They were ten feet from the opening when a commotion up ahead brought them to a halt. Two Ti-Ocks were quarreling. One was armored while another wore a simple, brown robe. They spoke in hurried and stern tones while gesticulating wildly. Other Ti-Ocks paused to watch the unfolding events. Many were on the opposite side of the quarreling pair and had a nearly unobstructed view of the two trespassers sneaking through their realm. If not for the shadows, they would assuredly have been seen.

As quickly as the argument began, it came to a halt. The armored Ti-Ock turned about and walked away while the robed one retained his position in the passageway until a few moments after the other one had departed. Then it, too, continued on its way as did the onlookers.

Holk wasn't sure who got the better of the other. He was just glad it was over and they were once again progressing toward the narrow opening.

After two more periods of motionlessness while pressed to the side of the passageway, they reached the opening and ducked through.

It was very narrow and had just enough clearance for Holk to walk erect without scraping his head. The light from the passageway lit the tunnel for a short distance. When it grew too dark to safely see the irregularities marring the floor, Streyan whacked a sunstone against the stone wall and they continued.

"We won't meet any Ti-Ocks in here," the lad assured.

"How much farther is this Cave of Winds?"

"Not far. Soon, you'll feel a breeze."

Sure enough, Holk soon felt the wafting of a cool breeze. The farther they went, the stronger it became. From a soft breeze, it grew to a blustery wind, then increased to a strong flurry that forced them to bend forward in order to not be knocked from their feet.

"Almost there," Streyan shouted. Hand braced against the side of the passageway, the boy struggled for each step.

Holk fared little better.

They came at last to where the passageway ended at a ledge that overlooked darkness. A sound like the wail of a thousand tortured souls shrieked from out of the darkness before them.

Streyan glanced back at Holk and grinned. "Want to see something really interesting?"

His initial response was no, but then he reconsidered as he didn't want to antagonize his guide. "If it doesn't take too long." He had very little time to idle away sightseeing. Kazzra had given him a day, and some of that had already been lost getting there.

The boy shook his head then brought the sunstone toward a section of the wall on their left that bore a pattern of faint sparkles that glittered in the sunstone's light. In a swift motion, he struck the pattern with the sunstone.

Instantly, the sparkles flared to life. From the point of impact a trail of sparkling light coursed along the wall and passed through the opening. Holk stepped forward and discovered how after it left the passageway the sparkling trail entered a cavern and divided. One branching trailed to the left, the other to the right.

Again and again, each strand split as they made their way along the walls of the cavern until scores coursed every which way. The darkness that had been so impenetrable began to give way to the light-trail's growing luminescence.

Staring at the cavernous ceiling where no less than a dozen light-trails meandered, Holk couldn't help but be awed. "Incredible."

"If you think that is something…"

Turning his attention back to the boy, he saw Streyan gesture to the center of the enormous cavern. In the ever brightening light put forth by the myriad network of light-trails, a massive vortex came into view.

A hundred feet tall, it filled the entire central area of the cavern. Holk had never seen its like before. Travelers would tell of vortexes that appeared in the summer months across the Plains of Arma, but he had never before encountered one.

"What causes it?"

Streyan merely shrugged. "I don't know. Kazzra once said that it had been here for centuries."

Holk turned a disbelieving look upon the boy. "It's never stopped?"

"No."

So awe-inspiring was the sight, that he almost forgot why they were there. "Where do we go from here?"

"*We* don't."

He cocked an eye at the boy. "What do you mean? Kazzra said for you to show me the way."

Streyan nodded. "But he also said that from here, you were to proceed alone." Motioning for Holk to accompany him, the boy moved to the edge of the ledge. A series of steps winding down the side of the cavern led to the rocky floor below. Streyan directed Holk's gaze to a pair of columns framing a dark opening not far from the end of the steps.

"There."

"I can get to the room where the Ti-Ocks make the mirrors?"

"Yes. The passageway beyond the pillars will take you to where you wish to go."

"Are you sure?"

The boy nodded.

Holk descended a step then paused to glance back over his shoulder. "What…?" he began but Streyan had already used one of his hand-helds and vanished.

A day. That's all the time he had before Kazzra would seek him out. There wasn't a moment to spare.

As he descended from the ledge, the steps gradually took him closer to the swirling vortex. Its winds grew ever more furious and whipped hard as they sought to knock this unwanted intruder from his feet and dash him on the rocks below. But Holk maintained his balance and succeeded in reaching the bottom.

The noise coming from the vortex was deafening this close. Despite the fact that it swirled in a cavern, the air itself held very little dirt. Other than a few specks striking with the force of arrows shot from bows, he reached the pillars unscathed. Once in the passageway beyond, the force of the wind greatly diminished. He whacked his sunstone against the tunnel wall and made his way from the Cave of Winds.

The passageway continued straight and uninterrupted for quite some distance before the first side-passage came into view. *The passageway beyond the pillars will take you to where you wish to go.* Had Streyan meant to keep to the tunnel? Or would he have to depart from it and take one of the others? Cursing the boy for not accompanying him, Holk decided to keep to the main tunnel.

After that initial branching, others appeared at regular intervals. First, one would appear on the right, then another on the left. Each proved to be dark and lacking in any clue as to where they led.

After passing the sixth tunnel, there appeared a light farther down the main passageway. Holk shielded his sunstone and proceeded in the dark so as not to give away his presence. The light, as it turned out, was from a torch burning in a sconce where another passage intersected his.

He paused before entering the light, listening to see if Ti-Ocks might be in the vicinity. Not hearing anything, he moved into the light and peered around the corner to the right, then the left. Both directions lay quiet and deserted. The one to the left soon fell to shadows once it passed beyond the light-radius of the torch. Down the right-hand passage was another area of light in the distance. It was too far for him to make out anything. He hurried through the convergence and continued on his way. Barely perceptible at first, the stench of Ti-Ocks grew more noticeable.

Another half dozen passages came and went before the light from a pair of torches came into view. As he drew closer, Ti-Ocks could be seen moving within the light.

The torches burned at a convergence of five passageways, his being one. One went left at a sharp angle while a matching tunnel branched off to the left. The final two were part of a fork that split the passageway he currently followed into two.

Down the right-hand tine of the fork, further lights and the movement of bodies could be seen. The left-hand held fewer lights and motion was at a minimum.

Both ways looked identical. Holk could not determine which way would be construed as a continuation of the tunnel. Cursing Streyan once more for not having accompanied him, he stayed back in the shadows as he worked to determine which way to go. At the present, the point seemed moot as any attempt by him to pass through the five-way intersection would precipitate discovery.

Time was not his friend. He couldn't afford to simply sit and wait for however long it would take the convergence of passages to clear so he could proceed. Whenever a Ti-Ock departed into one of the tunnels, another would emerge; sometimes more than one. And what if one decided to come his way? No, he had to get through and now. But how?

Time passed all too quickly as he worked on a plan to make his way through without being detected. One plan seemed to resurface more than the others. In his pack he still carried that piece of purple cloth. If he wrapped it around his upper torso and walked quickly...but no; there was far too much "humanness" left exposed for the deception to pass even the most cursory of glances.

Anxiety at the wasted time eventually forced him into action. He had to take the chance. Removing the cloth from his pack, he draped it over his head and held it tightly closed in front of his chest. He waited for a time when more than one purple-robed Ti-Ock was within the convergence of passageways, then stepped forward quickly.

Head down, practically running, he passed into the lighted area. Ti-Ocks glanced his way for he was the only one moving with such speed. One spoke to him in their guttural language, but he kept his eyes on the floor of the tunnel ahead and continued forward. A second Ti-Ock hailed him. Out of the corner of his eye, Holk saw the beast turn toward him.

Speeding through half a score of Ti-Ocks, he angled toward the darker of the two passageways of the fork. After what felt like an eternity, he passed beyond the light and entered the sheltering shadows.

A glance over his shoulder revealed several Ti-Ocks standing in a group looking his way. None seemed overly concerned with him; instead they appeared curious. Holk didn't stop to ponder the lack of pursuit or alarm. Accelerating to an all-out run, he quickly left the convergence of tunnels behind. Unfortunately, moving that fast brought him to the next illuminated area all too quickly.

This time there was an arched way on the right. Twin torches sat sentinel, one to either side. Pausing in the light's fringe, he peered through the arch to find many Ti-Ocks moving about. Tables, stools, and the odor of burnt meat brought to mind a dining hall. Tightening the cloth about him once more, he hurried past.

In the shadowed area between the dining hall and the next area of illumination, a Ti-Ock walked. Holk kept to the side of the passageway opposite that of where the Ti-Ock moved. When they came abreast, the Ti-Ock bowed, spoke several words, then continued on.

Holk couldn't believe he was making it through so easily. Could his disguise really be that effective? Or did they not care he was in their territory? Either way, he continued forward toward his goal.

Six more lighted areas were successfully navigated, and multiple Ti-Ocks bypassed without sign of the room wherein Ti-Ocks created their mirrors. Holk began thinking he may have taken a wrong turn at the five-passage convergence. *Maybe the right-hand tine had been the correct path?* When a sixth and seventh had been traversed, he considered the possibility that turning about may be required.

Wasted time!

A long, dark tunnel still stretched before him. There was another illuminated area, but it was far in the distance. *Go back or continue?* The thought of going back didn't sit well with him. Deciding to investigate this next area before backtracking, he raced forward.

During his trek toward the next lit area, the myriad of passages already passed played through his mind. If one had been the way he should have gone, would he be able to figure it out in time? Feeling the weight of fate settling upon him, he prayed that this would indeed prove to be the correct passage.

A single torch burned within a wall sconce next to an arched opening. Brighter light from beyond the archway lent its brilliance to that of the torch. Voices conversing came from the other side. As he drew near the light, he came to the realization that the voices spoke not the bestial tongue of the Ti-Ocks. Though the language was unknown, Holk knew beyond a shadow of a doubt that those speaking were human.

Surprise brought an abrupt halt to his progress. *Humans in a Ti-Ock controlled area? Unbelievable!* Shocked to say the least, he crept forward stealthily until he reached the end of the shadows. There, he could see partway through the archway to the other side.

A quartet of men sat around a table. They wore armor identical to that worn by the corpses encountered within cages in the silvery land. Their laughter and camaraderie for some reason felt out of place.

Could that be why the three Ti-Ocks failed to attack him earlier? He glanced to the sword hanging at his hip, the one with the red gem in the hilt. *Had they thought him to be one of these men?* It would also explain why he currently remained unmolested. Maybe it hadn't been the purple swath of cloth; but because of his sword.

Backing from the light, he considered what to do next. The Ti-Ocks might believe him to be one of these men, but the men themselves would see through his disguise in an instant. If he wished to continue the exploration of where this corridor led, he would have to risk detection.

As he weighed whether he should make the attempt or not, the silhouettes of two Ti-Ocks appeared out of the shadowy darkness of the corridor beyond the illuminated area before the archway. Holk moved to the side and slowly began backing down the tunnel.

He had almost resolved himself to returning to see if the other branching of the fork would prove to be the correct avenue when two Ti-Ocks entered the light. Each carried mirrors. One had two tucked under an arm while the other held three. Of the two mirrors the first Ti-Ock carried, one was twice the size of a hand-held and boasted a border of pearly magnificence. It had to be the same one that took him to the pool where he found Streyan.

Aha!

All doubt vanished. He was on the right track. Waiting until the Ti-Ocks drew closer, Holk stepped outward from the wall. Walking like he belonged there, he passed the mirror-carrying Ti-Ocks and approached the area of light. Pausing only a moment, he left the shadows and made to go by the archway. His eyes remained focused on the dark passageway ahead. Perhaps one of the men within the room called to him, but he didn't alter his stride or glance in their direction to find out. Once past and again in the protective darkness of the shadows, he quickened his pace.

Somewhere ahead laid the room wherein Ti-Ocks created the magical mirrors. And if they had already used the remainder of the creature... Shaking his head, he refused to allow such thoughts free rein. All would be lost if that were the case. Hoping to arrive in time, he ran.

—20—

Twice more he encountered Ti-Ocks bearing mirrors. Each time, they gave him little more than a brief glance as they passed by. Up ahead, another illuminated area broke the darkness. From an opening in the side of the tunnel, a Ti-Ock emerged. In its hands it held a single mirror.

Holk grinned. He had found the room. Slowing his pace, he assumed a casual stride as the Ti-Ock approached and made its way past. Once it was some distance behind him, Holk resumed his hurried pace. Coming to the area of light, he threw caution to the wind and strode forward purposefully. At the entrance, he turned and went through.

Four Ti-Ocks worked busily within. Two were shaving a piece from what was left of the massive creature-turned-solid. One held the narrow chunk of creature while the other used the thin, slicing rod. The piece they worked on was two-thirds of the way removed. A third Ti-Ock stood before the table with the three bowls and the fourth was transferring a mirror to the stack; now less than a fourth of its former size. Setting the mirror on top, it turned toward the door and came to a sudden halt upon seeing the intruder in their midst. It glared at Holk while making gestures toward the entrance and uttering Ti-Ock speech in a commanding tone. The interchange drew the attention of the two slicing mirror sections from the creature.

Its expression was not pleasant as it came forward. Gesticulating wildly, it came to a stop before Holk, pointed to the entrance Holk had just passed through, and spoke again.

"I don't think so," Holk responded.

Whether it understood or not, the tone of his reply was unmistakable. It barked a command while at the same time drawing a wicked-looking dagger from out of its robe. The two working on the creature broke off from their endeavor and moved to join it.

Holk grinned. "Fine with me."

In a movement perfected in long hours of drills, his sword came free of its scabbard and separated the hand holding the dagger from its wrist.

Crying out with pain and outrage, the Ti-Ock stumbled backward. The two Ti-Ocks had already drawn similar daggers and were closing in. The one at the table with the trio of bowls remained where it was. From what Kazzra had said, to break off once the process of mirror construction had begun would bring about lethal consequences. Exactly what those might be, the dragon had failed to specify.

The dagger-wielding Ti-Ocks moved in for the attack.

Holk lashed out at the one on his right and parted the material of its robe across its chest; blood welled forth. He then danced to the side as the dagger of the other shot forward, missing him by a hair's breadth.

The thrill of battle was upon him. Holk laughed as he lunged at the Ti-Ock on his left, then brought it around for a slice at the one on his right.

These robed Ti-Ocks had very little skill in battle. The one on his right left itself open when it came in for an overhand attack. Holk ducked beneath it, caught its downward plunging arm with his free hand, and thrust his sword blade up and through the creature's chest. As it slumped to the ground, he pulled his sword free and turned to face the other.

It thrust at his midsection.

Spinning out of the way, Holk made a full circle and brought his sword up to sever the creature's neck. The head tumbled to the floor. Movement out of the corner of his eye drew his attention to the entrance. There, the Ti-Ock whose hand he'd removed fled into the passageway.

Holk considered pursuing it, but time was rapidly running out. Exactly how much longer remained before Kazzra began the hunt, he didn't know. There wasn't a moment to lose. He turned toward the remaining Ti-Ock that stood at the table. With sword at the ready, he approached.

Before it on the table lay the mirror's reflective surface, the part that had come from the massive creature. A band of shimmering darkness surrounded it. Kazzra had explained that it would solidify and become the border. That was the final step. Once the border was complete, so too would be the mirror.

Kill the creature, or not kill the creature, that was his dilemma. If he killed it now, unpleasant ramifications from disrupting the mirror-creation process might arise. But waiting held its own dangers as the one that had fled would certainly summon reinforcements to take care of him. Indecision stayed his hand for precious moments. Then when he at last decided to strike, the border solidified and the Ti-Ock was gone. It had used the mirror to escape.

Holk didn't care. There was work to do and very little time in which to accomplish it. Sheathing his sword, he picked up the mirror from the table and tossed it over to the pile. After that, he hurried to where the remnant of the massive creature sat, and took hold of the rod used in slicing it.

It takes a gentle hand. The mirror must be perfectly even or you risk it shattering.

Kazzra's words returned as he mimicked how the Ti-Ock had used it. Pressing down ever so slightly, he felt the rod slide into the hard material of the massive creature. It felt like cutting a very well-done turkey.

Keeping a sharp eye on the rod's downward course, he maintained an even width. When the rod touched the table, the end-piece tipped outward and he caught it just as it slipped from the table. It was cold to the touch. He carried it across the room and placed it on the other table.

Nausea rose as his eyes passed over the liquids contained within the bowls. Fighting to keep it under control, he averted his gaze and proceeded to search the room. He needed something with which to grind a portion of his tunic into a fine powder. On a shelf at the rear of the room he found a small, stone concave bowl. Within the bowl rested a short length of stone with a rounded end. That would do nicely.

He tore a small strip of cloth from the bottom of his tunic and placed it within the bowl. Then with the length of stone, began grinding the cloth against the bottom of the bowl. Holk worked for several minutes before the sound of approaching Ti-Ocks drew his attention to the passageway. Setting the bowl with the partially pulverized strip of cloth on the table, he turned to the entrance and drew his sword.

Two armored Ti-Ocks, each bearing shield and their favored axes with the wickedly curved head, charged into the room.

Holk met them head-on.

One was slightly ahead of the other and launched an over-hand chop.

Holk dodged to the side and countered with an upward slice toward the descending arm. Before the blow could connect, the Ti-Ock's shield struck him aside. Dancing backward, he avoided being split in two by the second Ti-Ock's axe.

"This isn't very fair," Holk said as he maneuvered through the tables in an attempt to come at a solitary opponent. "You have shields and all I have is this sword." Unfortunately, they didn't care and came together so he would have to meet them simultaneously.

He feinted left, then darted right and struck a resounding blow upon the right-most Ti-Ock's shield. To his surprise, the sword taken from the entrapped corpse in the silvery land cleaved the shield in two and continued on to sever the arm holding it.

A roar filled the room as the wounded Ti-Ock stumbled backward, its life-blood draining away through the stump.

"Well," he said to his remaining opponent, "maybe this is fairer than I had supposed." Giving the Ti-Ock a grin, he came forward.

Downward came the axe. *If it worked on the shield...* Avoided the out-thrusting of the shield, he sliced upward to meet the axe's haft. The impact was jarring, but it resulted in the axe-head coming away. If not for a deft twist and sideward move, the axe head would have finished him for sure.

As it was, it scraped along his right shoulder leaving a red two-inch furrow.

Pain was part and parcel to combat, and if it wasn't life-threatening, it was to be ignored. Holk dismissed it and rounded on the now weaponless Ti-Ock. Thrusting, he had his sword knocked aside by the shield. As he brought it around for another attack, the Ti-Ock turned about and fled toward the entrance. Holk pursued it out into the passageway before coming to a quick stop.

In the lit area of the passageway some distance away, he saw many Ti-Ock warriors racing his way. He darted back within and glanced around the room. If only there was a way to block the entrance; but there wasn't. His gaze fell across the stack of mirrors and the dozen or so hand-helds sitting next to it.

There were far too many Ti-Ocks coming for him to handle; even with this newly acquired sword. He could always use one of the mirrors and flee. But Kazzra would soon be coming. He had no choice. Flight was not an option; he had to finish the mirror. But what to do…

Ti-Ocks boiled down the passageway. When they saw the flight of the one whose axe handle had been severed, a reverberation of bestial cries shook the very walls of the tunnel. They charged forward with blood on their minds.

The lead Ti-Ock approached the entrance and rushed to enter when it saw something with light shining forth slide across the floor through the entrance. Realization of its danger came too late. The hand-held mirror with the light-worm came beneath him and pain erupted as its leg was ensnared by the light-worm.

Instantly, the light-worm elongated and wrapped itself around the Ti-Ock's torso. When another Ti-Ock inadvertently bumped into the first, the light-worm split in twain and proceeded to coil around its second victim.

The Ti-Ock charge came apart as another light-worm exuding hand-held slid from the room. Latching onto yet another of the beasts, it elongated and began to feed.

Holk watched as Ti-Ocks became entrapped by the light-worms. A third mirror rested on the ground at his feet, its light-worm already testing the area surrounding it. When a Ti-Ock tried circumventing its light-worm ensnared brethren, Holk batted the mirror toward it with the tip of his sword.

It leapt over the hand-held and charged toward Holk.

As Holk moved forward to meet it, he saw the light-worm latch onto another that had followed the first.

Down came the axe and Holk merely dodged to the side. As the axe rose for another attack, he stepped backward as the shield came forward. His foot struck out and scored directly on the Ti-Ock's chest. The blow caused it to stumble backward and into the one entangled with the light-worm. Its roar echoed throughout the room as tendrils of light coiled about its body.

Holk quickly returned to the stack of hand-helds, used his sword to move another away from the rest, then brought his hand close and drew it back. Just as the others before, a light-worm emerged.

A glance to the entrance showed half a dozen Ti-Ocks writhing upon the floor, effectively blocking the rest from continuing the attack. Not sure how long this would last, Holk left the no longer needed hand-held where it lay and hurried back to the table where he resumed the grinding of the piece of cloth.

With bowl in one hand and the rock pulverizer in the other, Holk worked to reduce the cloth to mere powder. He kept an eye on the events unfolding at the entrance. Time seemed to pass quickly. One Ti-Ock ceased moving and the bands of light that had entwined it withdrew into the mirror.

The cloth in the bowl still had many large sections that according to Kazzra would render the mirror creation void. Pressing harder and twisting faster, he prayed that the Ti-Ocks would endure the lethal caress of the light-worms a little while longer.

Beyond the light-worms and their victims, dozens of the beasts waited impatiently for their brethren to perish so the light-worms would vanish and they could then reach the room. Holk doubted very seriously if they would fall prey to his mirror tactic as easily as had the others.

Twist. Twist. Grind.

Back and forth, the rock pulverizer ground the cloth against the bottom of the bowl. More and more of the cloth was being reduced to a powder-like state. Cloth was not like rock or bone, its reduction to fine particles took longer. A glance at the Ti-Ocks set upon by light-worms revealed another of the creatures had ceased to move and the light-worm attacking it returning to the mirror.

Kazzra had been unclear as to how much powder would be needed to complete the mirror's creation. Removing the pulverizer, he found a small amount of fine particles accumulated in the bottom. The bulk of the cloth remained in small, shredded pieces; all of which was unusable. Placing the pulverizer once more in the bowl, he continued grinding and moved to the table.

Once he began the ritual, he should be safe from Ti-Ock attack; for any disruption before its completion would have serious repercussions, or so Kazzra had indicated.

Glancing to the entrance, he saw another of the Ti-Ocks had perished and its light-worm gone. It wouldn't be long now. A few more twists of the pulverizer and he set it to the side. Praying that Kazzra's information would prove to be correct, he rested his hands on the table's edge, took a calming breath to steady his nerves.

"Okay, here we go."

You will find three bowls; two small and one large. First, form a border fully encompassing a thin section removed from the otherworld creature.

How wide of a border do I make?

It matters not; merely that the border is unbroken.

He reached for the largest of the three bowls. Nausea assailed him as his hand took hold of the edge, but he managed to bring it under control. Holk tipped the bowl and allowed its contents to drip and began forming the border. Slowly at first, but then quicker once he got a feel for its consistency for it was thick like molasses, the border took shape. When it was complete, he returned the bowl to its place on the table.

You will have scant moments after completing the border to add the contents from the other two bowls. A thin layer from the one on the right needs to be added upon the substance from the first bowl forming the border. Then take the bowl on the left and use its contents to create a thin layer directly upon the reflective surface.

As soon as the contents of the right-hand bowl dripped upon the border, a small tendril of smoke rose accompanied by an unpleasant, acrid odor. Then the border at that point turned dark and began to shimmer. Holk continued drizzling the substance upon the rest of the border until the entire mass had been transformed to a dark, shimmering material.

A glance over his shoulder revealed another of the Ti-Ocks had perished. Those waiting behind were edging forward. If another of those entwined with light-worms was to die, the way would be sufficiently clear for them to enter the room without risk.

Taking up the third and last bowl, he tipped it over the center and when the drops hit the surface, they appeared to be absorbed within the hard material, leaving behind only a small, oily residue. A rise in Ti-Ock speech from the passageway prompted a speedier delivery method. Large globs fell from the bowl, each being absorbed as had the first. Once the surface had a consistent, oily hue throughout, he returned the bowl to the table.

Finally, and this is where much is risked, take the Catalyst and place it upon the center of the mirror. Sprinkle the powder of the object from whence you wish the mirror to take you upon the Catalyst. You must ensure no part of the powder falls to the mirror's surface.

What happens if some does?

The dragon had smiled. In that case, I won't have to worry about hunting you.

Taking the black dodecahedral object which was the Catalyst from his pouch, he held it up before him, revealing the faces and the arcane markings engraved upon each. Which side should I have up?

It matters not, human.

Movement within the room drew his attention back to the here and now. The light-worms no longer barred the entrance. Ti-Ocks came to either side of him, their hooked axes threatening, but not touching him. Their faces promised swift death, or perhaps pain and torture, Holk couldn't be certain. Fear of what might happen if the mirror-creation ritual was interrupted, he kept still, all the while expecting bestial hands to take hold of him. None did.

Sighing with relief, he tried to shake off his nervousness. "Don't let them fluster you. Finish the job and get out of here."

He picked up the bowl with the finely ground portion of cloth. As he moved it to above the Catalyst, an undercurrent of Ti-Ock speech ran through those packed around him. His confidence did not improve when those nearest took three steps backward. *What did they fear might happen?*

Returning to the task at hand, he tilted the bowl ever so slightly before the shaking of his hands caused him to bring it back level. *Relax.* He closed his eyes and took several deep breaths. When he opened them, he kept his attention focused solely upon the bowl and the Catalyst. As the bowl tipped to once again deposit the powder within upon the black dodecahedral Catalyst, Holk ignored the many pairs of eyes boring into him, and the impending doom waiting to be unleashed.

A fingertip gently encouraged each spec to fall. One by one, they accumulated upon the uppermost surface of the Catalyst. Its darkness gradually turned gray. He wondered what would happen if even a single granule fell upon the reflective surface. *Dire consequences* were what Kazzra warned.

What do I do after administering the powder?

Watch and do nothing. Once the border has solidified and the reflective surface remains whole, it will be ready.

But how much of the powder was a question he desperately wished he had asked. Too much and particles would spill over the edge. The Catalyst was not all that big. When he felt no more could be applied without fear of spillage, he set the bowl aside.

For a few anxious moments, he feared more would be needed. But then the powdery substance sank into, and vanished beneath, the surface of the Catalyst. A murmur coursed through the assembled Ti-Ocks. Holk darted a quick glance to either side, but couldn't discern the cause. It probably had to do with the powder and the Catalyst. Returning his gaze to the soon-to-be mirror, he saw that no more powder coated the surface of the black dodecahedron.

From each of its eleven exposed sides, small bursts of light flared as the runes came alive. Once, twice, then after the third burst, they went dark and the Catalyst transformed in the space of two heartbeats from a hard object, to liquid. It radiated from the center and flowed outward to the edges, coating the entire reflective surface.

At its touch, the border turned from shimmering darkness to a reddish brown. Churning into itself, the substance of the border changed yet again to orange, then yellow, then a dark green. No sooner had a color come into being, than it shifted once again to another.

Knowing that he would have less than a moment to make good his escape once the border solidified, he positioned his hand above it. One touch and he'd be free of this place forever.

Dark green changed to light green that in turn changed to sky blue...

In those final moments of waiting, a thought flittered across his mind. *What happens after he uses the mirror?* Providing it works, and he does in fact arrive somewhere back home, then what? The mirror will remain in the possession of the Ti-Ocks. They will be able to follow! And if they do, would Kazzra be very far behind?

Sky blue...dark blue...black...purple...

Purple held dominance for a lengthier time before fading into amber. The cycle of change was slowing. It wouldn't be long before the process would conclude.

If he could not leave the mirror behind, then perhaps he could take it with him? But a moment's consideration was what fate had allotted him before the border turned from amber to a dark red...and solidified.

Both hands shot for the borders and grasped it just as a dozen points of pain erupted along his back, shoulder and arms. Claws dug into him as Ti-Ocks pulled him unceremoniously back from the table. Others latched onto the mirror and worked to wrench it from his grasp. An arm snaked around his neck and breathing became all but impossible.

Strength born of desperation maintained his grip on the mirror's edge despite the vicious onslaught. Ignoring the pain and the inability to breathe, he steadily edged his right thumb toward the reflective surface. Such an easy task was made nearly impossible considering that at the same time he had to maintain a firm hold so as not to lose the mirror.

The claws gripping him tore; those grasping the mirror wrenched; yet somehow he kept his grip on the mirror and his thumb moved ever closer. Almost there, he caught sight of two Ti-Ock curved-headed axes being raised, one to either side. The way they were positioned could only result in the severing of his hands when they descended. The Ti-Ocks sought to bring this struggle to a quick and bloody end.

His gaze returned to his thumb, now a mere half inch from achieving freedom. The strain on his hand had reached such an extent that attempting to stretch across the last bit of distance would surely cost him his grip on the mirror. But with the axes rising to end the stalemate, what choice had he?

When they reached their apex his thumb quickly shot toward the reflective surface only to have its goal yanked from his grasp.

Timed seemed to slow. No longer anchored by his grip on the mirror, he was no longer able to deny the claws pulling him and in that instant when the mirror was drawn away, he lost his balance and fell into the ranks of Ti-Ocks behind him.

In the heat of battle, tactics must be fluid. As he fell, Holk twisted until he faced the creatures, put one foot upon the floor, and lurched forward. Shouting a war-cry, he barreled into the mass of creatures; he and they went down in a tangled, snarling mass.

The snout of one reared before him and his fist found a home. Rolling to the side, he managed to come to one knee with sword drawn. Not after any particular target, he laid about him in a flurry of frenzied slices. Ti-Ock blood flew. For the briefest of moments, his enemies fell back. Screaming as a madman, which may not have been very far from the truth, he quickly scanned the room for the mirror. A single Ti-Ock held it above its head as it made for the passageway.

A score of Ti-Ocks, the greater majority wielding hook-axes, stood in his way; the unarmed ones edged backward and away from the impending fight.

No matter how many opponents stand in your way, only so many can come at you at once. Use the terrain to your advantage; reduce the avenues from which attacks can be launched.

Sergeant Wilkers' sage advice filtered through the haze of battle. Little good it did when you are in the middle of a room with opponents on all sides. Indecision turned to action when the shadow of a falling axe fell upon him. Twisting, he brought his blade up to meet it and hewed through the haft.

Screaming again, he brandished his sword to the creatures arrayed against him. Feinting toward those grouped farthest from the entrance, he then launched an attack in the general direction of the piles of mirrors, a place where at the moment the concentration of Ti-Ocks was thinnest.

Axes rose and fell. Each one came away with its head removed. A slice through a Ti-Ock's chest, a kick to knock another backward, and he had gained the side of the room and the mirrors.

A quick glance to the entrance revealed the mirror-toting Ti-Ock passing through and moving with all speed to the right.

Two enemies rushed forward with many more behind. He struck off the axe head of one and had to dodge to the side to avoid the blow of the other. That maneuver put him precariously close to the remaining hand-helds. Light blossomed forth as his proximity brought a trio of light-worms to life.

Sidestepping half a pace to avoid their grasping tendrils, he ducked beneath the path of an axe and brought his sword in under the creature's shield.

Crying out with pain, the beast fell back as its leg felt the bite of the sword from another world. Holk only had a moment to notice the deep gash that would have been a complete severing had he been better balanced when he attacked; then more opponents rushed forward.

Though he held his own, he was being pushed back toward the reaching tendrils of the light-worms. A feint to one, a kick toward a second and a moment's respite developed. Screaming, he made as if to attack, then stepped backward and struck the hand-helds with the flat of his sword.

Ti-Ocks roared in pain and fear as light-worms connected with them. Those able to avoid the grasping tendrils fell back rapidly.

A narrow avenue barred by a Ti-Ock quartet ran between the wall and the writhing gyrations of light-worm ensnared Ti-Ocks. Holk lashed out at a Ti-Ock converging on him from the opposite way. After shearing through its armor, Holk kicked out and sent it reeling back into its fellows.

Next to him sat the stack of large mirrors. Taking the topmost by its border, he flung it toward the four Ti-Ocks standing between him and the exit to the passageway. No sooner had the mirror left his hand than he reached for a second.

The lead Ti-Ock instinctively reached out to catch it. When it did, part of its hand came into contact with the reflective surface and it vanished. A second vanished like the first when another mirror hit it square on the snout. The other two, seeing what happened to their fellows, allowed the next three mirrors to sail past and land on the floor. Holk was surprised not to see them smash. Instead, they merely bounced along the floor until coming to a stop in the passageway beyond. The larger ones were apparently more durable than their smaller counter-parts.

Holk followed the cumbersome missiles with an attack. Meeting the first Ti-Ock head on, he used both hands in a cross-hand slice. Ti-Ock armor, and no small amount of the skin beneath, parted before the blade from another world.

As it fell backward, the remaining Ti-Ock paused momentarily. Its gaze flickered between its comrades undergoing the less-than-gentle caresses of light worms, and the human before him that had so readily dispatched the one before. When Holk shouted, brandished his weapon and charged; the Ti-Ock lost all stomach for the fight, turned tail and fled.

Holk was hot on its heels until it entered the passageway and turned to the left; he let it go. Glancing to the right, he saw the mirror-toting Ti-Ock pass through another of the torch-lit areas some distance farther down. It didn't appear to be in any hurry. With a grin on his lips and vengeance on his mind, Holk took out after it.

—21—

His prey didn't remain ignorant of its danger for long. It was alerted when a mob of maddened Ti-Ocks boiled outward from the room. Shouting their guttural speech, they set out in an axe-waving wave of death after the human. Seeing a shadowy presence with a glint of steel in its hand racing through the dark passageway toward it, the Ti-Ock clutched the mirror close to its chest, turned, and fled.

Holk exhilarated in the chase. His bid for freedom might come to an end at any time, he may end up dead beneath a Ti-Ock blade, but he didn't care. He felt more alive at this moment than before the ill-fated siege and subsequent flight through *The Devil's Kiln* that culminated in his coming to this place

Casting a glance over his shoulder revealed that he was keeping ahead of the Ti-Ock mob; maybe even gaining ground. Returning his gaze to the one with the mirror, he saw the gap between them steadily narrow. He kept focused on what lay before, not the danger following behind.

The Ti-Ock momentarily vanished from sight when it dodged into a side passage. As Holk came abreast of the opening and prepared to enter, an axe-bearing Ti-Ock barred his way; and the axe was coming straight for his head.

Unable to do more than dive beneath the blade, Holk felt the axe head slice several hairs before he hit the floor. Rolling, he reached a kneeling position barely in time to bring the sword up to block a downward hack. The sword edge bit into the haft but hadn't the momentum to completely cleave it in two.

As the Ti-Ock drew back the axe for another attack, Holk attacked. A quick roundhouse over his head and his sword connected with the beast's shin sending the beast to the floor minus the lower part of its left leg. Coming to his feet, Holk turned to follow the mirror-toting one and left the other to writhe on the floor.

This new passage held no torches, but wasn't completely dark. Unlike the main passage he had recently departed, this one exuded a small amount of light. Holk couldn't discern its source, but it was sufficient for him to see that it stretched for quite a distance. Far ahead, his prey raced with all speed down its dimly lit length.

The brief battle with the Ti-Ock had allowed his pursuers to narrow the gap. Not enough to catch him, but close enough that should he experience another such unexpected interlude, he would risk being overtaken. Dismissing the increased danger, Holk remained focused on the Ti-Ock with the mirror and worked to recover the lost ground. Slowly, he pulled away from those behind.

Mirror-Toter fled down another side passage; Holk didn't even slow. Keeping his sword before him, he braced for an attack that failed to materialize. No sooner had he entered the new passageway than he saw Mirror-Toter duck behind an iron bound door. When the door began to swing close, he increased his speed.

Hinges long in need of maintenance protested the movement of the ponderous door. A quarter of the way closed, it picked up speed.

Holk knew if that door closed, the chance of recovering the mirror would be all but gone.

Ten yards away, the door reached the halfway point and was closing in earnest. Six yards away, Holk knew he would never reach the door in time. Desperation times prompted desperate measures; he threw his sword toward the steadily narrowing gap.

The door was but inches from closing when the blade entered the narrow opening. A pain-filled howl followed, but the door slammed shut...then edged open a fraction.

Holk reached the door and dug his fingernails into the part of the frame sticking out and drew it open. On the ground beyond the door laid a purple-robed Ti-Ock. Protruding from its side was the hilt of his sword. The blade had entered just below the left shoulder. Lifeless bestial eyes seemed to stare accusingly.

There was no time to admire his handiwork. Passing through, he discovered a handle on the other side of the door. As he pulled it closed, the mass of axe-wielding, maddened Ti-Ocks slammed against the outer side. An iron bar used for securing the door was attached just above the handle. Throwing the bar into its wall recess, Holk secured the door.

He was in another of the mysteriously illuminated corridors. Mirror-Toter's shadow moved in the distance. Holk drew his sword from the lifeless Ti-Ock, wiped the blood off onto its robe, then sheathed it as he continued the pursuit. The sound of pounding from the other side of the door quickly changed to that of axes hewing away.

"Good luck," Holk laughed. The wood was very strong, and with the iron binding it, the Ti-Ocks could be at this for a long time; time enough for him to reclaim the mirror and make his escape.

Up ahead, the passageway enlarged, becoming wider and taller. As it broadened, the amount of light radiating from the walls increased. The Ti-Ock fled and Holk followed.

Steadily, the distance between them narrowed. So intent on his prey was he that when more of the purple-robed Ti-Ocks appeared in the distance, he failed to notice. When he did, he realized they came forward at a steady pace. There were four and each wielded two maces.

Mirror-Toter raced through their ranks. Afterward, they closed formation all the while continuing their advance.

Holk slowed as he drew close to these new adversaries. When less than twenty paces separated him from them, he noticed how the heads of the maces were oddly shaped. They were roughly spherical, about the size of an apple and faceted like a gem. Wary as to what this may portend, Holk slowed.

The line came to a halt when fifteen paces remained between them.

Advancing with caution, he caught sight of how the light emanating from the walls was being reflected by the heads of the maces. *What were they made of, glass?* Then it dawned on him. The heads were covered in small mirrored sections no larger than a coin. *Would they work the same as their larger counter-parts? Or did they portend some new deviltry.* If so, all they would have to do was touch him… Little time was given to ponder this new development for with a snarl and a series of barking commands, they charged.

They fanned out as they raced forward. Holk feinted for the center then dodge quickly to the left. A mirror-mace descended toward him and he met it with the broadside of his sword. The resultant clang rang throughout the passageway and the battle was joined.

As the second mace swiped in toward his side, Holk danced backward a step. Then when the Ti-Ock drew back its mace to resume its attack, he changed direction and skewered one of the other Ti-Ocks through the middle. The attack of a third forced him to twist off-balance in order to avoid the touch of the mace. Simultaneously, he drew the sword from the dying Ti-Ock and lurched toward the wall. Twisting so his back would hit the wall, he quickly regained his balance.

The three remaining fanned out; one faced him directly while the other two moved to either side.

Holk kept them at bay by slicing the air about him; first to one side, then to the other. Intentionally overextending himself while warding off the one to the right, he caught sight of the one to his left advance with mace held high.

In one fluid motion, Holk halted his attack, reversed the trajectory of his sword, and pinioned the forearm holding the mace.

Though in severe pain, the Ti-Ock had the fortitude to bring its second mace down against Holk's shoulder. To his surprise, he didn't vanish. As it pulled the mace back for a second blow, Holk grabbed the weapon's haft; then twisting his sword that was still impaling its other arm, the creature roared with pain and he wrested the mace from its grasp. Immediately, he struck it against the creature's forehead and the Ti-Ock vanished.

Two quick steps forward to put distance between him and the remaining two, Holk then turned about.

One was almost upon him. Lashing out with his sword, he forced it back but then pressed forward and followed through with the mace. The creature stumbled off-balance in its attempt to avoid the mirrored head. About to finish it off, Holk's attack was preempted by a blood-curdling roar from the remaining Ti-Ock.

Rushing in with little care as to its own safety, the creature attacked simultaneously with both maces. Holk brought up his sword and caught both weapons just below the head; then lashing out with his foot, he kicked the Ti-Ock backward. Off-balance for only a moment, it was sufficient time for Holk to follow through with a thrust that took it through the chest.

Seemingly oblivious to having a blade impaling it, the Ti-Ock continued forward. One mace came flying from the side. Holk managed to duck and avoided it; the mirrored head missing by mere inches. Its second mace came down in an overhand hack.

Holk brought up his mace, caught it haft-against-haft with the other, then in a deft maneuver slid the head downward to connect with the Ti-Ock's hand. When mace met flesh, the Ti-Ock vanished.

The remaining Ti-Ock rushed forward. But now that he had but a single opponent, and an unskilled one at that, to contend with it took but a moment before Holk had the creature lying on the passageway floor, its life's blood pooling on the ground beside it.

Ripping a strip from the creature's robe, Holk wiped the blood from his sword. Then with a second, he wrapped the head of the mace to guard against inadvertent contact. Before the cloth completely covered the head, he gazed at one of the mirrored facets and wondered where it was the Ti-Ocks had been sent; most likely somewhere unpleasant.

Once the head was securely covered, he slid it into his belt and searched farther down the passageway for sign of the mirror toting Ti-Ock. The time wasted in the fight with the quartet of mace wielders had allowed it to make good its escape; the passageway was empty. Cursing, Holk broke into a run as he sought his elusive prey.

The passageway continued widening and growing brighter. After the dead Ti-Ocks had vanished from view in the distance behind, the illumination filling the tunnel reached the equivalent of mid-day. Heat did not accompany the light; the air felt eerily cool.

Up ahead, the tunnel jogged around a bend to the left. As he rounded the curve and the passageway resumed its relatively straight path, something spied from the corner of his eye caused him to slow his pace. When he looked, all he saw was the brightness coming from the wall. Disregarding it as nothing, he continued on.

Not ten paces farther down, that same something was once again seen out of the corner of his eye. As before, when he turned to look, there was nothing to see.

Once, it could be his imagination. *But twice?* Unlikely. Scanning the walls failed to reveal the source of what had drawn his attention. Unwilling to waste time on what might still be a figment of his imagination, he hurried on.

Four more times his vision was drawn to the walls, and once to the ceiling. Each time, he failed to detect anything out of the ordinary. On the sixth instance, his eyes happened to be directed in the direction of the occurrence. A ribbon less than a finger's length of brighter light flashed for a moment before the spot on the wall resumed its regular luminosity.

Twin flares of light farther down the passageway drew his attention. Pausing but a moment, he moved closer to the wall to investigate. Reaching out his hand toward the spot, he quickly drew it back when a light-worm emerged followed shortly by two others.

Holk backpedaled to the middle of the passageway to put as much distance between him and the waving light-worms as possible.

Other ribbons of light almost immediately appeared in a growing circle radiating outward from the trio that had emerged.

Now he understood the source of the light radiating from the walls and ceiling of the passageway. They were infested with light-worms. As he resumed his pursuit of the mirror-toting Ti-Ock, additional light-worms emerged in what was quickly becoming a bright carpet of waving bands of light.

Were they indigenous to this part of the Ti-Ock territory? Or were they set there like guard dogs? By the time the passageway came to an end at a massive archway framed by a pair of massive columns, each comprised of eight brilliantly glowing square stone blocks set one atop another, Holk hadn't decided which. Either way, it made little difference. He had no where to go but forward.

Ten paces separated one column from the other. Holk slowed as he approached. Each block showed scores of light-worms moving beneath the surface. The combined illumination emanating from the sixteen blocks was so intense, that it obscured what lay in the shadows beyond the archway.

All that could be discerned were indistinct forms. Holk proceeded with caution.

In the hopes of escaping the notice of the light-worms within the stone blocks, he kept to the center of the archway. Even as he made to pass between the twin pillars of stone, what lay beyond remained indistinct. Feeling very exposed and worried of a light-worm attack, he passed through the arch.

Keeping the shape of the archway, a short passageway comprised of more light-worm infested stone blocks extended for a good ten paces before coming to an end. Holk hurried through and only had two moments where light-worms extended outward toward him. Each time, they failed to make contact. He was much relieved to pass out of the passageway and into one of regular, non-light emitting stone. How long this passageway may be was unknown for there was nothing but darkness. Holk drew his sword, struck his sunstone to banish the shadows, and continued on.

He didn't progress far before the tunnel narrowed and began circling to the right in a tight, downward spiral. Three revolutions brought him to where the darkness began to fade and light took its place.

Twice more he came full circle before being brought to a halt by a pair of rather sturdy looking doors. Ornate, runic engravings had been masterfully applied. Twin orbs of light glowed from where they were affixed to the walls on either side. Holk could see movement within each; a closer look revealed each orb held two light-worms.

Curiosity wanted him to reach out his hand to see if the orbs would prevent the creatures from emerging, but reason stepped in and forestalled such an ill-conceived action. Instead, he focused his attention upon the door.

Aside from the intricate pattern of runes, each door held a large ring that looked to be made of silver. Holk took hold of one and pulled gently. To his surprise, the door swung open.

Light exploded outward in such intensity that it caused him to dance backward in startlement and throw an arm across his eyes to shield them from the glare. Once they grew used to the brightness, he peered out from behind his arm and saw something that made his heart sink.

Beyond the doorway laid the beginnings of a vast cavern containing hundreds if not thousands of mirrors. Stepping forward, he opened the door to its fullest and gazed at the stacks upon stacks of mirrors. Some rose horizontally from the floor, others leaned against massive stalagmites. Scanning the room, he sought any sign of Mirror-Toter and his mirror.

As he turned toward the left, a light-worm emerged from the wall, and if not for a sudden duck and quick dash into the cavern, it assuredly would have had him. Now that he was several feet beyond the entrance, he could see the extent of the light-worm infestation. They were everywhere.

Hardly a square foot of any wall and ceiling lacked the creatures. Some crawled along the surface; some extended outward and waved in the air, while others would vanish beneath the stone only to reappear a moment later. The only part of the cavern that appeared to be unaffected was the floor.

Off to his left gaped the maw of a smaller cavern. Within, even more mirrors were visible. Not seeing anywhere else Mirror-Toter could have gone, Holk wended his way through the piles of mirrors toward it.

Not a very large cavern, this off-shoot of what Holk took to be the Ti-Ock's mirror repository was little larger than the passageway that had brought him there. A narrow path ran straight through a myriad of haphazardly stacked mirrors leading toward the far end where a narrow opening beckoned.

Holk moved to traverse the path, but only managed to take a couple steps before being assailed by an overpowering feeling of foreboding. Such was the power of the sensation that be broke out in a cold sweat and his hands started shaking.

His eyes drifted uncontrollably toward a mirror with a black border that leaned against a stack of fifteen others. The reflective surface drew his gaze and held it; fear rose at his inability to look away.

Losing the battle for control, his vision blurred as a scene of horrific proportions began unfolding within the mirror. His mind trembled at the sights; though indistinct, they produced an unreasoning and unbearable fear.

Unable to do naught but stare, he sought to break the connection by bringing up his sword and interposing the blade between his eyes and the mirror's reflective surface. The horror grew and his mind shuddered beneath the onslaught. Every inch was a battle; the terror drained his will and demanded that he drop his arm. From somewhere deep within, Holk found the strength to continue.

Not until the gemmed crosspiece filled his vision and no part of the horrific scene could be seen, did the mirror relinquish its control upon his mind. When it did, he felt his limbs go rubbery; closing his eyes he backed from the room.

Once in the main cavern, the unreasoning sense of fear and foreboding subsided until all that remained were whispers of nameless terrors. Wiping the sweat from his eyes, he gathered his courage then braced for a return into the smaller cavern.

This time he would not allow his gaze to wander. Holding his sword up before him with the narrow opening at the cavern's end directly behind it, he kept focused on the blade and entered.

The fear hit him again, but this time he was ready. There was intelligence behind the fear; he could feel it trying to gain a foothold within his mind. But with his concentration fixed firmly on the sword and the narrow opening that was his goal, he successfully fought the urge to turn his gaze upon the mirror with the dark border and safely traversed the room.

Beyond he entered a small junction where three other passages extending away like the cardinal points on a compass. Each was the same as the one through which he had just passed, the only exception being that these each bore eight mirrors mounted on the walls, four to each side. One of these passages had to lead where Mirror-Toter had gone. But which one?

Using his sunstone, he stood at the entrance to each and tried to ascertain the Ti-Ock's whereabouts. Where each passageway ended, a dark, open expanse began. *An additional mirror storeroom perhaps?* Thinking that to be a likely supposition, Holk turned his attention to the passageways themselves and the mirrors they held. None produced the unreasoning fear that had pervaded the small cavern just vacated. One being as good as another, he held his sword at the ready and passed into the one on his right.

He expected to feel something upon entering, but was relieved when nothing developed. Keeping his eyes firmly fixed upon the dark opening at the far end, he quickly sped through and discovered his supposition had been correct. Three tiers of mounted mirrors lined the walls; of Mirror-Toter and the mirror Holk had crafted there was no sign.

Turning about, he made his way back toward the junction. As he reached halfway through the intervening passageway, motion from up ahead made him quicken his pace. Mirror-Toter emerged from the passageway directly across from the one in which Holk moved. Seeing the human with sword drawn, it fled into the tunnel leading toward the light-worm infested repository. Holk let him go. It was not the Ti-Ock that he sought, but the mirror it no longer carried.

His gaze fell upon the shadowy entrance from which the Ti-Ock had appeared. Sensing that at last he may be free of this place, he hurried forward. Upon leaving the passageway and entering the junction, he came to a halt upon spying where Mirror-Toter had stopped. The Ti-Ock had yet to vacate the passageway and enter the repository. Their eyes met.

"Yah!" Raising his sword and yelling with every ounce of fierceness he could muster, he took one step forward.

Mirror-Toter turned and fled.

Holk didn't proceed any farther. It was the mirror he was interested in. Turning to the dark opening beyond which he was certain his mirror lay, he produced his sunstone and hurried forward.

The short passageway led into yet another room filled with mirrors. Holding aloft the sunstone, he searched for one with a dark red border. The search was not easy as the piles were haphazardly stacked and of varying heights. As those stacks nearest him failed to yield results, he moved deeper within the room.

When a mirror with a red border was spied, Holk would use the tip of his sword to move aside others in order to get a better view. The first one proved to be too rectangular, the second's border wasn't dark enough. A third proved to have the proper hue, and except for swirls of silver decorating two corners, could have been his.

Two-thirds of the way into the room, the glow of the 'stone pierced the deepest shadows in the farthest reaches. His eyes passed across a stack nestled against the rear wall. About to move to the next, he noticed a dark red corner protruding from behind. Grinning triumphantly, he moved forward.

A feeling of foreboding settled over him and grew stronger by the heartbeat. He glanced at the mirrors nearest him but failed to detect the source of the unpleasant feeling. Then a barely heard noise from behind caused him to glance over his shoulder.

Mirror-Toter stood at the entrance to the room. In its hands it clutched the mirror with the black border.

Like before, fear rose as his gaze was drawn uncontrollably to the reflective surface. Incoherent imagery grew to clarity and Holk knew terror the likes of which he never could have imagined existed. His mind quailed beneath the assault.

Whatever intelligence lay beyond the mirror knew that it had Holk and reveled in the knowledge.

Moving his sword to block the mirror from his sight proved beyond Holk's ability. The horror pierced his mind and subdued volition. Strength fled his body as would a lake after its dam gave way. Instead of rising, the blade dropped until his fingers could no longer hold it and the sword clattered to the ground.

Mirror-Toter laughed. At least so Holk interpreted the rapid burst of abbreviated grunting that coincided with an upturn at the edges of the creature's mouth. Stepping forward, it brought the mirror closer. He could do nothing but stand still; his limbs no longer obeyed his commands.

Fear will undo you, son. Is this what I taught you? To whimper and quail like a newborn child?

In a sea of madness, Sergeant Wilkers' voice found a kernel of sanity. Holk latched onto it as would a drowning man a wayward piece of flotsam.

Fear is of your own making. Understand it; control it; subdue it. Fear has no place on a battlefield.

Memories of his time with Sergeant Wilkers ebbed from the nether recesses of his mind.

...the drubbing given when Holk failed to perfect a simple maneuver...

...the first time Holk managed to leave a welt on the sergeant's chest...
...the look of pride on Sergeant Wilkers' face after setting four of Holk's peers upon him and seeing him prevail...

Holk latched onto that look of pride; concentrated upon it to the exclusion of all else. Sergeant Wilkers was an anchor, a safe harbor from the storm.

Mirror-Toter drew closer; the mirror but a shadowy haze obscured by his recollections of times past.

You know what you have to do, so do it. Are you going to allow fear to rule you?

No!

Fighting against the power of the mirror, Holk recovered marginal control over his right arm. With Sergeant Wilkers lending him strength, he managed to reach across his front to where the mirror-mace was hooked within his belt.

Mirror-Toter saw the movement and quickened its pace toward him; the mirror held out before it.

Numb fingers wrapped around the weapon's hilt and drew it forth. Still wrapped with cloth, Holk hadn't the strength to spare unwrapping it. Instead, he drew it back over his shoulder.

Now, son!

Releasing the vision of Sergeant Wilkers, Holk brought his arm forward and let go of the mace. It sailed the intervening distance to strike the center of the mirror with a crack.

The fear and terror vanished as the reflective surface shattered. So too did the hold on his limbs. Rubbery and weak, his legs buckled. As he hit the floor, a dark mist rose from the shattered remains of the mirror.

Mirror-Toter gave out a high-pitched squeal that could only be interpreted as fear, turned tail and fled.

Holk hadn't the strength to get to his feet. He lay on the ground and watched as the mist rose and came together. Once every wisp had merged to form a singular cloud, it began moving his way. He didn't know what it was, but was certain its touch was a thing best avoided. Glancing behind him, he spied the stack behind which his mirror had been placed. By sheer force of will, he turned onto his stomach and started crawling toward it.

He could feel the cloud behind him; could feel its malevolent energy drawing ever closer. Stretching out an arm, he would pull himself along the floor, then out went the other and he worked a little bit closer to his goal.

It was a race to see if he could reach the mirror before the cloud could reach him.

...stretch...pull...stretch...pull...

His legs trembled each time they pushed him along; arms screamed their protestation, but he continued toward his goal.

Whispered thoughts sought to intrude into his mind, undermine his will and bring him to a halt. Keeping focused on progressing across the floor kept him from succumbing to its spell.

He reached the edge of the mirror stack just as the sound of a boot scraping along the floor came from behind. Knowing it was foolhardy in the extreme, he couldn't prevent the reaction of looking back over his shoulder. Thinking he would find Ti-Ocks, he instead discovered a large warrior, completely encased within jet-black armor. From head to toe there was nothing showing what may lie beneath. At the same time, he realized the dark cloud had vanished. The armored warrior drew its sword and moved forward. Like the armor, it too was of darkest black and seemed to draw all life from the world.

Holk's own sword remained on the floor where it had fallen, now some distance on the other side of this new foe. Weaponless and weak, his only chance to survive was to reach the mirror. Spurred on by the nearness of his goal, he managed to quicken his pace.

The steps of the armored warrior echoed as it quickly closed the distance.

Reaching the rear of the stack, Holk grasped his mirror's border and worked to free it from where the stack of mirrors had it wedged against the wall. Yanking with one hand and pushing aside the stack with the other, he managed to get it free.

Wrapping an arm around the mirror, he rolled onto his back just as the warrior's sword struck the spot he had been but a moment before. Gazing up at the faceless helm, he prayed that Kazzra's instructions had been correct. With the sword rising to deliver another blow, he touched the reflective surface.

The dark warrior remained still for a moment as it gazed at the space where but a moment before Holk had lain. With a deft motion it sheathed its sword then turned toward the room's entrance.

There it found five Ti-Ocks; four bore the Ti-Ock's favored weapon; the fifth was Mirror-Toter. Mirror-Toter gave the warrior a grin and bowed.

"It is done, Master."

Black warrior no more, a small human boy-child strode toward the assembled Ti-Ocks. "Indeed, Kazzra."

The Ti-Ocks stepped back and bowed reverently as the boy-child passed between them.

Epilog

"When did you finish?"

"Yesterday afternoon."

At a table in the Blue Heron, a tavern within the village of Kran, two friends enjoyed a mug of ale at day's end.

One, with black hair and bearing the build of a blacksmith, glanced at his friend. "Heard your patron was, uh, crazy?"

Phillip, a well-digger, mason, and the village's jack-of-all-trades, nodded. "You could say that. Sat atop a box the entire time we dug the hole. He'd draw his sword every time one of us so much as got close to him."

"Hole? Thought he hired your team to dig a well."

Draining the last of his ale, Phillip nodded. "That's what we thought, too."

"But it wasn't?" Gazing at his own empty mug, Murg the Blacksmith signaled the barmaid for another round.

Shaking his head and chuckling, Phillip replied, "Nope. When we got down to where water began seeping in faster than we could remove it, he had us come out. You'll never guess what he did then."

"What?"

"Tossed that box into the hole and had us cover it with dirt."

"No."

Phillip nodded. "True, I say. Once the box had a few feet covering it, he had us roll a dozen boulders, each taking five men to move, into the hole and fill it up the rest of the way with dirt. Once we had the hole all but filled in, we laid down another layer of rock."

Murg shook his head. "Ever find out what was in the box?"

"No, but the way he was protecting it would seem to indicate it held something of value."

"Maybe the body of his wife was in it."

"I doubt that. We were digging that hole for quite a while. Had someone been in it…" he tapped his nose, "we would have known." Seeing the look of avarice his friend assumed, he added, "It wasn't gold, neither. Not heavy enough."

"How do you know if you never got close to it?"

"Saw the way he lifted it. Whatever was in there, it was none too heavy."

"Strange."

Phillip nodded. "Tell me about it."

"What happened to him?"

"Once the last layer of stone was in place, he tossed us a bag filled with coins, gold coins the likes of which I've never seen, and then walked into the forest."

Producing one of the coins, he handed it to his friend. One side bore the image of a sword, the other a curve-headed axe.

Murg took the coin, turned it to view both images, then tapped it on the tabletop. "Is it real?"

"Cranic claimed it was; had that checked first thing."

After a brief period of inspecting the coin, he handed it back to his friend. "So what's your next project?"

Tales grew of the man and the buried object. Several attempts were made to discover what was down there. But the manner in which the box had been buried stymied every would-be treasure hunter. The boulders were too massive and being at the water table made them impossible to move. Of the man, none ever discovered who he had been or where he had gone.

The End

Check out the other epically adventurous worlds of fantasy author

Brian S. Pratt

The Morcyth Saga

James, a high school senior, went looking for a job. But instead, he begins what turns out to be an adventure of a lifetime. Whisked unexpectedly to a world where magic works, he must learn to master its power, all the while searching for the meaning of why he was brought there and what he must do.

The Broken Key Trilogy

Four comrades set out to recover the segments of a key which they believe will unlock the King's Horde, rumored to hold great wealth. Written in the style of an RPG game, with spells, scrolls, potions, Guilds, and dungeon exploration fraught with traps and other dangers.

Ring of the Or'tux

In many stories you hear how *'The Chosen One'* appeared to save the day. Every wonder what would happen if the one doing the choosing bungled the job?

In *Ring of the Or'tux*, that's exactly what happens. Hunter was on his way to a Three Stooges' marathon when in mid-step, he went from the lobby of a movie theater to a charred tangle of stone and timber that once had been a place of worship. From there it only gets worse for the hapless *Chosen One*. First, an attempt to flee those he initially encounters (who by the way are the ones he was sent there to save), lands him into the merciless clutches of an invading army (those whom he was supposed to defeat).

The Adventurer's Guild

Jaikus and Reneeke are ordinary lads whose dream in life is to become a member of The Adventurer's Guild. But to become a member, one must be able to lay claim to an Adventure, and not just any adventure. To qualify, an Adventure must entail the following:

1-Have some element of risk to life and limb
2-Successfully concluded. If the point of the Adventure was to recover a stolen silver candelabra, then you better have that candelabra in hand when all is said and done.
3-A reward must be given. For what good is an Adventure if you don't get paid for your troubles?

Jaikus and Reneeke soon realize that becoming members in the renowned Guild is harder than they thought. For Adventures posted as Unresolved at the Guild, are usually the ones with the most risk.

However, when they hear of a party of experienced Guild members that are about to set out and are in need of Springers, they quickly volunteer only to discover to their dismay that a Springer's job is to "Spring the trap."

If they survive, membership in the Guild is assured.